apocalypse

apocalypse

"I am Time, the destroyer of worlds"
Bhagavad Gita

For Ivan,
a poet of ancient sunlight

Other books by Tim Bowler

Midget

River Boy

Storm Catchers

Firmament

Margaret K. McElderry Books

apocalypse

TIM BOWLER

Margaret K. McElderry Books
New York   London   Toronto   Sydney

Margaret K. McElderry Books

An imprint of Simon & Schuster

Children's Publishing Division

1230 Avenue of the Americas

New York, New York 10020

First published in England in October 2004 by Oxford University Press

First U.S. edition, 2005

Book design by Ann Zeak

The text for this book is set in Baskerville Book.

Manufactured in the United States of America

2 4 6 8 10 9 7 5 3 1

Library of Congress Cataloging-in-Publication Data

Bowler, Tim.

Apocalypse / Tim Bowler.—1st ed; p. cm.

Summary: Fifteen-year-old Kit and his parents must ground their sinking
sailboat on a rocky island inhabited by a primitive sect who believe the
stranded family has been sent by the Devil.

ISBN 1-4169-0370-4 (hardcover)

[1. Sailing—Fiction. 2. Shipwrecks—Fiction. 3. Survival—Fiction.] I. Title.

PZ7.B6786Ap 2005; [Fic]—dc22

2004020506

1

They came in the night in a long black boat.
They rowed out of the harbor at the south end of the
island, past the breakwater, past the cottages, and on
toward the bluff at the northeastern tip, still hidden from
view in the foggy murk. They pulled in silence, their hands
wet and cold in the chill before dawn, the only sounds their
grunting breaths, the grinding of oars, and the murmur
of water against the bow as it cut a path through the
milky sea.

The breeze was cool and no longer smelled of summer.
They pulled on, none speaking, and the rocky shore slipped
slowly by, just visible through the gloom. More wind came,
more mist, great clouds of it now rolling in from the north.
They rowed on, their eyes on the sea, the shore, the gray
haze, anything but each other.

At last they saw the bluff ahead, fog swirling around it
like smoke. They gave the outlying rocks plenty of room,
then brought the boat round into the cove at the top of the
island. They stopped for a moment to muffle the oars, then
set off again, past the rocky scar at the northwestern point

and away from the island itself. All sense of the land was gone now. There was only mist and sea, and themselves. They rowed slowly, watching, listening.

From somewhere in the mist came a deep, mournful cry. They stopped. It came again: a long, eerie moan, no human cry, nor that of any normal creature. They felt a swell in the water, a movement far down. The blades of the oars hung dripping. The cry came again, the same unearthly moan. It seemed to well up from the sea itself. But it sounded farther off this time.

They rowed hurriedly on, a panicky new vigor to their strokes, but now the wind had picked up and the surface of the sea was rippling with misty life. They drove the boat on, searching the darkness beyond the bow, and suddenly there it was—the great rock rising fifty feet above them, stony teeth around its base.

More mist rolled in, blocking the rock from view, but they had their bearings now and rowed on toward it. The wind freshened further; the swell grew greater. The mist parted overhead and they caught a glimpse of the moon, the first they had had since setting out. It was a cold moon, a dead, distant thing. But here, too, was the rock.

They could see the white water at the base where the seas washed over the teeth. They could see the gap that led between them to the tiny haven under the side of the rock. They entered the raging water, wrestled with the eddies that threatened to pluck the oars from them, then suddenly they were through and inside the sanctuary.

They moored the boat and started to make their way along the twisting ledge that spiraled up to the summit of the rock. Below them the sea moved and breathed like a fretful beast. They reached the summit and peered over the flat table of rock. The fog was so dense here they could barely see more than a few feet ahead. They took a few steps forward, then stopped, their eyes searching around them.

But all they saw was darkness and mist.

They linked arms and started to inch their way across the top of the rock. Nothing at first but the clear flat floor, then, as they neared the southernmost point, a rougher, more broken surface: potholes, cracks, fissures. They slowed down, aware of the edge somewhere just ahead.

There it was, and closer than they had realized. They stopped, clutching each other tight. From below came the heaving of the sea, a deep, unsettling sound. They turned and made their way back across the surface of the rock. Then suddenly the mist parted and they saw the man at the northernmost end. He was utterly still, sitting on a stump of stone. But his eyes looked straight into theirs.

They pulled the clubs from inside their belts and rushed forward. The man did not move, did not speak. The first blow knocked him to the side. The second felled him. They crowded round with mad shrieks and set about him with their clubs. He soon stopped twitching, but they carried on even so until they were spent. Then they stood back, breathing hard, and looked down at the body.

It lay there unmoving in a sea of blood.

They stared at it for a long time, spitting on it one by one. Then they bent down, picked it up, and flung it over the edge. It cannoned into the water with a splash and vanished from view. They watched for a while, searching the space where it had fallen, but all they saw was foam.

From deep in the mist came the long, unearthly cry.

"What was that noise?" said Dad from the cockpit. "Did you hear it?"

"Yes," said Mum.

"A kind of weird cry."

"I heard it."

"What do you think it was?"

"Don't know," she said. "But let's hope whatever made it isn't interested in us."

Kit listened to their voices from down in the cabin. He was lying, not in his usual berth up in the forepeak, but in Dad's bunk with a blanket over him. He was supposed to be sleeping, and he had been sleeping. But he'd heard the cry too. It had woken him from his dream. There was a long silence, broken only by the shiver of sails and the ripple of water against the hull. Then Dad spoke again.

"Wind's picking up."

"Maybe it'll blow away some of the mist," said Mum.

"Let's hope so. Can you ease off the jib a bit?"

"Okay."

Kit frowned, unwilling to doze off again. The dream that had fallen so fitfully upon him since he came below to sleep had been horribly disturbing. But what was more disturbing still was that he had had the same dream three times already on this voyage, and each time it had felt more real than the time before.

He rolled over onto his back, enjoying the extra space of Dad's bunk but little else; then he saw his father watching him through the open hatchway. Dad smiled and called down to him.

"Don't get any ideas about nicking my bunk on a regular basis. I'm only letting you have it this time because I'm feeling kind."

"Don't want it on a regular basis," Kit called back. "Might catch something."

Dad gave a chuckle, then Mum's face appeared in the hatchway.

"Kit?" she said. "You're supposed to be sleeping."

"I was, but that weird cry woke me. What do you think it was?"

"Don't know. But nothing to worry about, I'm sure."

"Okay." He yawned. "Mum?"

"Yeah?"

"I had that dream again."

Mum's face softened. "It won't happen, Kit."

"It might."

"It won't. I promise."

"How do you know?"

"Because I'm cleverer than you."

"Oh, yeah?" He raised an eyebrow. "How do you reckon that, then?"

"I'm older and wiser."

"Older, yeah. I'll give you that. By miles."

"Not by miles, Kit."

"By miles!" He snorted. "I'm only fifteen. You're at least a hundred and forty."

"Give or take the odd century."

"Yeah, sorry. I meant two hundred and forty."

She laughed but was quickly serious again. "It'll be all right, Kit," she said, and moved back to her former position in the cockpit.

He closed his eyes but even now found himself reliving the dream: the restless water, the dark shape moving through it, the clear sense that he was drowning. He felt a tightness round his heart and opened his eyes again. This was crazy. It was only a dream. Mum was right. It wouldn't happen.

He rubbed his chest for a while with the flat of his hand, then sat up, put his clothes on, and climbed up to the cockpit. Mum made a space for him between her and Dad. He sat down and looked about him. *Windflower* was still reaching on starboard tack as she had been when he first went below, but everything else looked different now that the fog had come down.

"Sure you've had enough sleep?" said Dad.

"I'm all right."

"That's not what I asked."

"I've had plenty of rest. I've been down there for six hours."

"But you weren't sleeping all that time," said Mum.

Kit looked round at her.

"Have you two been spying on me?"

"Dead right we have," she said. "And we reckon you only slept a couple of hours in all that time. And that wasn't proper sleep either because of your bad dream."

He said nothing.

"So what were you thinking of all the time you were awake?" she said.

"This and that."

"I know what that means," said Dad. "It means mind your own business. Okay, we will."

"It doesn't mean that. It means . . ."

But in truth he didn't really know what it meant. And he didn't know what he'd been thinking about down in the cabin. All he knew for certain was that he'd been worrying.

Maybe it was because this was *Windflower*'s last voyage. Now that Dad was officially bankrupt, the boat was going to have to be sold along with everything else when they returned. But they'd promised themselves that her last voyage would be a proper one, not just coastal stuff, but a real adventure. And so it had been, with weeks and weeks of almost nonstop sailing, most of it out of sight of land. They'd loved every moment of it, but the summer holiday was almost at an end now, and so, too, was the voyage, though they were still a good ten days from home.

But Kit knew it wasn't just the imminent end of the voyage that was bothering him. It was something else, something that had started a couple of days ago when the first of the dreams came. He'd felt frightened, not just by the thought of drowning, but by something in the sea itself. He'd never felt this way before, but there was something strange about the waters round here. They were unfamiliar to be sure, but that in itself couldn't account for his fear. Most of the voyage had been through unfamiliar waters—that was the whole point of the trip—and he hadn't had a problem. Until now. And he didn't like this night fog either. He looked round at Dad.

"Where are we on the chart?"

Dad glanced at Mum, then back at Kit.

"We're not sure," he said slowly. "The compass is playing up."

"What?"

"It's been playing up for quite a while."

"Quite a while?"

"Several hours."

Kit stared into the binnacle and saw the compass spinning wildly.

"Have you tried the spare compasses?" he said.

"Yeah. They're all doing the same thing."

"So we could be anywhere?"

"Yeah," said Dad. "But we should be safe. The nearest land is at least forty miles away by my estimation. And we're not crossing any shipping lanes here."

"But you don't know how far off course we've gone in this fog."

"That's true. So we need to be cautious." Dad glanced over the sails. "I think we'll reef her a bit more. The wind's picking up again."

It was indeed and the seas were growing larger, too.

Ordinarily *Windflower* thrived in rough weather, but Kit knew that Dad was right. It would be foolish to go racing through the night, especially when there was fog and they weren't sure of their position.

"Would it be safer to heave to?" suggested Mum.

"Might be an idea," said Dad. "But let's shorten sail anyway. She'll be more comfortable."

"Okay. Jib first?"

"Yep."

Mum eased off the jib sheet, then pulled in the reefing line. "Enough?"

"Can't see," muttered Dad, squinting toward the bow. "This fog's getting worse. I'm going forward. Take the helm, Sarah, can you?"

Mum took the helm and Dad climbed forward to the jib, his body turning to a gray shadow as the mist engulfed him.

"Jim!" called Mum. "Be careful!"

"I'm all right!" came the answer; then, "Pull in a bit more!"

Kit took the reefing line and pulled it in.

"That's enough!" called Dad, and a moment later he reappeared. Kit felt a sense of relief to have his father clearly in view again. Dad stopped by the mast and clung to it, balancing himself against the heel of the boat.

"How does she feel?" he called.

"Bit heavy on the helm," answered Mum.

"She'll be better when I've taken more off the mainsail."

"Okay."

"Any chance of fixing us a bite to eat?" said Dad, already bent over the reefing gear. "Something we can nibble as we go along? I'm starving."

"I'll make us some sandwiches," said Mum. "Kit? Can you take the helm?"

"Sure."

"Just keep her as she is."

"Okay."

Kit took the tiller from Mum and sat to windward, hunched against the cool air. Mum disappeared below and he soon heard the sound of her busying about the galley. Up at the mast, Dad was trying to ratchet the sail round the boom. Suddenly a squall struck. *Windflower* heeled sharply to port, her lee rail under. Dad clung to the mast and bellowed at Kit.

"Ease off the mainsheet a bit!"

Kit was already doing so, but it made little difference. The squall was growing stronger.

"More!" shouted Dad. "Get her on an even keel if you can!"

He eased the sheet out farther, and *Windflower* steadied for a moment. But now more squalls were coming in, and with them great clouds of mist. He saw Dad furiously working the ratchet, but the boat was heeling dangerously as the gusts swept over her.

Something hard knocked against the hull. Neither Mum nor Dad seemed to hear it but Kit caught the sound. Then he saw a piece of wood drifting past to leeward. It was barely a foot long, and in a second it would be gone. Yet in that second he saw what it really was.

A tiny carved boat.

On an impulse he scrambled to the port side of the cockpit, switched the tiller to his right hand, and reached out with his left to pick the model up. His hand closed round it; then he froze. Holding on to the carved boat was another hand, a hand reaching up through the sea itself, and below that, an arm, a body, a face, staring up at him through the foam.

And then it was gone, swept past and lost in the wake.

He heard Dad yelling at him from the mast.

"Kit! What are you playing at? She's coming up into the wind! Get her back on course!"

He struggled back to the windward side of the cockpit and wrenched at the tiller. But his mind was in turmoil now. All he could think of was the watery eyes staring up at him. Dimly he realized that *Windflower* was still shooting round to starboard into the wind, that he was somehow clutching the little carved boat, that Mum was hurrying up from the cabin, that Dad was shouting at him to bear away and get back on course. In a daze he stood up and yanked the tiller toward him. *Windflower* started to bear away to port, bear away to port, bear away to port.

"Not too far!" shouted Dad. "Straighten up or you'll jibe her! Sarah! Get the helm off him! Quick!"

From up in the bows came a *crash*.

Windflower gave a lurch and skewed round to port, throwing the mainsail across in a violent jibe. The impact and the swinging boom jolted Kit back to the present, but the movement of the boat still flung him off balance, and he fell with a thud against the coaming. Mum rushed over to him, but he pushed her aside and scrambled to his feet again, his eyes on the mountainous shape towering over them.

He'd run the boat into a rock, a huge, murderous thing. But it was the teeth at the base that were the greatest danger. *Windflower* was caught between a score of them, and with the wind now dead astern of her and the sails still full, she was pounding against the sharp tips as the swell dropped her. She could break up at any moment.

"Sarah!" roared Dad, now clinging to a shroud. "Port your helm! See if you can bring the bows round to starboard! But watch out! She'll probably jibe again! I'll try and push us off! Kit! Dive into the forepeak and see if we're shipping any water, but come straight back!"

"Dad!" he spluttered. "I'm sorry, I—"

"Never mind that now! Go and check below!"

He climbed down into the cabin and hurried forward, tears streaming down his cheeks. If *Windflower* foundered, he'd never forgive himself—and losing the boat wasn't the only thing that could happen. There was something far worse than that. But he didn't dare think of it. He found he was still clutching the little carved boat and flung it under his berth. Then he crawled into the bows.

It was worse than he'd expected. One of the planks was sprung, and a steady flow of water was oozing in. Another break could open her right up. He hurried back to the cockpit to find the situation worse than ever. Dad was on the foredeck, desperately trying to push the bows off the rocks with the boat-hook, but the pressure of the wind on the sails made it impossible.

"Jim!" called Mum. "You've got to take the mainsail down! It's keeping us stuck here!"

Dad ran back to the mast and fumbled with the halyard and topping lift. "Mind your heads!" he yelled, and a moment later the mainsail came shivering down. He seized the boat hook again and pushed, and this time the bows eased back a fraction from the rocks.

But now in spite of Mum's efforts at the helm, the wind was forcing the stern round to starboard. If they didn't do something quickly, the boat would be broadside onto the rock with the whole of her starboard side exposed to the teeth. Dad looked quickly about him, then bawled at Mum.

"Sarah! We'll try and get her off the other way! Let go the port jib sheet and pull in the starboard one! And helm hard to starboard!"

"Okay!" shouted Mum.

The jib flew out, then tautened and filled on the other side as Mum pulled in the starboard sheet. The bows started to move round to port away from the teeth. But the stern was still swinging to starboard, and Kit saw to his horror that the boat did not have enough way on her to pull clear.

"My God," said Mum under her breath. "The stern's going to hit." She threw a glance at Kit. "Are we shipping water?"

"Yes."

"Tell your dad."

"Dad!" he shouted. "One of the planks is sprung up in the bows! We're shipping water!"

"How fast?"

"Not fast yet but steady!"

"Go back and stuff all the mattresses and pillows you can find against the leak, and hold them there! I'll be down the moment I can!"

Kit scrambled below again, grabbed the mattresses and pillows from the bunks, and crawled with them into the forepeak. The water was coming in faster now. He thrust the pillows over the leak, then the mattresses on top, and held them in place. But it was no good. The water was still seeping in around them. There was a sudden, rending *crash* from the stern, followed by a shout from Mum.

"Jim! The rudder's gone! I can't steer!"

Kit felt the tears start again. This was the end. They couldn't stop the water coming in, and they wouldn't be able to pump or bail fast enough to keep her afloat. And now the stern had crunched into the teeth and the rudder was gone. *Windflower* would founder against the rock, and he was the one who had brought her here. He felt the stern lift in the swell, and hang there. He held his breath and waited for the next crash. The stern fell again.

But there was no crash. Instead a shout from Dad.

"Roll up the jib! Roll up the jib!"

He heard the sound of the jib rolling up and wondered

what was going on. If they were drifting, Dad must have decided they'd be safer without any sails set. He listened, his hands and arms now soaked as the water seeped in around the pillows and mattresses. There were no more crashes, only the lifting and dropping of the hull and the smack of the sea against the side. Suddenly the forehatch opened, and he saw Dad peering down at him.

"Kit? Is it working?"

"No."

"I'll come and take a look."

Dad started to climb down through the forehatch.

"What's happening with the rock?" said Kit.

"The wind's blown us past it, but one of the outlying teeth messed up the rudder."

"So we're drifting?"

"Yeah." Dad squeezed next to him and ran his eye over the damaged plank. "Damn! It's coming in faster than I feared. We'll have to rig a fothering sail over the leak or she'll go down. And we'll have to be quick about it." He grabbed one of the sail bags. "We'll use the storm jib," he said, pulling it out. "It's thicker than the other sails. Pass me those coils of rope."

Kit handed him the ropes.

"Right," said Dad. "Now come with me on deck, but be very careful. The boat's pitching like hell. And put your life jacket on."

"There isn't time for that."

"Just do as you're told."

Dad wasn't wearing a life jacket and neither was Mum, but Kit said nothing. Dad climbed up through the forehatch with the sail and ropes. Kit put his life jacket on, then joined his father on the foredeck.

Dad was right about the sea. It was more lumpy than

before, and the wind had risen further in the last few minutes. The darkness was clearing a little and so was the mist, but visibility was still poor. The rock couldn't be more than fifty yards upwind of them, but all they could see of it now was the foaming white of the teeth that had savaged *Windflower*. And here she was, rocking rudderless in the swell. Mum clambered across from the cockpit.

"Are you going to try a fothering sail?" she said.

"Yes," said Dad. "But there's no telling if it'll work. You'd better put some water and provisions into a couple of kit bags. We may have to abandon ship and take to the dinghy."

"Okay."

Kit glanced at the dinghy in her place between the cabin top and the mast. *Splinters* was a sturdy little boat, but she was hardly suitable for a voyage in rough weather with three people and a stack of provisions. He prayed it wouldn't come to that. Mum hurried off and Dad turned back to him.

"Now listen, Kit. You're to keep one hand on the boat at all times, you understand?"

"Okay."

Dad knelt down, balancing himself as best he could on the shifting foredeck, and tied the ropes to the corners of the storm jib.

"Right," he said. "Let's go."

They stretched out over the edge of the bow, waves smashing up into their faces, and spread the sail across the leak. *Windflower* bucked suddenly as a larger wave rolled in.

"Keep hold of the boat!" yelled Dad. "Don't let go!"

Kit clung on, one hand on the sail rope, the other on the forestay. Another wave crashed in, drenching them both. He hung on and waited for his eyes to clear. When they did, Kit saw to his horror that Dad had been washed half over the side and was slipping into the sea.

15

"Dad!" he shouted.

He clutched at his father but missed, then heard a pounding of footsteps on the cabin roof. The next moment Mum leaped across the foredeck and threw herself onto Dad's disappearing leg.

"Jim!" she yelled, struggling to pull him back. Kit let go of the forestay, sprawled across the foredeck, and seized Dad round the waist, and somehow they manhandled him back onboard. He lay there for a moment, breathing hard, one hand tight round the anchor chain. Mum bent over him.

"Jim," she said. "Jim, are you—"

"I'm all right."

"I thought you'd—"

"I'm all right, I'm all right." Dad rolled upright again and gave Mum's arm a squeeze. "Thanks," he said, then turned to Kit. "And you, lad. Well done." He took a deep breath. "Right, let's finish this thing."

Mum moved back but only as far as the mast, her eyes fixed on the two of them. Dad grabbed his end of the storm jib, waited for a smoother patch of sea, then nodded to Kit. "Now," he said. And they pulled the ropes tight, drawing the fothering sail back over the leak, and then made fast.

"Do you think it'll work?" said Kit.

"Don't know," said Dad. "But we'll soon find out." He turned to Mum. "How are you getting on with the kit bags?"

"I was just getting started when you decided to go for a swim."

"Well, can you carry on with that now?"

"Okay."

"Put a compass in as well. I know they're not working, but put one in anyway. And a chart. And some warm clothing and waterproofs. When you've sorted that, get pumping. I'm going to try and rig an oar over the stern so we can steer.

Kit, dive into the cabin and pass me up the sweep. Then find yourself a bucket and bail like hell."

But Kit didn't answer him. He was staring through a gap that had suddenly opened in the mist.

"Dad," he said. "There's an island."

They stared. And there, about half a mile beyond the bow, was a small but unmistakable island. They couldn't see it clearly yet, for though the mist had gone, some of the night still lingered. But dawn was on its way, and by its spreading light they could see the outline of a hill, and cliffs, and what looked like a cove at the nearest point.

"Come on," said Dad. "We'll see if we can get *Windflower* over there. If it's all rocks, we can't do much for her, but if there's some kind of a beach, we might be able to run her ashore."

They hurried to work: Mum to the kit bags, Dad to the stern locker for more ropes, Kit down to the cabin. But the hopes he had felt rising at the sight of the island fell at once. A pool of water now covered the bottom boards, filled by a steady flow from the bows. It was hard to tell whether the fothering sail was making any difference or not. He saw a plastic food box floating down toward him, and a mug, and a sponge, and some of the mattresses.

And the little carved boat.

The image that he had tried to forget came back to his mind: the body below the surface, the arm, the hand, the face, the eyes, and with that image came the other thing, the thing he had not dared to acknowledge until now.

The recognition.

It made him shiver to think of it, yet there was no doubting what he had seen. He had seen the face of a man, not a boy, yet it had been a face so like his own he had felt he was looking at an older version of himself. A face drowning not just in water but in another dimension.

Mum joined him in the cabin and started collecting things for the kit bags.

"Come on, Kit," she said. "No time to waste. Your father's waiting for the sweep."

The long oar was easy enough to find. It was floating right in front of him. He picked it up and steered it out through the hatchway into Dad's waiting hands.

"Thanks, Kit," said Dad. "Now get bailing."

Kit filled a bucket, carried it up to the cockpit, and tipped the water over the side into the sea.

"Not that way," said Dad, already busy lashing the oar to the horse. "It'll take too long. Just tip the water straight into the cockpit. The self-draining system will get rid of it."

"Okay."

He hurried back, filled another bucketful, and tipped it into the cockpit, and then another, and another, trying as he did so to push aside the thoughts that plagued his mind. Dad now had the steering oar in place and was testing the blade over the side. Mum had finished with the kit bags and was hard at work at the pump. To Kit's relief, both had slipped into their life jackets.

He went on bailing, bailing, bailing. He was almost grateful for the monotony of it. He could hardly bear to watch what was happening, and at least this gave him something mindless to do. He heard the sound of the jib being unrolled and then the sheet trimmed, and then Mum's voice.

"How does she feel?"

"Sluggish," said Dad.

"Is the oar working?"

"Just about. But it's difficult. The broken rudder's giving us some negative drag, and I keep having to compensate for it. This rolling sea doesn't help either."

Kit carried on bailing, trying to push all thoughts from his mind save the need to clear the cabin of water. But there seemed little hope of that now. It was coming in too fast. He felt the bows plunge as *Windflower* drove into a trough. He waited for her to come up again, but to his horror she stayed down as though locked there. He stopped bailing and waited, panic filling him, then slowly, ponderously, she rose once more to the surface. As she did so, he saw a stream of water run down from the bows into the pool in which he now knelt.

"Kit!" called Dad.

He turned and saw his father craning over from the cockpit.

"Nip into the bows and tell me what the leak looks like."

Kit crawled through the water and studied the broken plank. It was obvious that the fothering sail wasn't working very well. Water was finding its way in easily, and the movement of the hull in this deep, rolling sea was clearly making things worse. He hurried back to Dad.

"It's coming in faster than before. The storm jib's not making much difference."

"It's the motion of the boat," said Dad. "The waves are picking us up from behind and pushing the bows down into the troughs, so the water's getting in round the edge of the sail." He frowned. "We'll give it a bit longer and see if we can keep the water level down enough to stay afloat. But if it gets much deeper in there, we'll have to launch the dinghy and abandon ship. Get back to your bailing. And give it everything you've got."

Kit returned to the bailing with all the energy he could manage. Yet the ever-increasing flow of water seemed to mock his efforts. He filled the bucket and reached up and tipped it into the self-draining cockpit, yet when he turned back to the floor of the cabin, the pool of water seemed only to have deepened. The little carved boat brushed against his legs.

"Go away," he muttered to it. "Go away, go away."

He picked it up and threw it into the forepeak. It reappeared at once, floating blithely back. He dipped the bucket again and tipped the contents into the cockpit, and then dipped again, and tipped again, and so it went on, as he worked to keep *Windflower* afloat. And while he worked, he heard Mum's ceaseless action at the pump and the scrape of the oar against the hull as Dad struggled to keep them on course for the island.

But Kit was sure now that they weren't going to make it to the island. A glance through the forward cabin windows showed *Windflower* still some distance from it, and she was slowing by the minute. Hampered by the rolling sea, and by the water she was carrying, and by her reduced sail, she was moving more and more awkwardly.

He knew there was little else they could do. If Dad hoisted the mainsail, the boat would speed up but she'd also ship a skinful of water and maybe go down within seconds. It had to be this snail's pace if they were to have any chance at all. Yet even this didn't look as though it was going to save her.

"We'd better launch the dinghy," he heard Dad say.

"Kit and I can do that," said Mum. "You stick with the steering oar. You're probably the only one of us who can work it."

"All right."

"Kit!" called Mum. "Stop bailing for a second and come up here!"

Kit hurried up to the cockpit.

"Help me launch *Splinters*," she said.

They climbed over the cabin top and unlashed the dinghy.

"Give me the painter," said Mum, and they eased *Splinters* over the side. Mum dumped the kit bags in her, then guided the dinghy round to the stern and made the painter fast.

"Thanks, Kit," she said, and returned to the pump.

Kit glanced quickly at the island. It was still some way off, but in the last few minutes they seemed to have made a small amount of headway toward it. And one thing was clear now in the growing light of day: The thing that had looked like a cove was a cove. And inside was a shingly beach. If they could just get *Windflower* to that and run her up on the shore . . .

But once again his hopes were shattered by the sight of the water in the cabin. The pool had deepened further, and he knew the situation was now critical. They would have to make a decision soon about whether to abandon ship. He looked for the bucket and saw it floating around with boxes, mugs, oars, the spare boat hook, and as always the wretched carved boat. He grabbed the bucket and started bailing furiously. It seemed to make little difference, but he kept at the work until his body ached. After a while he heard Dad's voice again.

"All right, Kit. That's enough now. Come up."

"But—"

"I said come up! Don't argue about it! It's not safe down there now. The water's got too deep. I need you up here. We may have to take to the dinghy any moment."

He climbed up to the cockpit and looked around him. To his surprise they were barely two hundred yards from the mouth of the cove. To port was a large bluff and to starboard, at the other extremity of the cove, a long rocky scar running out for about fifty yards into the sea, a narrow platform barely three feet across and scarcely visible above the surface of the water. A fearsome thing, but Dad had seen it and was giving it plenty of room.

They limped closer. The features of the island grew clearer. There was a rocky shore and a hill rising high above the cove.

The slopes were mostly grassy, but they were studded, too, with rocky outcrops and a high stony ridge at the peak and what looked like the dried-out beds of long-gone streams that had once cascaded down. The cove itself ran no more than a few hundred yards to its innermost point, the small shingly beach that Dad was aiming for.

Kit stared about him. There were no signs of present habitation, but as they drew closer to the mouth of the cove, he saw on the rocky embankments of the two shores the remains of old stone cottages. No roofs or windows or doors, just shells and broken-down walls. They sailed on, *Windflower* rolling as before and the jib now fluttering as the wind grew fickle under the sloping sides of the cove.

"Come on, girl," murmured Dad. "Just get us there."

Kit held his breath and *Windflower* struggled on. He watched the ruins slip by and the shingle beach draw nearer. Below him in the cabin the water swirled as it pulled the hull deeper and deeper. He saw the little carved boat bobbing among the other things. He remembered what he had seen, and on an impulse turned and gazed out to sea.

The mist had cleared and night was gone. All was gray. The sea was gray; the sky was gray. Half a mile astern was the great rock. It, too, was gray: a deep, foul gray. He saw waves rolling in toward the island, long waves with angry crests, and nearer than that something else, something just a few yards astern of them: a dark shape slipping beneath the surface of the water like a vast moving shadow. He stared hard at it, trying to see it more clearly, but it eased away toward the sea and was gone. From somewhere beyond the cove came a long, eerie cry, the sound they had heard during the night. He shivered and turned to Mum and Dad.

But as he did so *Windflower* grounded on the beach.

Dad raced forward to the bow, took a line, and jumped with it into the shallows. Then he waded to the shore, ran up the shingle, and made the end fast to a stump on the rocky embankment. Mum rolled up the jib and hurried with Kit to the foredeck. Dad came breathlessly back down the beach and stopped at the water's edge.

"Get the line round the windlass and take up the slack," he called.

"Okay," said Mum. She bent down and took hold of the line.

"Take a couple of turns," he said, watching her from the beach. "Or maybe three."

She wound the line round the drum and started to work the lever. The rope tightened and tightened.

"More," said Dad, feeling the line with his hand. "More." The windlass clanked on.

"Mum?" said Kit. "Do you want me to do it?"

She threw him a baleful glance.

"Sorry," he said.

"That'll do!" called Dad eventually.

Mum stopped and leaned back. Dad stepped into the shallows and waded back to the boat.

"I can't believe she made it," he said. He stopped by the bows, the water up to his waist, and ran his hand down the damaged side. "The fothering sail's still in place. I can feel it."

"Do you think it helped?" said Mum.

"Must have done a bit. But it was a close thing. I thought we were going to lose her."

"I thought we were going to lose each other."

Kit felt himself flush.

"I'm sorry," he said. "This is all my fault. I feel terrible."

"You mustn't," said Mum. "The conditions were dreadful last night. Anyone could have gotten into difficulty."

"It wasn't the conditions. It was my fault. You know it was."

"Easy, Kit," said Dad, straightening up. "No point beating yourself up. I've lost count of the times I've done something stupid at the helm."

"But you never ran a boat into a rock, right?"

"Maybe not, but I've still done lots of stupid things. It was a tricky situation last night. Don't blame yourself anymore."

Kit shrugged. He knew they were trying to be kind, but it didn't alter the fact that the only reason they were in this predicament was because of him.

"What can I do?" he said. "I want to do something. I want to be useful."

"You can carry on bailing," said Dad. "Get the water out of the cabin."

"What are you going to do?" said Mum.

"Put a kedge out astern," said Dad. "I'll do that in *Splinters*. And I want to tidy up a few things. I can't get at the leak till the tide goes down farther and she rolls over on her side. We'll have to make sure she goes to sleep the right way. Still . . ." He glanced around him. "She'll be afloat for a while yet, I reckon."

"How do you know the tide's going out?" said Kit.

"Look again."

Kit stared over the little beach and then saw what Dad meant: the trails of weed, still moist, that the tide had left behind on the shingle.

"Jim?" said Mum. "Do you want any help with the kedge?"

"No, I'm all right, thanks. You might as well help Kit with the bailing."

"Okay."

"Dad?" said Kit. "Can you fix the leak?"

"I can do a temporary job to stop any more water coming in."

"How?"

"I'll pack one of our spare pieces of plywood with cloth and mastic and screw it over the broken plank. That should keep her dry, though I wouldn't want to take her too far like that."

"What about the rudder?"

"I suspect that's going to be more serious. But one thing at a time. Let's sort out the other things first."

"Okay," said Mum. "Anything you need before we go below?"

"The ladder would be nice."

"Oh, yeah. Sorry."

Mum fitted the ladder to the side of the boat, then turned to Kit.

"Come on," she said. "Let's get rid of all that water." And she climbed below.

Kit hesitated. He was desperate to get the water out of

the boat, but he wanted to do this on his own. He felt it should be his job and nobody else's, since he had caused the problem. And he needed to be by himself to think. He saw Mum waiting for him in the cabin, bucket in hand, and climbed down to join her.

"That's my bucket," he said.

His feeble joke was rewarded with a smile. She handed him the bucket, found another for herself, and they set to work together, filling up and tipping out into the cockpit as he had done before, only this time without the stress of imminent disaster. A few moments later Dad climbed through the forehatch to fetch the kedge and its cable, then he was gone again and there was a sound of oars as he rowed out in *Splinters* to lay the anchor over the stern.

"All right, Kit?" said Mum after a while.

"Yeah."

"Does that mean no?"

"Yeah."

"I thought so." Mum tipped another bucketful over into the cockpit. "Still feeling guilty?"

"Yeah."

"I don't want you to."

"I just do."

"Okay." She paused. "But there's something else, isn't there?"

"Yeah."

"What is it?"

He dipped his bucket, stretched up and tipped the water over into the cockpit, then settled himself again at the bottom of the cabin.

"What is it?" said Mum again.

"I saw something when I was at the helm. Just before I lost control."

"What?"

"A little carved boat floating past us."

"You didn't say."

"There wasn't time. Everything happened so quickly."

"What happened to the boat?"

"I picked it up. It's here in the cabin somewhere."

"Here in the cabin?" She looked around her. "Where?"

"It's . . ." He looked about him, searching the chaos. And wasn't that just typical? Before, when he was bailing and didn't want to see the damn thing, it kept bobbing into view. Now when he did want to see it, he couldn't find it.

"Is that it over there?" said Mum. "By the mast?"

She was right. It was wedged among some plastic boxes and one of the spare life jackets that had floated down from the bow. He crawled forward, fetched the model boat, and brought it back to Mum. She took it from him and looked it over.

"It's not very well made," she said, turning it round. "Very roughly carved. But there's no mistaking what it's meant to be. Look, the bottom's been weighted to keep it the right way up when afloat."

It was true. Whoever had made it had bored tiny holes inside the top of the keel and then forced little stones into the gaps to act as ballast.

"So you reached over the side to pick this up?" said Mum.

"Yeah."

"And then lost control?"

"Yeah."

She held his eyes for a moment.

"There's still something else, isn't there?" she said.

"Yeah." He looked down again at the model boat. "I reached down to pick it up and saw . . ." He took a deep

27

breath. He couldn't tell Mum this. And there was no point. She'd never believe him.

"What did you see?" she said.

He bit his lip.

"Kit? Tell me. What did you see?"

He saw the image in his mind again and tried to push it away. He felt Mum's fingers under his chin, gently lifting his face until their eyes met again.

"Come on, Kit," she said. "I need to know."

"I saw a man underneath the water. He was reaching up from below. He had a hand round the model boat. I saw his body. I saw his hand. I saw his face."

Mum's expression didn't change. But he saw what he expected. He saw the doubt appear in her eyes. He saw her try to conceal it from him. He saw her smile. And then he knew for certain. She didn't believe him.

"Are you sure, Kit?" she said. "*Windflower* was moving fast. And there was a mist."

"I know what I saw. I saw a man. But I didn't just see any man. I saw a man with my face."

There was no point in holding anything back now. She didn't believe him anyway. So he might as well tell her the whole lot.

"I don't think that's likely," she said.

"It's not likely. But it's what I saw."

"He didn't have your face, Kit. He can't have had your face."

"He had my face. He was like a man-version of me. Fast-forward me thirty years or whatever and that's what I'll look like. I felt I was looking at myself."

"But even if he looked like you, Kit, he wasn't you. Okay? I mean he maybe had a face that looked a bit like yours, but that's all he had." She smiled at him, then reached out and touched the thing he hated most about himself: the long black birthmark that disfigured his neck and cheek. "He didn't have that, I'm sure," she said quietly.

He looked hard at her.

"Yes, he did," he said.

He saw the color drain from her face.

"Are you serious?" she said.

"Yeah. That's why it freaked me out. That's why I lost control of myself. I didn't know who I was." He looked away. "I still don't."

"I can understand." She stroked his arm. "It's no surprise you lost control at the helm. Seeing something like that would unsettle anybody. But, Kit, think for a moment. You saw the model boat. You reached down and picked it up. And here it is. Okay, that's real. But this other thing . . . this face . . . you have to consider the possibility that it might have been your imagination."

"It wasn't my imagination. I saw what I saw. Someone as ugly as me."

"You're not ugly, Kit."

"Yes, I am. There's no point pretending."

"Kit—"

"I know, I know. You and Dad don't think I'm ugly. But I do, okay? And just about everybody else I know thinks so too. They don't have to tell me. I can see it in the way they look at me."

"Kit, listen—"

"And I did see the face in the water."

Mum frowned. "I know this is hard. And I'm not saying it wasn't vivid and frightening. But, Kit, think of these horrible dreams you've been having lately. You've been overwrought, haven't you? And I know you've been worried about Dad and the bankruptcy and all that."

He said nothing. There was nothing to say. He'd known after all that she would take this line. And he didn't blame her. She was only saying what he might have said to someone else in similar circumstances. Except that in this case there was one thing he knew that she didn't: He hadn't imagined the face.

And now he had to deal with that.

They went on bailing, both silent now as though they each needed a moment to be busy and to think. He felt little relief at having told her his story. She would now be convinced that he had imagined the face and that it was further evidence that he was still in a state over the bankruptcy, and she would tell this to Dad later when they were alone together, and he would agree with her. There was little more to be said now. So he went on bailing and lost himself in that.

Dad returned in the dinghy and could soon be heard moving about the deck. A few minutes later he climbed down to join them, bucket in hand.

"I've taken off the steering oar and tidied up a bit," he said. "And now I'm ready for a spot of bailing. Since you two have obviously been doing nothing down here."

"Don't know why you bothered turning up," said Mum. "We've practically finished."

Dad chuckled, then looked around him, his face suddenly sad. "What a mess," he said. "What a bloody mess." His eye fell on the engine, still partly under water. "That's well and truly wrecked, isn't it? Not that it was ever very reliable."

"Is there no chance of it working?" said Mum.

"None at all. The salt water will have done it in. It's a job for the engineer." He turned back to them. "You all right, Kit?"

But Kit hardly heard him. His thoughts were still on the

images pulsing through his mind: the man, the face, the rushing water—and now the dark moving shape he had seen below the surface as they entered the cove. He couldn't mention this. It would be met with the same incredulity as his description of the man. Then he remembered something they could all relate to.

"Did you hear that weird cry?" he said. "As we came up to the beach? It was the same sound we heard last night in the mist."

Mum and Dad looked at each other.

"I heard it," said Mum eventually.

"So did I," said Dad. "I've no idea what it was. Never heard anything remotely like it in all the years I've been sailing."

"It was scary," said Kit.

"I wouldn't worry about it," said Dad. "Just because we don't know what it was, there's no reason to suppose it's anything dangerous."

"Maybe it's some kind of porpoise or whale," said Mum. "Or a bird."

"It wasn't any of those things," said Kit. "And you know it."

"Whatever it was, I agree with Dad. There's no reason to suppose it's anything nasty. It might just be a trick of the wind or something." She caught Kit's expression and smiled. "I know. I'm shooting in the dark."

They went on bailing, then suddenly Dad stiffened.

"She's starting to settle. God, that's sooner than I expected. Come on! We need to make sure she rolls the right way."

They hurried on deck and looked over the side. The water was much shallower than it had been and the tide had fallen farther down the beach, and now Kit felt what Dad had picked up: the subtle tremor in the hull as the shingle

31

moved against the keel. She was definitely starting to settle.

"Come on," said Dad. "Let's give her a bit of help."

They stepped out onto the starboard gunwale, Mum and Dad holding shrouds, Kit the backstay, and then leaned out over the edge as far as they could go. *Windflower* dipped her starboard side a fraction under their combined weight. Kit hung there, peering down through the shallow water at the shingly bed below.

He didn't really know why they were doing this. *Windflower* almost always rolled onto her starboard side at low tide. But there was just a chance she could go the other way, so perhaps it was as well to make sure. Dad really needed to be able to get at that leak.

He felt the tremor again in the keel. He dipped his weight farther over the side and saw Mum and Dad doing the same. *Windflower* seemed to be easing over now, just a fraction. He looked beyond the beach at the rocky embankment above and then the foothills of the great peak that dominated the cove. They would have to pitch the tents somewhere on the grassy verge. It would be strange not sleeping in *Windflower* tonight.

"She's going!" called Dad.

And so she was. Within minutes she had dipped her starboard side and rolled over into the shallow water.

"Come on," said Dad. "Just a few more things and then we can rest."

Moving about the boat was more difficult now with her lying on her side, but they carried on bailing until she was dry. Mum and Kit pulled out the tents, climbed up the embankment and pitched them on the flattest part of the slope that they could find. Then they brought the kit bags in from the dinghy and set about carrying ashore the cooking and camping gear and the stores they needed for the night.

All the while Dad busied himself over the broken plank. Finally he called them down and showed them the plywood patch he had screwed over the leak.

"It doesn't do much for her looks, I'm afraid," he said. "But if it keeps her from drowning, I reckon she'll forgive me."

Kit stared at the patch. Dad was right. It didn't do much for her looks. It was a blemish on the side of such a beautiful boat. A bit like a birthmark, he thought, and felt his hand stray over his neck and cheek.

"What about the rudder?" said Mum.

"Well and truly messed up," said Dad.

"Can we sort it?"

"Not on our own. We'll need some help. Let's just hope there are some people on this island."

"Well, that can wait for now," said Mum. She hooked her hand round Dad's arm. "Come and see our camp. And let's have some breakfast."

So they ate, and then they turned in—Mum and Dad in their tent, Kit in his—and slept.

But Kit soon woke. He had dreamed again, the same dark dream, and it had prodded him awake as usual. All the ingredients were there—the restless water, the moving shape, the sense of drowning—and also the man's face, the face that felt like his own. But suddenly these figments seemed more than just images. They seemed so real to him, he was starting to wonder if he was truly awake or lost in some twilight region of his mind. He felt the tightness round his heart again.

He rubbed his chest and took some slow breaths, and tried to calm down. But it was no good. Everything felt wrong now. He wriggled to the opening of his tent and lay there on his stomach, staring out over the bay. The sun had risen above the horizon, but only a pale, chilly light came from it. And there was a curious coldness in the air.

He picked up his watch and looked at it. To his surprise the hands were at meaningless angles and seemed to be stuck. The second hand was not moving at all. Yet he knew the battery was fine. He put the watch down, crawled out of the tent, and stood up. Below him the water in the cove had a dull, coppery sheen. The rolling seas that had driven them in toward the shore seemed to have gone, and the surface was now calm, though tiny waves rippled across from time to time. The wind had dropped to a light breeze.

Half a mile offshore was the great malevolent rock. He stared at it with loathing and felt another stab of shame at the thought of what he had done. The pictures of the dream still ran through him. And now another one pressed itself upon his mind. He had forgotten about it till now. He couldn't see it clearly. He had a sense of water as usual, but there was something else, something long, a kind of spear shape, and then a tiny form at the end.

None of this made sense. But nothing much made sense right now. And now there was this business with his watch. He bent down and peered through the opening of Mum and Dad's tent. They were fast asleep, flat on their backs. He pulled aside one of the flaps and reached in as quietly as he could for Dad's watch. A flash gizmo if ever there was one and if anything was going to be working, this would be. But it was not. As with his own watch, the hands were out of sync and not moving at all. He checked Mum's watch. Exactly the same.

He didn't like this. He didn't like this at all. The compasses had gone funny and now the watches. He thought for a moment, then ran down the embankment, jumped onto the shingle, and hurried across to *Windflower*. She was still lying

34

on her side and the tide had left her dry, though the water was only a few feet below her. He climbed in and made his way down to the cabin. He had to check the radio and the mobile phones. If they weren't working either, then something was seriously wrong.

They were dead. No reception, no power, nothing. He clenched his fists and closed his eyes, and for a moment felt as though the solid world he thought he knew no longer existed. He opened his eyes and found his muscles were clenched tight. He took some slow breaths. They didn't work. He was more tense than before. He saw a small bottle of mineral water nearby and took a couple of sips. The water was warmer than he liked, but he felt his nerves settle a little. He replaced the top, thrust the bottle into his pocket, then clambered back to the shingle and stared out beyond the cove.

And felt his muscles tighten again.

Over to the left by the point he could see the long rocky scar that stretched out into the sea. At the end of it was something small, something dark. The picture from the dream rushed back at him. The spear shape, the dusky image at the tip. He started to walk back across the shingle. He was trembling now and couldn't stop himself. He reached the embankment and climbed up it to the top, then, after a long hesitation, set off along the shore toward the point.

4

Something small, something dark.

He could see it in the distance. He stared at the scar beyond the mouth of the cove and tried to make out what the shape was. But it was too far away. He thought of Mum and Dad sleeping in their tent. He probably shouldn't be doing this. They wouldn't want him wandering off. But it was either wake them up and bring them with him or check this out on his own. And waking them up was out of the question. They needed to rest.

But that wasn't the real reason for keeping quiet and he knew it. There was no point in kidding himself. He just needed to do this on his own. It was part of the dream and the dream wasn't something they could believe in. Not that he blamed them for that. He wasn't sure he believed in it himself.

He was passing the first of the ruins now. They were strange little places, each one just a single room. They were so broken down, it was hard to imagine anyone had ever lived in them. He wondered how old they were, how long ago they had fallen into disrepair. There was a sadness about them that seemed to hang over the whole place. He glanced across the cove to the ruins on the other side. They looked in an even worse state. Some of them were just piles of stones.

Once again he felt the coldness in the air, and as he walked on, he became aware of subtler chills, strange icy patches that seemed to cling to him for a few seconds and then slip away. He shivered at their touch. They didn't feel natural. He had thought at first that they were just pockets of cold air he was walking through, but now he was starting to feel that it was they that were moving through him rather than the other way round.

He stopped and ran his eye over the water in the cove, the rocky embankment, the ruins, the bluff. Another chill passed into him, held him, then moved out the other side and was gone. He shuddered and walked on, quickly now, anxious to check out what was on the scar and get straight back to Mum and Dad. The ruins fell away behind him, and he pushed on toward the point. The shape on the scar grew clearer, and he suddenly saw what it was.

A man's body.

There was no doubting who it was. It was the man he had seen peering up at him through the water, the man with his face, his hair, his birthmark, now sprawled over the end of the scar, half-in, half-out of the sea, completely naked and almost certainly dead.

Another chill passed through him.

He tried to think what to do. It would be stupid to approach the man. There was too much danger, not from the man himself—he was obviously no threat—but from the scar. The tide had fallen since he saw it earlier, but the water was still close to the top of the platform, and an unexpected wave could sweep him off easily.

Then he saw the twitch of an arm.

He narrowed his eyes and stared. But the body was still again. He frowned and watched. Perhaps he'd been wrong. The body remained motionless, still sprawled in its original position, the face turned slightly toward him, the cheek against the rock. He saw another twitch of the arm, an unmistakable movement this time, and now that same arm was stretching out as though the man was trying to climb out of the water.

Kit scrambled down the embankment to where the sea lapped against the shore. He had to help this man. He didn't know how. But he had to do something. Before him the scar stretched out over the water, a long platform of rock. He tested the surface with a foot. It was wet and slimy with weed. He stared down toward the body at the end and took a deep breath.

He ought to be able to do this. It was only about fifty yards, a flat surface, a straight walk. The sea had calmed down; the tide level had fallen. He just needed to take it slowly and keep his wits about him. He took a step onto the scar, then another, and another, and suddenly he was walking, one slow step at a time, away from the shore.

He saw no further movement from the figure, but his eyes were wandering now. Something told him he had to watch the sea. He could sense something in it, something he had felt several times in the last few days since they brought *Windflower* to these waters and the dreams started. He stopped and looked about him, aware of the sea, aware of the man, aware of the slender rock on which he was standing.

There was no sign of danger.

He walked on down the scar. He was halfway along it now and the man's features were growing clearer—long black hair, just like his; the birthmark on the neck and cheek; a similar build, only that of a man rather than a boy; and now something else: angry bruises over the back, down the arms, over what he could see of the buttocks, though these were mostly covered by the water.

Again he stopped. He was sure he'd seen a movement in the face. Then he saw it again, just a flicker but enough to dispel doubt. The eyes were watching him. He knew it. He remembered the bottle of water in his pocket and pulled it out.

"I've got some water!" he called to the man.

No answer but again the flicker in the eyes.

"I've got some water!" he called again. "I'll bring it over to you! I'll—"

But to his horror he heard a rush of water nearby. He turned in panic to see a wave sweeping in from the sea, a long wave with a foaming crest. He dropped the bottle and threw himself down on the scar, scrabbling for something to hold on to. All he could find was the outer edge of the rock and that was slippery with weed. He squeezed his fingers tightly round it and braced himself.

The wave broke with a crash, and to his relief surged only across the inshore segment of the scar, leaving his part untouched. The top of the rock glistened where the water had rushed over it. He scrambled to his feet again and scanned the sea. A short distance away a blurry form was slipping below the surface, the same form he had seen when they entered the cove at dawn. He stared at it, trying to catch a clear view, but it was so shadowy and swift there was no telling what it was. All he knew was that it was at least as big as a whale.

And that it was no whale.

The shape disappeared from view. He heard another rush of water and saw a new wave rolling in. He threw himself down again and gripped the edge of the rock. The wave drove in and swallowed the inshore section of the scar once more. But this time the water passed within five feet of him. He stood up, shaking. He couldn't stay here. The next wave would surely carry him off. He threw a glance back at the man.

"I'm sorry," he called. "I can't help you. It's too risky here."

There was no response. But he knew the eyes still watched him. He sensed an energy in the sea, a deep, dangerous energy. He was still shaking. He knew he should run back. He was utterly exposed here. At his feet lay the bottle of water. He bent down and picked it up. From somewhere close by came the eerie cry he had heard before. He stared over the sea again, searching for danger, and he knew it was all around him in this soft, seductive water. He looked at the shore; he looked at the man; then carried on walking down toward him.

Again he felt the energy in the sea. He pushed it from his mind and walked on, his face set, his hand squeezing the bottle tight. He drew close to the figure and saw the eyes clearly now. They were watching him without expression. He stopped before the man and looked down. It was like looking at himself. He saw his own face, his own body, his own birthmark, his own ugliness. Yet this man couldn't be him. He had to be someone else.

"Who are you?" said Kit.

The man did not answer. He simply looked back. Kit bent down and held out the bottle. The man did not take it, did not move at all. Kit unscrewed the top.

"Here," he said, and he steered the bottle toward the man's mouth. The lips parted to receive it, then suddenly the man's hand came up, placed itself over Kit's fingers, and pushed them upward to tip the bottle. The man drank long and deep.

"Who are you?" said Kit again.

Still no answer. Instead he felt the man's hand squeezing his own, pulling his arm to the side, guiding him round toward the shore. He resisted and stared back into the misty eyes. They looked up at him just as they had done through the sea. And now they seemed to speak.

Go, they said. *Go.*

"I've got to get you back to the shore," Kit murmured.

Go, said the eyes.

He heard the heaving of the sea. He heard the eerie cry again. He closed the man's fingers round the bottle.

Go, said the eyes.

He looked around him. Over to the right a wall of green was scything across the sea.

Go, said a voice inside his head.

He started to run back across the scar. The shadow reappeared beneath the surface of the water, tracking him as he went. He put on speed and raced on, reckless with fear now at the sight of the approaching wave. His foot skidded on a patch of weed, and he tumbled onto the rock. He hauled himself back up and hurtled on toward the land. He was close now, but so was the wave. He could hear the rising of its body, the rippling of its crest. He sprinted over the final yards and scrambled up the embankment to safety. Behind him came a crash. He turned to look back and saw the scar fizzing with foam.

The body at the end was gone.

He stared, now shivering uncontrollably, over the sea. There was no sign of the man or the vast moving shape, and the water was still again, unnaturally still. It was as though no turbulence had ever passed this way. But the restlessness in the sea remained. He could sense it. He glared at the water. It had so many secrets, and all of them frightened him.

He heard the click of a rock behind him and whirled round.

But all he saw was the deserted embankment running down the cove, and over to his right, on the other side of the point, the coastline of the island stretching away: a rocky shore with low cliffs and what looked like caves all along its foot. Then he caught a flash of gray over by the rock face.

Someone was there, peeping out from the nearest of the caves, someone with short, sandy-colored hair. It looked like a girl about his age, but he couldn't be sure. He took a step down toward the cave. At once the figure broke clear and started to run away down the shore. He was right. It was a girl about his age. She was slender and slight and was wearing little but a kind of rough gray smock and a short gray skirt. Yet in spite of her bare feet she leaped from rock to rock with such agility and skill, it was as though she were dancing.

"Wait!" he shouted.

She didn't stop, didn't even look behind her. She simply went leaping on from rock to rock. Suddenly he was hurrying after her. He had to try to speak to her. She might be able to help them, or at least tell them where they were. And she would surely know who the man was. But pursuit was far from easy. Where the cove had a more or less even embankment, this outer shoreline consisted of great boulders with rock pools or other awkward gaps between them. Running was almost impossible. He had to climb down one boulder, cross to the next, climb up and over that, and so on to the next—a ponderous way of getting along the shore.

To the girl, however, it looked almost like play. She seemed to bounce from boulder to boulder as though each one were a trampoline. He had never seen anyone make such great, confident leaps. He stopped. It was obvious he was never going to catch her. Then suddenly he realized he was still in with a chance. She was coming to a point where even she could go no farther.

A short distance ahead of her the boulders came to an end. Beyond that was a sheer section of cliff with no rocks at its base for about fifty yards. So unless she was going to swim across to the next patch of rocks, she was going to be stuck there. He started to move forward again, making his way slowly toward her, trying to smile as he did so, though it was hard. His thoughts were still on the man.

She had stopped now and was watching him as he approached. He felt a sudden ridiculous urge to try to jump the way she had done, to show her that he could do it too. But he stopped himself. This was hardly the time for bravado, and he could easily miss his footing and hurt himself. Besides, the more he rushed, the more he was likely to frighten her even further. And there was no hurry anyway. She had nowhere to go from where she was.

Then he saw that he was wrong.

She had been watching him like a cat, but now, with the same quickness that seemed to characterize all her movements, she ducked and darted through a small opening in the rock face that he hadn't seen.

"No!" he shouted. "Please don't go in there! I just want to talk to you!"

He hurried on, climbing from boulder to boulder, but he was starting to feel increasingly uneasy. This girl was only slight, but she was agile and quick and could well be much stronger than she looked. She was also clearly wild. If cornered, she might attack him. He reached the end of the boulders and the opening in the rock where the girl had disappeared. It was about his height but barely a foot wide. He peered through but saw only blackness.

"I won't hurt you," he called. "I'm a friend."

There was no answer. He glanced over to the right at the sheer section of cliff. At its base was the mouth of another larger cave, this one so wide and so low-lying that the sea washed in through it. He saw a wave disappear inside it and a moment later heard the crash of breaking water. He turned back to the opening before him.

"I won't attack you," he called. "I promise I won't attack you. I just want to talk to you."

Again no answer from inside. He heard another crash of water over to his right. He moved a little closer to the opening.

"The thing is," he said, "I came here with my mum and dad. We nearly got shipwrecked on that big rock off the island. But we managed to get our boat into the cove and up on the beach. So we're stuck here. And I just . . . I just wondered if you could tell us where we are. And if there's anybody here who can help us."

Again no answer. Again the sound of breaking water.

"I've also . . ." He hesitated. "I've also just seen a man die. He was lying on that rocky scar off the point. He was half-dead and he got washed into the sea. He must be one of your people."

Again he saw the man's eyes. He saw the lips parting to drink. He saw the hand close round his fingers. He could almost feel their touch again. He thought of the bruises on that naked body and wondered what this girl might know.

But it was clear she wasn't going to answer him. Perhaps she didn't speak his language. Perhaps she couldn't even hear him. With the crash of the waves she might not even know he was out here.

He crept right up to the opening.

"Please don't be frightened," he said. "I promise I'm a friend."

He stared into the blackness, searching for some sign of the girl, some sign of what was inside. There was no sound from within. He paused, then slowly put his head through the opening. Still only blackness but gradually it eased, and he started to pick out some of the features of the girl's hiding place. It was a low chamber that seemed to run into the cliff for a few yards and then twist away to the right. There was no sign of the girl here. He paused again.

"Are you in there?" he called.

He didn't expect an answer and none came. He took a step into the chamber, and then another, and slowly continued as far as the point where the passage twisted round to the right. Some light was coming through now and he could see the ground falling before him. The walls and floor were moist with condensation. He carried on down the passageway, watching for the girl, listening for her, but hearing only the sound of waves crashing as if in some cavern just ahead.

And there was indeed a cavern just ahead. It was the great cave he had seen at the base of the cliff. This passageway was no more than an artery that fed into it. He could see water rolling in from the sea below him. He felt his way down to the end of the passageway and stopped. Before him was an immense vault. To his right was the mouth that opened onto the sea, to his left a huge tunnel stretching up into the belly of the cliff.

There was no sign of the girl.

He tried to see where she might have gone. There was only one place: the great ascending tunnel. To reach it she would have had to inch her way along a narrow ledge that ran from the point where he was standing around the wall of the cavern. That decided it. He'd risked enough already this morning. The girl could wait. But he gave her one final shout.

"I just want to talk!"

The only answer was a thunder of waves.

He turned and made his way back through the passageway and out to the shore. He was desperate to see Mum and Dad now. He needed to talk to them. He needed to know they were all right. He started to climb back across the boulders, then stopped. He didn't know why, but he was certain he was being watched. Slowly he turned and ran his eye over the rock face.

Nothing.

Then he looked up.

And there on the cliff top was the girl looking down at him. He had no idea how she had climbed up there. All he could imagine was that the tunnel from the cavern must run all the way through to the top of the cliff. A dangerous climb and one he was glad he hadn't attempted. He stared up at the girl with a mixture of fear and respect, then opened his mouth to call to her again.

But with a toss of her sandy hair she was gone.

"Kit!" came a shout.

5

It was Dad. He was standing by the point, beckoning furiously.

"Come here!" he bellowed.

Kit frowned. He'd been hoping to get back before Mum and Dad woke up. He set off toward the point, dreading the conversation that awaited him. Dad started it before he'd even arrived.

"What the hell do you think you're playing at? We've been worried sick about you!"

Mum appeared round the side of the point and hurried across to join Dad. Kit reached them a moment later.

"Well?" said Dad.

"I'm sorry," said Kit. "I didn't mean to worry you. I thought you were asleep."

"What's that got to do with it?"

"Well, I . . . I thought—"

"You didn't think anything." Dad glowered at him. "That's the problem. You didn't use your brain. If you had done, it might have occurred to you that this is an unknown place with unknown dangers, and it's a pretty stupid idea to go wandering off on your own."

"Yeah, I know. I'm sorry."

"It was stupid, Kit."

"I know. I'm really sorry."

"Kit," said Mum. "Until we know more about this place, we must stick together. Do you understand that?"

"Yes."

"If you think we're being unreasonable, say so."

"You're not being unreasonable."

"We were really worried about you."

"I'm sorry. Honestly. But listen, I've got some things to tell you."

"Like what?" said Dad.

Kit turned to him. "I've seen that man again. The one I told Mum about. I don't know if she's . . . I mean . . . mentioned him or anything."

"She's told me what you told her," said Dad. The tone of his voice was enough to convince Kit that his father believed in the man exactly as much as Mum did. But he'd expected that.

"Well, I've seen him again," he went on. "He was lying over the end of that scar."

He nodded toward it as casually as he could, but a shudder still passed through him at the sight of it. It looked so innocent now. The water was placid, almost beguiling. Yet the memory of what it could do was all too fresh. Dad looked over the scar, then back at him.

"He was lying over the end of that thing?"

"Yes."

"How was he lying?"

"He was sprawled over it. He had his face pressed down against the top of the rock."

"So you couldn't possibly have recognized him."

"But I did recognize him."

"You couldn't have done. It's too far from the shore. According to your story, you've only ever had a fleeting glimpse of this man. The only way you could be certain it was him lying there would be to get nearer to him. And that would mean walking out along the scar."

Kit said nothing.

"And you didn't do that, I hope," said Dad.

"Of course not."

"Are you sure?"

"I'm not stupid."

He shifted from one foot to the other. Mum spoke.

"Kit, are you lying?"

"No, Mum."

She held his eyes for what seemed a long time.

"Kit, you won't forfeit our trust if you own up. You'll only forfeit it if you don't."

He dropped his eyes.

"Did you walk along the scar?" said Mum.

"Yes."

He waited for the shouting to start. But instead he felt Mum's hand on his shoulder.

"Tell us what you saw."

He looked up at her again.

"It was him. I promise you. I know you both think I've imagined this. But I saw the same man. He was naked. He had bruises over his body. I thought he was dead at first, but then I saw his arm move. That's why I went out along the scar. I thought I could maybe help him."

"What happened?" said Dad.

"I gave him water. I had a little bottle with me."

"Did he speak to you?"

"No, he just drank some of the water and looked up at me with these weird eyes he's got, and then . . ." He thought of the waves, the cry over the sea, the moving shadow. The dash to safety.

"And then?" said Mum.

"I saw the sea was getting up. So I ran back to the shore."

"You did the right thing."

"But I left the man there."

"You still did the right thing."

"I left him to die!" Kit looked from one to the other. "I got back to the shore and looked round, and he was gone. A wave washed him off."

"You actually saw it wash him off?" said Dad.

"No, but . . ." He stopped. For a moment they had been starting to believe him. He knew it. But now the doubts were back in their eyes. "Why would I make this up?" he said.

"I don't know," said Dad. "Why would you?"

"Don't either of you believe me?"

Neither spoke, and that was answer enough. He looked away.

"I've seen a girl, too," he muttered.

"A girl?" said Mum.

"I suppose you don't believe that, either."

"Kit," she said. "Don't be angry with us. We both accept that you've seen something that's upset you."

"Somebody, you mean."

"All right, somebody. We don't doubt that, okay? But what you're describing is hard for us to get our heads round. You must see why."

"I suppose."

"Now, what about this girl?"

He told them everything this time, even his hunt in the cave.

"I'm glad you didn't go farther in," said Mum. She looked at Dad. "She must be some climber. And the cavern must be the start of a blowhole."

50

"Sounds like it," said Dad. "If we go up to the cliff top, I expect we'll find the opening where the tunnel comes out." He thought for a moment. "I don't know about this guy Kit keeps seeing, but if there's a girl, then there's got to be other people on the island too. I think it's time we did some exploration."

"Okay," said Mum. "But let's get a bit more food inside us first. We don't know when we're going to eat again. We can finish off those rolls and some of the fruit."

They made their way back to the cove, ate a hurried second breakfast and set off up the slope.

"Seems to me," said Dad, "that the obvious thing is to make straight for the top of this hill. I know it's a bit of a climb, but it should give us a view of the whole island."

"Makes sense," said Mum. "But I wish it weren't quite so high."

"I know what you mean," said Dad, puffing already.

Kit said nothing. He was still feeling raw, not just about the hideousness of what had happened to the man, but also about Mum's and Dad's reactions to his story. He wasn't even sure they believed him about the girl. They were acting as though they did but he had a feeling they were just humoring him. He felt another of those strange pockets of cold air enter him, hold him, and then slip away.

He glanced at Mum and Dad. They showed no sign of having felt anything and were pushing on determinedly up the slope. He decided to say nothing. They'd probably only think he was making this up too. He climbed slowly after them, wary of this unfamiliar ground. The hill had looked straightforward from below, but close up he could see that the slope was littered with clefts and bumps and tiny potholes that could trip him or turn an ankle if he wasn't careful. It was hard ground, too; the grass was withered and interspersed with rocks and the dried-out river beds he had noticed when they first entered the cove, all of which made the ascent more difficult.

But somehow he was making progress up the hill. He was high enough now to look down on the top of the cliff at the point where the cavern lay. A rough path ran along it, bordered by bushes and scrubby vegetation. Close to the cliff edge was what looked like a gaping mouth in the ground. It had to be the top of the blowhole the girl had climbed through to escape from him.

He stopped and ran his eye over the hill, the cliffs, the cove. There was no sign of anyone apart from the three of them. He tried to work out his bearings. The sun had risen over to his right, so that must mean that the cavern was on the west side of the island and that the cove faced north. Whoever lived on this island had to be somewhere to the south, on the other side of this great hill.

"Kit!" called Mum.

He turned and saw Mum and Dad waiting for him farther up the slope. He hurriedly caught them up.

"You all right?" said Mum.

"Fine."

"You sure?"

"Yeah, don't fuss."

"Okay." She gave him a smile, then nodded down toward the slope. "Look at those dried-out streams. This island's had a difficult few years."

"A difficult few centuries more like," said Dad. He pointed to the eastern shore. "Look over there."

Kit stared down the slope and saw more bushes, more scrubby vegetation, and also the thing that had attracted Dad's attention: a large, oval-shaped hollow with what looked like discolored grass in it.

"What's that?" he said.

"A silted-up mere," said Dad.

"A mere?"

"Kind of a marshy lake. Some of the streams from this hill would have run down into it. You can see the tracks they made all down the slope. That mere was probably one of the water sources for the community that lived here. When it dried out, the people would have had to pack up. Unless they had another water source on the island."

Kit thought of the girl again. There had to be another water source. There had to be a community here.

"Let's go on climbing," he said.

"Okay," said Mum.

They carried on up the slope and now he was the one forcing the pace. He felt a sudden, desperate urge to reach the top, to look over to the south and find out where the girl lived.

"Hey, Kit!" called Dad from behind. "What's got into you? First you dawdle, now you can't go quick enough!"

He didn't answer, didn't slow down. He had to find out about the people who lived on this island. If he could just meet them and see the girl and maybe get them to tell him who the dead man was, then Mum and Dad would have to see that he'd been telling the truth. He hurried on toward the summit. The ground was growing rockier now, though there were still patches of grass and even some slightly marshy hollows where water had clearly once been plentiful. He saw the top just ahead and forced himself on until he reached it.

It was worth the climb for the view alone. He stood on the highest point, a large rectangular plateau of rock, and turned full circle, scanning every direction. He could take in practically the whole island from here. It was only small, probably not more than about three miles long by one mile wide. To the north he could see the cove, the bluff, the scar, the great offshore rock; to the east and west low cliffs all the way along the shoreline; and to the south an undulating valley that stretched from the base of this great hill toward another much smaller peak about two miles away.

There was no sign of any people in the valley. All he saw was a confusion of bushes, trees, and mangy vegetation intermingled with boulders, screes, rocky hollows, cairns, and what looked like twisting tracks caused by the natural contours of the terrain. What lay at the southern tip of the island he could not tell; it was hidden behind that other peak. Mum and Dad arrived, both out of breath, and joined him on the plateau. Kit turned to them.

"I still can't see any people," he said.

They all stared down into the valley.

"Neither can I," said Dad after a moment.

"No sign of any water, either," said Mum.

"There's another silted-up mere," said Dad, shielding his eyes from the sun with cupped hands. "In fact there're two. One down there on the eastern slope—see it?—just above that bit where the cliff juts out. And I'm sure that's another one at the base of the other hill."

Kit could see them, two dried-out patches of marsh that had once been lakes fed by streams.

"But where are the people?" he said. "There must be a community here."

He saw Mum turn to look at him.

"I did see the girl," he said. "I'm not making this up. I did see her."

"Then we're bound to find her," said Mum. "And her people."

"But where are they?"

"There's only one place they can be," said Dad. "They're

not hiding in this valley. I'm pretty sure we'd see some sign of them from up here. And they'd need to be near a water source. So if there's one on the other side of that hill over there, then that's where they'll be."

"Come on, then," said Kit. "Let's find them."

And he set off down the slope toward the valley.

It was a matter of honor now. He had to prove to Mum and Dad that the girl existed, that her people existed, and if possible that the man existed. The sooner they checked out what was on the other side of that hill, the sooner he would be proved right. He tramped on down the slope.

"Kit!" called Dad. "Don't rush ahead! Slow down!"

He slowed down reluctantly, and let them catch up.

"We need to keep together," said Dad. "We don't know the island, remember. And the slope's treacherous. You don't want to go down it too fast."

He soon found Dad was right. Going down this side was much harder than climbing up the previous one. It was steeper than it had looked from the top, and the potholes and clefts were more numerous. Mum and Dad were making a zigzag descent and he did the same, studying the ground below him for stumbling points.

Slowly they drew closer to the floor of the valley. The sun was brighter now but the air was still cool, though noticeably less chilly than it had been around the cove and with none of those strange icy patches that seemed to pass through him. He glanced around him. There was a different character to this part of the island. It was less forbidding than the cove, perhaps by virtue of the trees and bushes, withered though they were.

He wondered what time it was. He hadn't bothered to put his watch on, since it wasn't working, and Mum and Dad weren't wearing theirs either, presumably for the same reason, but it had to be close to midday. They carried on down the slope and at last the ground flattened out, and they found themselves at the bottom with the bushy fringe of the valley before them.

"I suggest we make straight for the hill," said Dad. "We can explore the valley some other time if we want to." He glanced over the various tracks in front of them, then nodded toward the nearest one. "This looks like the most direct route."

But it turned out to be a circuitous one. The uneven nature of the land, the twisting paths, and the constant appearance of rocky impediments or patches of vegetation kept forcing them off to the right or left. Sometimes, too, the trees were close enough together to form miniature woods that they had to skirt or pick their way through.

Yet in spite of the obstacles they kept the hill in view and pushed on. Around the middle of the valley they came face-to-face with one of the cairns they had seen from the big peak, a scruffy, misshapen thing barely higher than Kit's shoulder and with several stones knocked askew. They walked on past it but soon came upon another, this one slightly larger and better preserved.

"I wonder how old these are," said Mum.

"Don't suppose we'll ever know," said Dad. "But I wouldn't be surprised if they go back a few centuries. Look at those stones. They're really old and crumbly, like the ones used in the ruins back at the cove. I'd say this place has a long history of settlement, even if it's come to an end now."

"Or coming to an end," said Kit.

Dad glanced at him.

"You really are convinced there are people here, aren't you?"

"Yeah."

"Well, you may be right. But I'll tell you one thing. Even if there is a community on the other side of that hill, they won't be here much longer. The island's dying. Anyone can see that. Everything's starved of water."

They walked on, passing more cairns on the way, and gradually drew closer to the hill. Kit had been hoping there might be a way round the base, but he quickly saw there wasn't. The eastern and western slopes fell almost directly over the shoreline and conjoined with boulders, screes, and other rocks rising in massive formations from the cliff tops.

"We'll never get past all that stuff," said Dad, echoing his thoughts. "We'll just have to climb to the top of this one too."

But it turned out to be much easier than the other peak. Not only was this hill about half the size of its companion, but the ground was less treacherous too. There were fewer potholes and the grass was softer underfoot. Kit could even feel traces of moisture in it. Perhaps there was water here after all. The closer they drew to the top, the softer the ground became, though rocky outcrops still covered much of the terrain. He was starting to feel nervous now. Within the next few minutes he would be proved right or wrong. He reached the summit and looked down.

Below him was a tract of grassland sloping away toward the south. Most of it was divided by drystone walls into enclosures, some with sheep in them, some with goats, some with geese. Other enclosures had been given over to the cultivation of crops. On the eastern side was a mere fed by a stream that ran down to it from higher up the slope. Below the enclosures was a cluster of stone cottages, most of them no bigger than the ruins in the cove, though two were larger and a third—slightly apart from the rest—was of substantial size. At the southernmost point of the island was a harbor formed by a rocky promontory to the right and a stone breakwater to the left. Moored inside were some long black boats.

"I told you," Kit murmured, as much to himself as to Mum and Dad.

"You were right," said Mum. "But where is everyone?"

He'd been wondering the same thing. They'd found a settlement but no people. No smoke was rising from the chimneys. No voices could be heard. Even the animals were silent.

"Come on," said Dad. "Let's see if we can find someone here."

They set off down the slope toward the village, Kit watching not just for people but especially for the sandy-haired girl. But she was nowhere to be seen. Mum nodded to the mere over to the left.

"So there is water on the island."

"Yes, but not much," said Dad. "It's going the same way as the other meres. Look at it. It's starting to silt up. There's water in the middle, but you can see the marsh encroaching from the outside and moving in toward the center. Give it a bit more time and you'll see reeds and grass and vegetation and other stuff growing all over it. And the marsh'll keep pushing in toward the center until the whole mere's useless. If the people here are depending on that for their water, they're in big trouble."

"The animals don't look too healthy," said Kit. "And neither do the crops."

"That's hardly surprising," said Dad. "The ground's ruined because everything's drying up."

"But where is everyone?" said Mum.

As she spoke, a tall man with fiery red hair and a thick beard emerged from the nearest of the cottages. He looked about fifty. He was wearing a coarse gray shirt buttoned up to the neck and heavy gray trousers with high boots. He stared at them in silence, his expression anything but friendly. Dad smiled and called down to him.

"Hello there!"

The man gave no answer. More figures started to appear from the other cottages, bearded men clothed in exactly the same way as this one and women with thick gray dresses down to their ankles and shawls over their heads. There was no mistaking the hostility in their faces. Dad forced another smile.

"Forgive us for this intrusion," he said quickly. "But our boat ran into the rock off the north end of the island. She nearly foundered but we managed to beach her in the cove. We'd be grateful for any help you can give us."

None of the islanders replied. Instead they turned into a huddle and started muttering. Kit did a quick count. Ten men, eight women. No sign of the girl or any other young person. Of the men, half looked to be in their forties and the rest in their fifties or sixties. The same was true of the women, though one, a bent old creature for whom the word *crone* might have been invented, had to be at least eighty.

They looked thin and underfed, yet also tough and determined; and he didn't like the aggressive gestures from both the men and the women. Suddenly the red-haired man turned and, to Kit's horror, pointed straight at him. An angry murmur ran through the group.

"Kit," said Dad out of the corner of his mouth. "I don't like the way they're looking at you. Move behind me. You, too, Sarah."

"I'm standing right next to you," she said.

"So am I," said Kit.

Dad opened his mouth to answer but before he could do so, the men and women broke up and hurried off to their cottages. A few seconds later they were back with clubs in their hands.

"My God!" said Mum.

Dad took a step toward them, his hand held high.

"Now wait! We mean you no harm! We come in friendship!"

But at that moment the islanders charged.

6

"We come in friendship!" shouted Dad.

His words had no effect. The islanders rushed on, led by the red-haired man. Dad threw a glance at Mum and Kit.

"Run for it!" he snapped.

But suddenly another voice cut through the air.

"Brand!"

To Kit's relief the red-haired man ground to a halt. The other islanders did the same, but it was clear they were struggling to restrain themselves. He looked from face to face. Some were snorting like animals, some simply stared with a kind of glazed loathing, and there was no disguising the fact that he was the focus of their attention.

He shuddered. He'd never seen a hatred like this before. It was as deep as it was inexplicable. He saw hands twitching round clubs, fists beating against thighs. Some of the women had bent down to pick up stones. He searched for the person who had called out to stop the charge.

It was an old man, now walking up from one of the cottages farther down the slope. He, too, was bearded and dressed in the same manner as the other men, but he was much older, probably in his seventies or eighties. Like the other islanders, he looked gaunt and underfed, but his gait was surprisingly brisk, and he clearly had some authority here.

Exactly how much was hard to tell. The islanders had stopped at his command, but none had turned to look at him. Their eyes remained on Kit. The man made his way to the front of the group and took up a position at their head. Dad spoke in a low voice to Mum and Kit.

"I'll try and talk to this guy. But keep your eyes on the group."

He took a step forward and at once the red-haired man raised his club.

"Brand!" said the old man sharply.

Slowly and with obvious reluctance the islander lowered his club. A ripple of tension passed round the group, and Kit sensed a clash of allegiances. One thing was clear: If this old man was in charge, he was only just in charge.

"We mean you no harm," said Dad. "We only wish to ask for help."

Another ripple ran round the group, an angrier one this time, followed by suspicious glances in their direction. Mum leaned forward and whispered urgently to Dad.

"Jim, we've got to get away. They're not going to help us. And they're looking daggers at Kit."

"I know," he whispered back. "But we mustn't run, okay? That might provoke another charge." He raised his voice and spoke to the old man. "It's clear that we've disturbed your community. We apologize for that. We have no wish to intrude upon you. We'll return to the cove now and leave you in peace. But if there is any way you can help us repair our boat, we'd be most grateful. Once again, we apologize for disturbing you."

And with a formal bow he turned and ushered Mum and Kit toward the slope. They set off back up the hill, Kit pushing ahead as fast as he could. Dad caught him by the arm and slowed him down.

"Easy, Kit. Try not to look like you're hurrying." Dad glanced over his shoulder. "Oh, God, they're coming after us."

Kit looked back and to his horror saw the islanders surging forward again. But now a dispute seemed to have broken out among them. The old man was arguing with several at once, in particular the man called Brand. Yet even as they argued, they kept coming on.

"Keep moving," said Dad. "And get ready to run if I give the word."

They hurried on up the slope, all three watching over their shoulders. The argument among the islanders had now intensified, and many were gesticulating at the old man. Then suddenly they stopped, and the old man stepped forward alone.

Mum, Dad, and Kit stopped too, and watched.

"I think he wants to talk," said Mum.

"I don't think he wants to talk," said Dad. "I don't think he wants to have anything to do with us."

Kit had been thinking the same thing. It was obvious from the old man's manner that although he intended to speak to them, he found the task distasteful. He approached them as though they were plague victims. His eyes avoided theirs; his face wore an expression of disgust; his body was half turned to the side as if he wished to present as little of himself to them as possible. He stopped several feet from them.

"Thank you for speaking to us," said Dad.

The old man did not answer. He simply stood there, his eyes fixed on the ground. Farther down the slope the other islanders looked on. Kit studied the man. He looked frailer close up and though his beard covered much of his face, the ravages of hunger were clear to see. Dad waited patiently, then, when the old man remained silent, spoke again.

"Forgive me, but . . . do you understand me?"

The old man did not look up. But he answered this time.

"I understand you completely."

His accent sounded strange. It was harsh and clipped. Kit couldn't place it at all. And there was something about the way he'd said "completely" that suggested he was talking about more than just an understanding of Dad's words. Dad spoke again.

"My name's Jim Warren. This is my wife, Sarah. And my son, Kit."

The old man said nothing.

"May I ask your name, sir?" said Dad.

"Names are of no importance."

The old man spoke the words with a kind of blunt finality that seemed to suggest nothing further needed to be said on the subject.

"I see," said Dad slowly. "Even so, it would be useful to know how I might address you."

"Names are of no importance."

This time Kit heard impatience in the old man's voice. There was a silence, and it was clear that Dad was at a loss for what to say next. But the old man spoke first.

"Your boat is in the cove?"

"That's correct, sir."

"How serious is the damage?"

"The rudder's broken. I can steer with an oar but not very easily."

"Does your boat have a leak?"

"I've managed to patch it up for the moment."

"Then my advice to you is that you sail away immediately."

Again the tone of finality. Dad looked at the old man, but he continued to stare down at the ground.

"Very well," said Dad, after a pause. "We'll sail away. But perhaps you could advise me on our position. We've lost our bearings and our compasses aren't working for some reason. We know the cove faces north, but which way should we sail to get to the nearest land?"

The old man shrugged.

"What difference does it make? North, south, east, west—you have come from evil and you will return to evil whichever way you sail."

Kit felt a wave of anger run through him. The old man's contempt for them was bad enough. This open insult was too much to bear.

"How do you know we've come from evil?" he snarled.

"Kit," said Dad quietly. "Don't get involved."

"How do you know we've come from evil?" Kit ignored the warning glances from Mum and Dad and glared at the old man. "Eh? How do you know?"

"I have nothing to say to you," came the reply.

"You don't know anything about us."

"I know everything I need to know."

"What's that supposed to mean?"

"Kit," said Mum quietly. "Leave it."

"I'm not leaving it!"

"Kit!" warned Dad.

But Kit fumed on.

"You talk about evil like we're the bad guys here. What about your people coming to attack us? There's three of us and a whole stack of you. And you've all got clubs. Isn't that evil?"

"Kit!" said Dad. "That's enough!"

65

"Go back to your world," said the old man coldly. "And leave us to ours."

"We will," said Dad quickly.

The old man started to walk away. Kit felt Dad's hand close round his arm and pull him toward the hill. But he tugged himself free. He had one last thing to say to the old man, and he was going to say it no matter what.

"I saw a man die this morning!" he yelled.

The old man stopped but did not look back.

"He was lying on the scar by the cove," said Kit. "But a wave washed him off. He had bruises all over his body."

"I have nothing to say to you," said the old man.

"He must be one of your people."

Kit felt Dad's hand round his arm again. This time he didn't pull away. The old man continued to stare down the slope toward the other islanders. Then he spoke.

"But all our people are before you. There are no others on this island."

Kit thought of the girl again. "But—"

"No one is missing," said the old man. "We are all here." He turned briefly toward them. "You will be safe for twenty-four hours. After that I cannot say."

The eerie cry that Kit had heard before sounded across the sea. He looked round at Mum and Dad, then turned to the old man again.

"What was that sound?"

"I heard nothing," said the old man.

"It was a cry. It came from the sea."

"The sea makes many sounds."

"I heard it too," said Mum.

"So did I," said Dad.

The old man sniffed the air.

"I heard nothing," he said, and moved off down the slope.

Kit felt Dad's hand pull at his arm again.

"Come on, lad. Let's go."

They set off up the slope toward the top of the hill, all three glancing over their shoulders. But the islanders had not followed. They were still standing there in a group, watching in silence. The old man joined them and watched too. A stillness hung over the village.

"I'll be pleased to get over the brow of the hill," Mum murmured. "The sooner those people are out of sight, the better I'll feel."

"They're probably thinking the same thing about us," said Dad.

They reached the top of the hill and turned one last time. The islanders were still there, watching.

"Come on," said Dad. "Let's get away from this place."

They made their way down the other side of the hill in the direction of the valley. Kit felt a powerful urge to run down the slope, dangerous though it was. He felt exposed on this open ground, and he knew he wouldn't feel secure until there was a good distance between them and the islanders. But he checked himself and picked his path carefully, watching the ground ahead for tripping points. The valley drew nearer with its welcome profusion of trees and bushes and other hiding places. He glanced back up the slope to the top of the hill, half expecting the islanders to be there watching, but he saw no one. Dad stopped them at the valley floor.

"We'll keep to the hollows and wooded areas on the way back, okay?"

"Okay," said Mum. "Do we need to climb that big peak again?"

"No, we can skirt round the base, I think. The sides aren't as sheer as the ones on this little hill."

There was a silence. Kit looked at Mum and Dad and saw for the first time how pale they were. He swallowed hard. Somehow he hadn't realized that they'd been as frightened as he was, and perhaps most frightened of all *for* him.

"I'm sorry," he said. "About the outburst."

"It's okay," said Dad.

"I couldn't help myself."

"It's okay."

"He just got to me, that old man."

"I know."

"And he heard the noise, that cry from the sea. He kind of flinched. I saw him."

"So did I," said Mum.

"The islanders heard it too," said Dad. "I saw them look at each other, and a couple of them turned toward the sea."

"What's making that sound?" said Kit. "It freaks me out."

"I don't know," said Dad. "But if it's any consolation, it freaks me out too."

Kit glanced up the slope again, but there was still no sign of anyone. He turned back to Mum and Dad.

"Why do they hate us?"

Mum and Dad exchanged glances.

"Okay," said Kit. "Why do they hate me?"

"I don't know," said Dad. "But I don't intend us to hang around long enough to find out."

"Is it safe to put off in *Windflower*?" said Mum.

"It's got to be safer than staying here."

"But can you steer the boat? You said the broken rudder was causing a drag and making it hard to use the oar."

"It was, and it's going to be a problem. I'll just have to do my best." Dad looked about him. "What's really bothering me is the weather. The wind's picking up again and it's still from the north. We could have big problems clawing *Windflower* out of the cove. And even if we do get her out, I'm not sure how she'll fare in heavy weather. I don't fancy handling her in a storm with just an oar and a dodgy rudder causing havoc underneath the hull. We'd better pray for a calm sea and a wind that's steady but not too strong."

"And preferably not from the north."

"Exactly."

But it quickly became apparent as they made their way across the valley that this prayer was not going to be answered. Not only did the wind remain resolutely in the north, but it strengthened with each passing minute. By the time they had scrambled across the hollows and crags at the base of the great peak and made their way round into the cove, it was clear that there would be no chance of setting off today.

They stood by the tents and stared down at the water. Gusts were now shivering over it. *Windflower* was afloat again and seemed to be having no difficulty riding the waves that came scurrying in from the sea, but Kit knew it was too risky to set off in these conditions. Dad shook his head.

"I can't believe this wind's picked up again so quickly. It was quite calm earlier."

"It picked up just as quickly last night," said Mum. "When we were sailing through the fog."

Kit frowned. Last night seemed such a long time ago now. He found himself wondering what this night would bring. He looked up at the sky. The sun was hidden behind a bank of cloud, and there was an ashen quality about the light, as though a veil was being pulled over them. It couldn't be later than mid-afternoon, yet it felt like dusk.

They made a hot pot and sat down on the grass in front of the tents to eat it. Kit noticed that Mum and Dad were glancing up the slope as much as he was.

"Do you think the islanders'll come for us?" he said.

"Don't know," said Dad. "I certainly hope not. The old man gave us twenty-four hours. With any luck they'll leave us alone for tonight, though I don't doubt there'll be trouble if we're not gone by the end of tomorrow. They obviously don't like strangers here."

"But why?" said Mum.

"Some religious thing. Got to be. Those drab gray costumes they're all wearing. All that stuff about evil. I bet they're some kind of religious community who've retreated to this island to keep themselves pure and untainted by the world outside."

"They didn't seem very pure to me."

"Nor me," said Kit.

"Even so," Dad went on, "I reckon that's what they are. And pretty fanatical, too. They're probably one of those groups that embrace poverty and the simple life."

"Simple?" said Mum. "Primitive, more like. They're running out of water, they're underfed, their clothes are frayed, the cottages are falling down." She thought for a moment. "I still don't get why they're so unfriendly. I thought the whole point of the religious life was to learn to love your neighbor."

"Well, they obviously don't buy into that here," said Dad. He glanced up the slope again. "I'm pretty sure we'll be all right tonight. The old guy's authority's a bit shaky, but I reckon if he's told them we're going to sail away in the next twenty-four hours, they'll leave us alone. But we need to be on our guard in case some of the hotheads like that Brand character decide to come for us."

"I didn't like the look of him at all," said Mum.

Kit listened in silence. He hadn't liked the look of any of the islanders. It wasn't just the man called Brand. There had been other men who had looked every bit as dangerous, and women, too: tough, hard-bitten women who had glared at him with as much venom as the men. He glanced down at *Windflower* rocking in the swell.

"So what are we going to do?"

"What I suggest," said Dad, "is that we separate the things we need for tonight and then pack everything else aboard *Windflower* to be ready for an early departure in the morning. And let's just hope the wind's kind enough to let us out of the cove."

"So we're still sleeping in the tents tonight?"

"Yeah, we can't sleep aboard *Windflower* with her rolling over at low tide."

"Can't we kedge her out to deeper water?"

"We could, but she's moored nice and snug. I don't think there's any point in moving her." Dad patted him on the arm. "I know you're worried about the islanders, but I'm pretty sure we'll be okay."

"I haven't seen anyone," said Mum. "And you'd think if they were after our blood, they'd have been here by now. It's not as if they don't know where we are."

"That's true," said Dad.

Kit said no more, yet he remained uneasy. They finished their meal. Mum made some tea and they sat there, sipping in silence. The sky clouded over further, and once again Kit felt a sense of premature dusk. He saw a shadowy form down in the cove and narrowed his eyes. It was over by the farthest of the stone ruins, and it was moving toward the bluff. He stared at it, but to his annoyance a splinter of light from what was left of the sun now broke through the clouds and scattered the image. When the gray returned, he found the shadow was gone. He felt another of those strange chills pass through him.

"It's cold," said Mum.

He looked sharply round at her. "Did you feel it?"

"Feel what?"

"The cold."

"I just said I felt cold."

"No, I mean . . . a different kind of cold, a kind of . . ." He frowned. "A kind of cloud of cold air passing through you."

"I just felt cold, Kit." Mum started to gather up the plates. "No big deal about it."

He said nothing and looked back toward the cove. There were no more shadows, no more patches of cold air, for the moment at least. Dad stood up.

"Come on. Let's sort out what we need for tonight and get everything else aboard *Windflower*."

They stowed all the nonessentials, then checked *Windflower* over again to make sure the mooring lines were secure. The sun dipped farther; the gray in the sky deepened. They returned to the tents and sat down again on the grass. Darkness slowly descended. Suddenly Kit gave a start.

"What is it?" said Mum.

"I thought I saw a figure."

"Where?"

"Down by the bluff. I saw one there earlier. Least I think I did."

"You should have said."

He didn't answer and went on staring toward the bluff.

"There!" he said suddenly. He pointed. "Heading past the first of the ruins. Can you see it?"

"No," said Mum.

"Dad?"

"No." Dad watched for a moment, then shook his head. "There's no one down there. You're imagining it."

"But—"

"You're imagining it." Dad pulled out the big flashlight, switched it on, and shone the beam down over the far side of the cove. "See?"

It was true. There was nobody there. Kit didn't know whether to feel relief or disappointment.

"We must keep our eyes open," said Dad. "But we mustn't let our nerves make us see things that aren't there." He switched off the flashlight and darkness settled round them again. "We might as well turn in," he said. "We didn't get much sleep last night, and we've got an early start."

Kit stifled a yawn. He'd been exhausted for hours and the thought of sleep was tantalizing, but he was afraid of closing his eyes. Maybe he'd been mistaken about the figure moving by the bluff, but the islanders were real enough, and they could be lurking anywhere.

"I'll stay up and keep watch for a bit," said Dad. "You two can turn in."

"Are you sure?" said Mum.

"Yeah, but listen—it might be best if we sleep in our clothes. Just rough it for tonight, okay? In case there's, you know . . ."

"Any trouble."

"Yeah."

Kit said nothing. He could feel another chill passing through him. He held his breath and waited, trembling, until it was gone.

"Kit?" said Mum. "Are you okay? I saw you shiver."

"Just cold."

"All right." She gave him a kiss. "Go on. Turn in. You'll be warmer in your sleeping bag. And try not to worry. Everything'll be fine."

He crawled into his tent, burrowed inside the sleeping

bag, and pulled the top right over his head so that he was cocooned inside. He was warm now, almost too warm. He lay like this for some time, listening to his own frantic breathing. He was still trembling.

He closed his eyes and tried to urge sleep upon himself, and somehow it came. Yet it was a fitful sleep troubled by dreams of roaring winds and tearing seas, of Brand and the islanders flailing clubs, of the dark shape moving beneath the water, and of the man lying on the scar, the man who had looked into his eyes and then been washed away.

Suddenly he was awake. He was sitting bolt upright, the sleeping bag thrown back, his head pressed against the roof of the tent. Once again he was trembling. He stared about him, unsure what had woken him. He felt another chill enter his body. It seemed to envelop the whole tent.

"Go away," he murmured. "Whatever you are, go away."

The chill left him. He found he was clenching his fists. He made himself unclench them, then crawled to the door of the tent and pushed his head out. The wind seemed to have eased a little, but it was still from the north. He glanced to the left. Dad had turned in and there was a sound of snoring from the other tent.

Out here all was dark. He saw no moon or stars, just dusky clouds and dusky sky. Yet for all that the water in the cove had a strange luminosity. He saw a wave rolling in from the sea, a long wall of water no more than three feet high yet somehow out of place among the snapping wavelets in the cove. It drove in toward the shore, rocking *Windflower* as it passed under her, then spent itself on the shingle. There was a hissing sound on the beach, then the wave fell back and the water in the cove relaxed. Yet he sensed once again the restlessness in the sea.

Then he saw a shadow moving toward him.

7

He stiffened. It was a figure, but whether it was a man or a woman he couldn't tell. He watched closely. It had been heading straight for him, but now it stopped, then a moment later set off up the slope as though anxious to gain the higher ground. Suddenly he saw who it was.

The girl.

It was the quick movements that gave her away. He couldn't see her face yet, nor much of her body, and he wasn't sure she had seen him. He kept his eyes fixed upon her. She was still in view for the moment, but if she climbed much higher, the edge of the tent would cut her off. He wondered whether to call Mum and Dad.

But there seemed little point. He was sure this girl meant no harm. She was probably just curious. And he was too: curious to know who she was and why the old man had not acknowledged her existence earlier. One thing was clear: She wasn't like the other islanders. They had a uniformity of dress and manner, a sense of community. This girl didn't seem to belong to anyone.

She had stopped again and he found he could make her

out more clearly. She was so slender, so slight, yet so strong and agile. Again he was reminded of a dancer. He still wasn't sure whether she had seen him. She started to move up the slope again, and he eased his head farther out of the tent to keep her in view. She caught the movement at once and bolted into the darkness.

"Damn!" he muttered.

He scrambled out of the tent and stared after her. She was racing up the slope toward the eastern side of the hill. He glanced at Mum and Dad's tent, then back at the girl, and tore after her. He knew this was the last thing Mum and Dad would want him to do. But he had to find out more about this girl. She wasn't an enemy. He was convinced of that. And he sensed a desperation about her. She might be wild, but she also seemed very much alone.

She was well ahead of him already. He knew he'd never overtake her, but if he could just get a little closer to her, it might be possible to call out and persuade her to stop and talk. He wanted to know about the islanders. He wanted to know about her. He wanted to know about the eerie cry and the dark shape he'd seen moving beneath the water. She might even know about the strange man.

But any hopes he'd had of getting closer to her were fading. She'd seen that he was pursuing her and put on speed. She hared up the slope toward the rocky brow that bordered the eastern foothills of the great peak. Once she'd passed that, he knew he'd lose her. Dad had taken them that way when they returned from the valley, and there were loads of places where she could hide.

He struggled on even so, determined to keep her in view. She was close to the brow now, and he could see her hair bobbing about as she danced over the rough ground. She reached the top of the brow, stopped on the rock, and turned.

He stopped too, fighting to catch his breath. Above him the great hill reached up into the sky, tawny clouds drifting over it. He looked at the girl. She was standing there, motionless. He called out.

"I only want to talk to you!"

She didn't answer but didn't move away, either. He had the feeling she was no longer afraid of him—if she ever had been. He called out again.

"I promise I won't hurt you!"

Again she didn't answer. He took a step forward, but she turned at once and dropped from view. He cursed himself and rushed up the slope to the brow. Below him the eastern shore stretched away. Like so much of the island it was a mixture of rock, grass, and scrub with hollows and clearings and withered trees. Cairns littered the terrain. He didn't suppose he'd ever see her among all this.

But he was wrong. There she was, running down among the outcrops over to the right. He sized up the ground at the base of the brow. The girl had jumped, but he knew he'd never manage it. He climbed down as quickly as he could and set off after her.

But now he'd lost sight of her completely. He reached the outcrops where he had last seen her and stopped by the lip of a small hollow. She was somewhere close. He was sure of it. He could almost sense her watching him from some hidden place, perhaps even silently laughing at him. He stared about him, but all he saw were murky shapes.

He started to make his way down toward the cliffs. He wasn't quite sure why he was doing this. There seemed little point in looking further. The hillocks, rocks, hollows, and trees offered her a hundred places where she could go to ground. He heard the sigh of the surf as he drew closer to the sea. He reached the cliffs and looked down. They were not high at this point but they were sheer. He felt his head swim and stepped quickly back.

He stared about him again. Still no sign of the girl, yet as before he sensed her near him. He was starting to feel vulnerable now. He was pretty sure she wasn't dangerous, but this was her turf, not his. He started to make his way up the slope again. He should go back now. There was nothing to be gained by hanging around here, and Mum and Dad would only worry if they woke up and found him gone.

Suddenly he heard a sound farther up the slope.

A human sound. A kind of squeak.

He stopped and listened. It seemed to have come from somewhere to the left. He looked that way and saw a large outcrop blocking his way. He skirted it and moved on up the slope. All he heard now was the surf breaking on the cliffs behind him. Then he caught another sound. A loud smack.

He shuddered. Something was wrong and he was sure it involved the girl. He scanned the ground to his left and saw a patch of rocks farther up. He ran toward them as softly as he could. From the other side came a sharp cry. He threw himself against the largest of the rocks, inched toward the edge, and craned his head round.

Before him was a small clearing bordered by cairns and boulders. The girl was pushed up against a large flat-topped slab on the far side. Two men stood over her. He recognized them at once, even in the darkness. They had been close behind Brand during the confrontation at the village. They both looked about forty. One was swarthy and muscular, the other rat faced and lean with a scrawny beard. The swarthy one had the girl by the arm.

She was punching furiously at him with her free hand. He reached out and smacked her hard on the cheek. She gave a cry of pain and lashed out with both feet. One of the kicks hit the man on the knee. He gave a shout and stepped back, but his companion grabbed the girl before she could wriggle free.

She kicked out again, but he was too strong and forced her back over the surface of the rock. The swarthy man had recovered now and was moving forward again. He gave her another smack in the face, then elbowed the rat-faced man to the side and took his place over the girl.

Kit looked desperately about him. He couldn't fight these men any more than the girl could, but he had to do something. The swarthy man was pulling up the girl's skirt. She writhed and kicked out again. He mumbled something to his companion. The other man reached down and held her more firmly.

Kit ran into the clearing and stopped. He had no idea what he was going to do, and he was terrified. If the men turned, he would be in full view. But they were still unaware of him. Their attention was all on the girl. The swarthy man pushed his trousers down to his knees. The girl gave a scream.

Kit looked about him again. Nearby was one of the cairns. He ran over to it, seized a stone from the top, and hurled it over in the direction of the men. It clattered against one of the boulders on the far side of the clearing. Both men looked quickly in that direction. Kit ducked behind the cairn, then crawled to the side and peered round it.

The rat-faced man had taken a step back. The other was holding the girl by the thighs and had her legs spread on either side of him. He stared about him for a few seconds, then muttered something to his companion, who wandered out into the center of the clearing, his face moving from side to side as his eyes searched the darkness. The swarthy man watched him for a moment, then turned back to the girl.

Kit seized another stone. He knew he'd be spotted this time, but there was nothing else for it. He stood up and flung the stone toward the figures by the slab, praying it wouldn't hit the girl. It struck the swarthy man in the small of the back. He gave a scream of rage and pulled back from the girl. Kit started to duck, but the rat-faced man had seen him and was racing across the clearing toward him. The swarthy man was not far behind, tugging the resisting girl and struggling with his trousers at the same time.

"Run!" she screamed.

Kit ran toward the outcrop at the top of the clearing, clambered round the largest boulder, and stopped a few feet up the slope, keeping the rock between himself and the others. The rat-faced man stopped on the other side and glared up at him. The swarthy man arrived, his hand locked round the girl's wrist. She was still full of fight. He had literally had to drag her across the clearing yet she was still kicking and struggling to escape. The two men glanced at each other, then started to edge round the rock, each from different sides.

Kit turned and fled toward another outcrop farther up the slope. The swarthy man was no threat, being encumbered with the girl, but the rat-faced man was close behind. Kit reached the outcrop first and clambered over it to find himself facing a small hollow. He leaped into it, ran across to the other side, and scrambled up it to the higher ground. Then he stopped and turned.

The rat-faced man appeared at the far edge of the hollow and stopped, too, glowering across. A few moments later the second man joined him, still clutching the girl. She was struggling more fiercely than ever, but she caught Kit's eye and screamed again.

"Run!"

He didn't run. He knew he couldn't. If he left the girl now, they'd rape her for sure and maybe kill her too. He had to help her if he could, though he didn't know how. The rat-faced man jumped into the hollow. Kit took a step back up the slope. On the far side of the hollow the girl was still battling to break free. He saw the swarthy man squeeze both her wrists in an iron grip. But the other man was the danger right now. He was already edging across the hollow. Kit squared up to him, determined not to be fazed.

"Don't think killing me will do you any good. My dad's got a gun and he'll come looking for you."

The rat-faced man merely sneered and carried on. Kit felt a wave of hatred well up inside him, hatred for this man, hatred for his friend, hatred for their community. He put on a sneer of his own.

"I suppose you killed that man, too."

There was no answer.

"Eh?" said Kit, now brazen with defiance. "The man with the birthmark? Don't tell me you don't know who I mean. I saw him. He was naked. He had bruises all over him. And now he's dead. I suppose that's your doing."

The man reached the near side of the hollow and stopped there, scowling up the slope at him. Kit scowled back as fiercely as he could.

"You're evil. You and your friend. And your community. That old man from the village went on like it's me and my parents who are evil. Well, in my book it says rape's evil. It says killing's evil. So that makes you evil, not us."

He saw the rat-faced man tense for a spring and stepped quickly back. But at that moment the girl made a move. She stamped on the swarthy man's foot and kicked him hard in the shin. He gave a bellow, released one hand, and threw his arm back to strike her. Before he could do so, she bent down to his other hand and bit him hard in the wrist. He gave a shriek of pain and let go, then clutched at her again.

But she was gone.

Kit turned and ran, and this time kept running. The girl was so quick he felt sure she would get away. He tore up the slope, scrambling over rocks, around hillocks, through scrub. He heard the rat-faced man's savage breaths behind him.

Then suddenly they stopped.

He carried on a few more yards, then turned and looked back. The man was bent over some way down the slope, catching his breath. Kit stopped and searched the terrain below them. At first he saw nothing but ghostly shapes, then by the moonlight now shimmering through a gap in the clouds he made out two figures racing toward the cliffs. The girl was in front, the swarthy man behind. Both were moving fast, but the man was closing. Kit felt a flicker of panic. The girl was such a fast runner he had felt sure she would leave the man trailing.

But she was in trouble. He could see that now. She was limping. He watched in horror. The man was close now but so too was the cliff. She would have to stop soon and turn to the side. But she raced on toward the edge, the man reaching out to catch her.

And then she jumped.

"No!" shouted Kit.

He put a hand over his mouth and stared. The man drew up at the cliff edge, swayed there for a moment, then caught his balance and stooped to look over. The rat-faced man set off down the slope. Kit dropped to his knees and watched, trembling. The swarthy man went on staring over the edge for some time, then finally he straightened up and looked about him. A few minutes later the other man joined him and the two looked over the edge together.

Kit was still trembling. He could barely think. The men had turned now and were staring back up the slope. He had no idea whether they could see him. But he no longer cared. All he felt was guilt: guilt for running *Windflower* onto the rock, guilt for bringing Mum and Dad to this terrible place, and now guilt for something even worse. This girl's death was his fault too. He had run after her. He had chased her into the path of these men. He stared with loathing at the figures below him.

"I hate you," he spluttered. "I hate you almost as much as I hate myself."

The men turned and set off along the cliff top toward the southern end of the island. Kit spat in their direction.

"Yeah, go back to your village. Bastards!"

He watched them all the way along the cliff until they disappeared from view.

Of the girl he saw nothing more.

8

He made himself stand up. He had to get back to Mum and Dad. He had to tell them what had happened. Yet the pictures in his head paralyzed him. He saw the girl, the cliff, the sea. He saw the sheer drop.

"Tell Mum and Dad," he said. "Do it now."

He forced himself to move. But even as he stumbled up the slope, he found a new thought pushing itself into his mind.

"That's stupid," he said, and tramped on.

But the thought kept coming, and with it more pictures, pictures of the girl as he remembered her best: racing, jumping, dancing over rocks. He thought over what he had just seen. She had not hesitated. There had been no struggle on the cliff. She could have turned to the side, but she had run straight toward the edge and jumped from the very spot where he had stood only a short while ago.

He remembered how his head had swum. Yet he also remembered how the cliff at that point had not been high. It was dangerous enough, to be sure, and only a nutcase would jump off it in normal circumstances, but a wild girl like this who seemed capable of almost anything and who knew the island well might just do such a thing if the situation was desperate enough.

He climbed to the top of the brow and stared back down toward the cliff. It still didn't seem possible that she could have survived the fall, and even if she had done, what chance would she have on that unforgiving coastline? Once again the thought he had been trying to ignore forced itself into his mind.

And this time he knew he could not resist it.

He found Mum and Dad fast asleep. Both were snoring and clearly had no idea that he had been away. He mouthed a silent apology in their direction for what he was about to do next and an equally silent prayer that they wouldn't wake for at least a couple more hours. Then he hurried down to the beach.

Windflower and *Splinters* were afloat. The dinghy was moored by a long painter running to the shore, but this was slack as the tide was now high up the beach, and the onshore wind was keeping the boat pressed against the shingle. He untied the line, climbed aboard, and rowed out to *Windflower*. The breeze had definitely eased a little, but it was still gusty and still from the north. Dad would have big problems tacking *Windflower* out of the cove in the morning.

It wouldn't be easy in *Splinters* either but he was determined to try. He laid her alongside *Windflower* and made fast, then climbed aboard, fetched the dinghy's sailing gear from the cabin, and climbed back into the little boat. A squall rushed across the cove, bringing with it a ripple of waves. *Splinters* rocked from side to side as they passed. He clutched both gunwales and stared anxiously toward the sea. It looked a dark, unwelcoming place.

"Come on," he murmured. "You've got to do this."

He stepped the mast, shipped the rudder, pushed down the centerboard, and—after some hesitation—hoisted the sail. It flapped so loudly he felt sure the sound of it would wake Mum and Dad. But neither appeared on the embankment. He turned back toward the sea. The water in the cove was fairly calm, though still ruffled now and then by the gusts whipping in from the north, but the sea beyond the mouth looked choppy and unpredictable.

"Go," he told himself. "Just go."

He cast off the painter, hauled his wind, and set off on the first tack. It only took him a few yards before the beach loomed up ahead. He went about and headed across to the other side of the cove. Another short tack, but all would be short in this cramped space. So far *Splinters* felt comfortable enough. She was no speedster with her single sail and ungainly hull design, but she was at least seaworthy and he had plenty of confidence in her abilities.

He just wished he had as much in his own. Sailing at home was one thing, but out here on this unknown shore—and in the darkness—it was foolhardy in the extreme. But he knew he had to do this. If the girl was alive at the base of that cliff, she would need help.

He went about again and headed back toward the other side of the cove. *Splinters* was heeling sharply and seemed to be moving well, but she was making little headway toward the sea. There was so little room in which to maneuver. The opposite shore rushed toward him. He tacked and set off the other way, then tacked again, and again, and somehow after many more tacks brought the dinghy, as close hauled as he could get her, to the mouth of the cove.

But he knew that this was where the dangerous part really began.

First he had to deal with the scar. It was now buried

from view, not just in the darkness but beneath the sea itself. The high tide had turned it into a hidden sword waiting to cut the life from any vessel unlucky enough to stray too near. But he would have to take *Splinters* fairly close if he was to create the room he needed to tack his way out to sea.

He glanced quickly at the shore. He could see the point where the scar reached out into the sea, but after that nothing at all. It was just possible that with her shallow draft *Splinters* might sail right over it, but that wasn't a risk worth taking. He thrust the helm down and went about. *Splinters* plunged across the mouth of the cove toward the bluff on the other side.

He could see straightaway that he wasn't going to weather it on this tack. The seas were smashing into the bow and forcing the boat back toward the cove. He took the dinghy as close to the bluff as he dared, darting his eyes this way and that as he searched for outlying rocks. He saw white water ahead and drove the helm down again.

Splinters spun round onto the other tack and headed back toward the scar. He felt fairly certain that he'd weather it this time, but he tacked again as he drew near to make sure. The bluff was down to starboard now, but he went on beating out, determined to give himself plenty of room under his lee.

Finally, when he was convinced it was safe, he bore away and set off toward the eastern shore of the island. The bluff soon slipped past to starboard, rocks foaming around its base. *Splinters* was rolling now with the wind dead aft, and she seemed uncomfortable with the motion. To make matters worse, the waves were lifting the stern and trying to roll the hull round as they passed under her.

He sailed on, scanning the shore for the section of cliff where the girl had jumped. It was hard to make out the features of the coast in the darkness. The moon that had broken through to reveal the girl's final moments on the cliff top had disappeared again behind the night clouds, and apart from the white water breaking on the rocks and around the base of the cliffs, all was dark.

But this was not the only problem. If it was hard to see the shore, it was even harder to see the squalls. There was little likelihood of spotting the gusts racing up behind him or the more dangerous waves until the very last moment, and by then it was too late. The stern was already lifting and the hull twisting round. He met each movement of wind and sea as best he could, but he was feeling increasingly vulnerable. It seemed only a matter of time before he reacted too late and the boat skewed round into the path of the oncoming waves, one of which would certainly capsize her.

He craned forward suddenly and peered to starboard. He was sure he recognized the coastline over there. He stared at it, trying to watch the sea yet at the same time study the land. The sheer rock face, the low cliff—it had to be the place. He glanced over his shoulder at the dark waves rolling up astern. Somehow he'd have to jibe and sail across them.

He chose his moment, then hauled the mainsail over and set off toward the shore. To his surprise *Splinters* seemed more comfortable heading this way, in spite of the fact that she was shipping more spray from the seas breaking against her starboard side. But she was moving too fast. He couldn't go racing like this toward a dangerous shore.

He eased the sheet a fraction, and the dinghy slowed down to a more manageable speed. He had no doubts about the place now. This was definitely the spot. He could even make out the point where the girl had jumped. He stared through the darkness toward the base of the cliff.

That, too, was becoming easier to see as he drew closer, but the sight of it did nothing to strengthen his hope that the girl had survived. There were rocks all the way along. He hadn't seen them from above because they were hidden by the overhang of the cliff top, but from down here they stood out like fangs. Whether the angle of the girl's jump had taken her clear of them he could not tell. Then he saw something else that he had missed from above.

The darkened outlines of caves. They were quite large though none came anywhere near the size of the great cavern he had seen on the western shore. But they were caves nonetheless and a possible refuge for the girl. He thought of how intimately she must know the island, how confident she seemed in the things she could do, and how brave she was. Surely she hadn't tried to kill herself. She had far too much spirit for that. She might well have tried to escape from the men by jumping down to these caves. But whether she had killed herself in the process was another matter.

Then he saw her.

She was barely fifty yards away, standing on a ledge in the cliff face just to the side of one of the cave openings. Water was breaking on the rocks below her, but she seemed unconcerned by this; indeed, as he watched she jumped down to another ledge that was even closer to the sea. Suddenly she waved.

But it wasn't a greeting. He could see that. She was trying to direct him to the right. He stared that way and frowned. All he could see were massive rocks. She must be out of her mind. He wasn't going to take *Splinters* over there. But she went on waving him in that direction. He searched the shore again but still saw no place to land.

Suddenly she leaped off the ledge onto a boulder below her. He could see water breaking over the outer edge of it, but she ignored this and jumped straight over to another boulder farther up. She was heading to the right, picking her way from rock to rock with reckless skill, sometimes jumping through breaking spray. He saw no trace of the limp she had had earlier.

He hauled his wind and brought *Splinters* round to keep the girl in view. But he was growing desperately uneasy. The boat was now close to the shore with the biggest rocks just a short distance up to starboard. The girl was still jumping and scrambling toward them. He bellowed across the water.

"I can't land there! It's too dangerous!"

But it was clear she couldn't hear him with the waves crashing. She reached the biggest of the rocks, climbed to the top, and then waved him toward it. He knew he had to make a decision. He stared at her, trying to read some other interpretation into her gestures, but there was no mistaking what she meant. He squeezed his hand round the tiller and steered toward the rock. The sound of breaking water was intense now, and spray was showering him as he drove in. *Splinters* was moving too fast again. He eased off the sheet–too much. She fell back, wallowing in the lumpy seas.

"Damn!" he muttered.

He hauled the sail back in, and *Splinters* surged forward again. The girl was barely thirty feet from him, still waving from the big rock, and now as he sped toward her he saw for the first time what she was really pointing him toward: a slender channel round the inshore side of the rock that seemed to lead between it and another rock jutting out from the foot of the cliff. He checked the gap. It was barely enough for *Splinters* to squeeze through, and what was inside it he could not tell.

He had to trust the girl.

He gauged the distance between *Splinters* and the gap. There was still just room for him to go about and escape to the sea. He saw the girl's face above him on the rock. He saw her arm waving him on, and he knew there was no turning back. He felt his hand tremble round the tiller. The gap drew closer. He steered toward it, then at the last moment pushed the helm down.

Splinters slid head to wind and, with what momentum she had left, slipped through the gap between the rocks. He jumped forward, pulled up the centerboard, and braced himself to fend off whatever lay ahead. But he quickly saw that he had no need to fear. *Splinters* was floating in a small pool of still water, sheltered all around by a fortress of rocks.

He saw the girl looking down from above and smiled up at her.

"Thank you," he said.

She did not answer but went on watching him in silence. He tied the painter to a spiky rock, then lowered the sail and clambered out into the pool. The water came up to his thighs. He waded to the inshore rock, climbed round it, and made his way to the ledge that ran along the base of the cliff. He saw the girl jumping across to join him.

He waited for her warily. For some reason he felt suddenly nervous of her. He was sure she meant him no harm, but she was so unlike anyone he had ever known and her physical abilities were almost scary. She stopped for a moment on top of the big inshore rock, then with typical abandon leaped off it to land perfectly on her feet just a yard from him.

He looked at her in the darkness. Close up she seemed even more slight, yet he could almost feel the strength within her diminutive frame. There was an animal quality about her, especially in the way she moved. Everything about her was quick. Even now when she was still, some part of her seemed to be moving, and moving fast. Perhaps it was her eyes. He studied them. No, it wasn't the eyes. They were fixed on him.

It was something else, something he couldn't see, some hidden essence of this girl that was never, ever at rest.

She did not seem hurt by the fall from the cliff. But she was completely wet. Her skirt and top were sodden. Her hair, her face, her arms and legs, her bare feet all glistened. She was like a creature from the sea. He tried to think of something to say. But she turned suddenly and set off along the shore toward the caves.

He followed. She didn't look back but didn't run ahead, either. He sensed she was moving at a speed that felt unnatural to her, a slowness that he presumed was a courtesy to him. No doubt she was taking him to one of the caves. But she passed the first and the second and the third without even glancing in and continued along what was now becoming an increasingly uneven ledge. What was more disturbing, however, was that he could see waves breaking over it just ahead. To his relief the girl stopped a few yards before that and turned to face him. He stopped too, wondering what she was going to do next.

She nodded upward.

He stared up the cliff and saw a small hole in the rock just above head height and about shoulder width in diameter. He looked back at the girl.

"You don't mean in there?" he said.

But she was already climbing up the rockface toward it. He watched her with a queasy fear growing in his stomach. The climb to the hole wasn't the problem. It was what was inside that scared him. He hated narrow tunnels. He glanced back at the caves the girl had ignored on the way here. There had been plenty of room in any one of those. Why did she have to take him into this drainpipe of a place? They were only going to have a talk.

And yet perhaps it made sense. Perhaps her instinct for

self-preservation told her this was the safest option. He had already seen how much danger she was in on the island. The caves would be an easy place to enter not just for the two of them but for others who might have worked out, just as he had done, that she'd survived the jump. There could be a boat on its way here right this moment.

At least this tunnel was less vulnerable. The men might not think of checking in there, and even if they did, they probably wouldn't be able to squeeze through it. He looked up and saw the girl pulling herself in head first. She didn't look back or speak but simply wriggled on out of sight. He frowned. It was probably safe, but he still hated the thought of the tiny space that awaited him. He just hoped the tunnel didn't run far before it widened into something bigger.

He climbed up the rock to the opening and peered through. It was dark inside and there was no sign of where the passage led, but he could just make out the girl's feet scrabbling over the rock ahead of him. He eased himself into the tunnel and followed. It was close and dark and he hated it. He was also convinced that the girl had miscalculated. She was slender and this was probably easy for her, but he was larger and the sides of the tunnel pressed tightly around him. A few feet in he found he could scarcely move at all.

He tried to calm himself. He could feel panic starting. From somewhere ahead came the sound of the girl's body scraping over the rock. She seemed unaware that he had stopped. He tried to think. It didn't matter if he took it an inch at a time. As long as there was room to wriggle, he would be all right. He forced himself on, trying not to let his fears overcome him, and it did indeed feel as though he was moving an inch at a time. Then at last the passage widened before him, and he found himself looking up into a small cave. The girl was standing a few feet away. He stood up with relief and struck his head on a low-lying rock.

"Shit!" he said, and then laughed.

It felt good to laugh, if a little strange. The girl didn't respond. He saw a dull, wispy light falling over her face. It was hard to tell where it was coming from. A few feet away was another larger tunnel twisting almost vertically up into the rock. The girl set off toward it.

"So are we climbing now?" he asked.

She didn't answer and simply started to clamber up the inside of the tunnel. He let her get some way ahead of him, then followed. It was an easy climb with lots of rough edges. After about twenty feet she disappeared from view above him. He reached the same point and found himself at the lip of a long flat chamber. So this was where the light was coming from. He could see it seeping in through holes in the cliff face. He thought of the approaching dawn and Mum and Dad back in the cove. He hoped they were still asleep. But he'd have to get back soon.

The girl was standing by a small unlit fire of driftwood and dry weed. Close by was what looked like a rough bed made from wool and animal hide. There was no sign of any food or water or anything remotely sanitary. She clearly didn't live in this place for any length of time. It looked more like a bolt-hole, probably one of many she had.

He climbed into the chamber and stood there, watching her. She stared back in silence, clearly as wary of him as he was of her. He tried to think of some way to make her feel less threatened by him.

Sit down, he told himself. Make yourself smaller.

He sat down. The girl went on standing there, staring down at him. He cleared his throat.

"I'm Kit," he said.

She didn't speak.

"That's my name," he went on. "Do you . . ." He searched her face for some change of expression. "Do you understand?"

He saw her nod.

He breathed out, still watching her face. Suddenly she sat down. But it was nothing like the way he had sat down. Where he had stiffly arranged himself on the floor, she simply dropped to the ground and pulled her legs round her body in what seemed like one movement. He could hardly believe the speed of it. One moment she was standing, the next she was cross-legged and as relaxed as a cat. And it was almost like watching a cat. Watching a cat watching him.

"What's your name?" he said.

She spoke at last but not to answer his question.

"Tell me about the man you saw," she said.

9

Her voice sounded strange. He had heard it briefly when she'd shouted to him to run, but that had not been enough to convey its character. It was deep for a girl's voice, and the words moved as quickly as her hands and feet. He knew at once which man she meant.

He thought of that first terrifying glimpse of the face beneath the water. He couldn't reveal that. Mum and Dad hadn't believed him, and if the girl didn't either, it would be a sorry start to the conversation.

"He was lying on the rocky scar just off the cove," he said. "That time you first saw me, remember? You bolted and I ran after you. You went into that big cavern and climbed up the blowhole to the cliff top."

He waited for some acknowledgment of this, but she gave none.

"He was naked," he went on. "He was just lying there, half-dead." A picture of the man floated into his mind. It made him shudder. "He had bruises all over his body. And he had . . ." He looked down, suddenly self-conscious.

Something touched his neck, something cold and wet. He

looked up with a start and saw her tracing a finger round his birthmark. She caught his eye and took her hand away.

"Yeah," he said. "He had a birthmark just like mine. He even looked like me. A right ugly bastard."

She said nothing and he took that as polite agreement.

"It freaked me out to see him," he said.

She looked at him blankly.

"Freaked me out," he said. "Scared me, frightened me, gave me the willies."

But he could see she understood him now.

"Anyway, he was lying there, half-dead. I didn't know what to do. I didn't want to walk out over that scar. It's pretty dangerous and I'm not like you. I'm not very brave."

The compliment fell flat on its face. He wished she would say something. He was starting to feel awkward. He bit his lip and went on.

"I walked out onto the scar. It was a bit scary, but I got to the man and offered him some water. I had a bottle on me. He drank a bit, then . . ." He remembered the rush of water, the restlessness in the sea; a restlessness he could feel even now from inside this chamber. "Then these . . . these big waves started rolling in. It got really dangerous, and I had to run ashore. I just made it before one broke over the scar. When I looked back, I saw the man was gone. The wave must have washed him off." He paused. "Then I saw you."

He saw more light filtering in from outside.

"Do you know who the man is?" he said.

She looked away with a brisk movement of the head. He studied what he could see of her face. The mouth was tight, the eyes narrowed. It was clear she was thinking fast. He sensed that she knew the answer to his question, but whether she would give it to him was another matter. She turned back suddenly.

"Why are you here?" she said.

So she wasn't going to tell him. He wondered for a moment whether he should refuse to answer her questions, since she obviously wasn't going to answer his. But there seemed little point. He was leaving soon and there was no harm in telling her things. And the more he told her, the more she was likely to trust him and perhaps tell him things in return. Though there wasn't much time left for this. He'd really have to go soon.

"We nearly got wrecked," he said. "We ran . . ." He checked himself. "I ran the boat onto that big rock off the north end of the island. Nearly sank her. But we got her into the cove and repaired the leak. We'll be leaving in a couple of hours."

"Perhaps," she said.

He stared at her. It was a strange thing to say and she'd said it in a strange voice.

"No perhaps about it," he said. "We're leaving."

He tried to read her expression, but her face told him as little as her words. He was starting to find her evasiveness irritating.

"I suppose you're not going to tell me your name," he said.

He didn't expect a response. He remembered the mantra the old man had trotted out when Dad asked him the same question. *Names are of no importance.* Probably the girl would say the same thing. If she said anything at all.

"My name's Ula," she said.

He felt his mouth drop open. He quickly recovered himself and smiled.

"That's a nice name. How do you spell it?"

"I don't know."

"You . . . ?" He checked himself just in time. The girl was

wild. She wouldn't be able to read or write. It would be tactless to pursue this. Then she spoke again.

"No one on the island can spell. There is no need for it."

"No need for it?"

"No."

"Doesn't anybody here read or write?"

"No."

"What about books?"

Nothing registered in her face.

"You must have books here," he said. "Haven't you?"

Again nothing from the girl. He wasn't even sure from her expression that she knew what books were. He saw a tension in her face and quickly smiled again.

"Thank you for telling me your name."

No smile came back, but he sensed an infinitesimal shift in her feelings toward him; a shift toward trust, small but perceptible. He hesitated.

"What's the name of the old man? The leader of the community."

"His name is Torin."

"And the old crone? That really ancient woman I saw in the village?"

"Her name is Wyn."

"What about the two men? The ones who attacked you?"

"The one with black hair is called Uddi. The other is called Zak." She spoke the names without emotion. Her eyes flickered over him for a moment, then she said: "Thank you for helping me."

He made no reply. He was thinking of Uddi and Zak. So that was what they were called. He pictured them in his mind and felt hatred pour through him again.

"Why are you in danger from them?" he said.

"I am in danger from everyone."

"Not from me."

She said nothing. He saw light and darkness play over her face. But the darkness was waning.

"Why are you in danger from everyone?" he said.

"Because I am an outcast."

"Why?"

Again she said nothing. He took a slow breath.

"What will happen if they catch you?"

"They will kill me." She ran her eyes over his face. "And they will kill you, too. You are in danger as well."

"From everyone?"

"From everyone."

"But not from you?"

She paused.

"Not from me."

He heard a wave crash against the cliff outside. He looked at the girl. There was so much he wanted to know and so much she wasn't telling him. But he had to get back. The islanders were clearly even more dangerous than they'd seemed before. He had to make sure Mum and Dad were all right. And then they had to get away from this place.

This place.

Strange that he hadn't thought of asking her the obvious question. But he could ask her now, before he left.

"Does this island have a name?"

"It's called Skaer."

He'd never heard the word before. Nor had he seen it on any of the charts he'd pored over with Dad.

"Where's it near?" he said.

"I don't know."

"You don't know?" He stared at her. "You must have some idea of the places around you?"

"Why?"

"Well, you must have been to some of them."

"I have never left the island."

"What?"

"I have never left the island."

"Never?"

"Never."

He shook his head.

"I can't believe this. How old are you?"

"I don't know."

"Now look . . ." This was getting ridiculous. All this stuff she claimed not to know. She had to be lying. "You must have some idea how old you are," he said.

"We don't count ages on Skaer."

"You look about my age."

"Then I am about your age."

"Or you could be about sixteen."

"Then I am about sixteen."

He frowned at these cryptic answers. She watched him in silence for a moment, then went on.

"I am the last person born on Skaer. The last person who will ever be born here."

"What do you mean?"

"The Skaerlanders are dying. It's not just that there have been no children for many years. The island itself is dying. The trees, the crops, the animals. Even the fish around the island. There is some food and water but not much. And it's getting worse each day."

"But don't you get supplies from outside? I mean, the people here must trade, don't they?"

"They have not traded for a long time. They did once but it's all finished now. The Skaerlanders don't like the outside world. And the outside world doesn't like them."

"But you can't live without some contact with the outside world."

"To the Skaerlanders this island is their world. It has been their world for many centuries. Ever since their ancestors first settled here. But it's a world with no future." She paused. "Only a past."

"What do you mean?" he said.

But she turned her head away. He watched her for a while in the hope that she might eventually answer, but it was clear she had no intention of doing so. He stood up.

"I've got to get back to the cove."

She stood up too, and they faced each other.

"That limp you had," said Kit, "when you were running down to the cliff—did you put it on?"

He saw from her face that she didn't understand him.

"Did you pretend?"

She nodded.

"And was it to lure the man toward the edge?"

She nodded again. He gave a low whistle.

"You're dangerous."

She said nothing.

"You are," he said. "You're dangerous."

There was a long silence. It was Kit who broke it.

"We won't see each other again."

"Perhaps."

"You said that before. Why perhaps?"

She flicked back her sandy hair. "You have to get back to the cove."

"You're not answering my question."

"You have to get back to the cove."

"You're still not answering my question."

He saw her mouth tighten.

"I'm sorry," he said quickly. "I didn't mean to push you."

He remembered why he had first come out here and said, "Listen, do you want me to take you to the cove in my boat? Or somewhere else?"

"I don't need your help. I can climb up the cliff."

He shuddered at the very thought. But he knew this girl was not like other people, nor was she to be argued with. If she said she could climb up the cliff, then she could. She spoke again suddenly.

"Thank you."

He had not expected her to say that. He gave her a smile and though he didn't receive one in return, he saw a faint softening round her eyes. But it was not to last. With her usual quickness she turned away and set off out of the chamber. He followed, glad to be heading back to the open air. He had been dreading the crawl through the narrow tunnel, yet for some reason it felt easier this time, and he was soon back on the ledge at the base of the cliff. Dawn had broken and sea and sky were now a pale gray. The wind was still from the north. He turned to Ula.

"Good-bye," he said.

She nodded. Nothing more. He held out his hand. She seemed confused by it, but eventually took it in hers. Her hand was small and cold, but the grip was firm and there was no mistaking the strength in it. He squeezed it gently in his own. He had two final questions he wanted to ask. He didn't suppose she'd answer them, but it was worth a try.

"Ula?" he said. "What's the long dark shape I've seen moving beneath the water? And what's that strange cry I keep hearing?"

She looked away toward the sea.

"Go back to your boat," she said.

And so he did. He was relieved to find that *Splinters* had come to no harm among the rocks. The surf had gone down a little, and launching the dinghy proved easier than he had expected. Soon he was clear of the shore and heading out to sea. He glanced back and saw Ula standing on the ledge watching him. He waved to her and after a moment saw a small wave back. He knew she still didn't trust him. But it was clear that she had long since ceased to trust anyone. And having seen something of the danger she was in, he couldn't blame her.

But now he had dangers of his own to contend with. The rolling seas that had made *Splinters* so uncomfortable on the way down the shore had gone, but the wind had turned freakish. Not only was it gusting without warning but it was constantly veering and backing so that while it was still more or less from the north, the squalls came at him from different angles.

He went on grimly beating up the coast and finally drew level with the bluff at the northeastern point of the island. He was desperate to see Mum and Dad now. He needed to know they were all right. And he had so much to tell them. He knew he had stayed too long with the girl. He had let curiosity keep him there. But he was nearly back now. It was just possible they were still asleep. And if they were awake, they'd see *Splinters* was gone and hopefully assume he'd just gone for a row. As long as they hadn't gone off looking for him, everything should be all right.

He checked the bluff. He was pretty sure he could weather it on this tack. He set off toward it, scanning the water around it for rocks. He knew there were quite a few and he could see the bigger ones already, but *Splinters* was moving well and showed every sign of getting upwind of them. Not that he planned to take any chances. If he had any doubts, he'd take a couple more tacks to make sure.

No rush just yet, though. He could take *Splinters* much

closer in before he had to make a decision. Another squall struck. The boat heeled sharply, and he shifted his weight to balance her. She settled back on an even keel and punched on toward the bluff. Half a mile to starboard he saw the great rock that had been the cause of their misfortune. He hoped he would never see it again after today.

But now he saw something else.

Another rock fifty yards ahead. It was long and dark and it barely showed above the surface of the water. Frothy seas were breaking over it. He stared. There was something strange about the rock. He had been steering toward this point for several minutes and in all that time had seen nothing but sea. Yet he should have seen the rock before now.

Then suddenly it vanished.

A shiver ran through him. He let go the sheet and stopped the boat. He wasn't going near that spot. Whatever had been there was no rock. He searched the water for some further sign of the thing, but all he saw was waves and foam. *Splinters* was now wallowing in the swell, her sail flapping. He hauled in the sheet but only enough for the boat to pick up the speed she needed to go about. He had no intention of going any closer to the bluff. He'd take at least two more tacks and come back into the cove from the other side. He thrust the helm down and set off out to sea. But even as he did so, he sensed a presence close to the boat.

He was being followed.

He didn't know what it was or where it was. But he could feel it, one moment here, one moment there. He thought of the dark shape he had seen before. And suddenly he glimpsed it beneath the boat, long and sleek, too far down to make out clearly, but close enough to give more than a hint of its vast size.

It disappeared again, yet still he felt it close to the boat.

The sail was flapping again. He had been neglecting the sailing. He had to focus, even with this thing swimming around him. He forced himself to concentrate on the boat again. She was still heading out to sea, but he'd easily make the bluff now if he went about. There was no point in avoiding it anymore. Whatever had frightened him over there was now out here.

He tacked and raced back toward the island, trying to squeeze every bit of speed that he could from the boat. And *Splinters* seemed to respond. He drew closer to the bluff. He was well to windward of it, and there was no danger from the rocks. But a greater danger lurked just a wave-distance away. He could see the moving shadow crossing his wake, then his bow, then doubling back to his wake. He tried to keep his mind on the sailing.

From somewhere behind him came the long, eerie cry.

He shuddered and looked back. About thirty yards astern he saw a tumult of water, a swirl of spume; then nothing but gray sea. He sensed that the shadow was gone but he wasn't going to hang around to make sure. He turned back to the island and sailed on. The bluff was now high above him to port. Over to starboard was the scar, visible again now that the tide had fallen. He saw waves breaking over it in a mass of spray. And there in the cove was *Windflower,* exactly as he had left her.

But not all was as it had been.

He stared in horror. The tents had been torn to pieces. What shreds of them remained were blowing about the hill like rags.

Of Mum and Dad there was no sign.

10

He raced *Splinters* in to the beach, pulled up the centerboard and lowered the sail, then ran up the shingle and made fast the painter.

"Mum! Dad!" he shouted.

There was no answer.

He looked frantically around him, searching for a glimpse of them. Nothing. Hideous possibilities rushed through his mind. He ran over to where the tents had been. Some of the guy ropes and pegs were still there, and a few scraps of the tents. He bent down and examined them. It was no freak wind that had done this.

It was a blade.

He pictured Uddi and Zak. They were dangerous enough to do anything, and he had provoked them. Yet again he was to blame. While he was sailing round the coast to see Ula, they must have come here. They probably never went back to the village at all. Walking that way was just a blind. Or maybe they did go back, but only to fetch Brand and some of the others. He had no doubt there were plenty of other islanders thirsty for blood.

He'd failed Mum and Dad in every way.

"Don't let them be dead," he muttered. "Please don't let them be dead."

He tried to think. It was just possible they weren't in the tents when the islanders arrived. Perhaps they'd woken up, found him missing and gone looking for him, then the islanders had turned up and destroyed the empty tents in a fit of rage. He didn't really believe this, but it was something to clutch at.

"Come on," he said.

He pelted off round the cove, his eyes racing everywhere. He searched the ruins, the bluff, the scar. He peered over cliffs and into caves. He checked on board *Windflower*. He checked everywhere he could think of. He ran and ran and ran. And then finally he stopped.

He'd been searching for at least two hours, and he was back at the place where the tents had been. He was breathless. He was close to panic. And to make matters worse, he could feel those icy patches moving through him again. He shivered and looked about him, trying to put some face to the things, but they had no face. All they had was hungry air that slipped and slithered through him.

He started moving up the slope. He knew where he had to go now. But first he had to climb the great hill. He would be able to see more from up there. He should have done this earlier, but he hadn't been thinking straight. Another chill passed through him. He carried on walking. He was in a daze now. He could feel his emotions breaking up, but he forced himself on. Climbing seemed to help. Not only did the chilly presences leave him as he drew farther from the cove, but the height seemed to clear his head a little.

Yet clarity only sharpened the pictures cascading through his mind. He saw Mum's face, Dad's face, Uddi's face, Zak's face. He saw the faces of the other islanders. He saw the face of the strange man. He saw Ula's face. He saw a black wave and a black form slipping beneath the water. He saw tumult in the sea.

He saw death. Death in a thousand forms.

He saw the valley stretching below him.

He had reached the plateau of rock at the very top of the great hill. He had no memory of the last half of this climb. He had been lost in mad visions. He was alone and he was crying and he felt close to collapse.

"Don't," he murmured. "Don't go to pieces."

He stared over the valley. It stretched away toward the little hill at the southern end of the island. There was no sign of anyone moving among the rocks, trees, and vegetation. He set off down the slope into the valley.

He felt strangely resigned to what would happen. He had no doubt the islanders would kill him on sight. They had wanted his blood the first time they saw him. But if Mum and Dad were dead, he wanted to be dead too. And if by some miracle they weren't, then he might at least be able to find out what had happened to them and maybe even do something to save them.

He looked uneasily about him as he descended the slope. He was visible from countless places up here. But he saw no one. He reached the base of the valley and started to make his way across it. The sun broke out from behind a cloud, and a trickle of warmth started to filter over the land. It did nothing to take away the cold despair inside him, but it helped a little and he felt a tiny renewal of energy.

He trudged on across the valley. He had no idea which way he was going. It certainly wasn't the route that Dad had taken yesterday. There were more cairns this way and more areas of scrub. He supposed he should have kept closer to the trees for the sake of concealment, but again he wasn't thinking straight and the part of him that believed Mum and Dad were dead had ceased caring.

He reached the base of the small hill and stopped. The feeling of resignation vanished and fear took its place. It wasn't fear of death. He knew that. He was almost looking forward to death. It was fear of the manner of death. There was no guarantee it would be quick.

He clenched his fists and started to climb. And as he did so, he became aware for the first time of the strangeness of the sea. Why he had not noticed it before, especially when he was on the great peak, he did not know. But now, as he ascended this smaller hill, he saw how unnaturally still the water was. It shouldn't be still at all. The wind had picked up and was blowing thunderously from the northwest. Gusts were raking the water even as he watched, yet the surface remained unruffled.

He shivered. He had never known a sea like this. It didn't seem possible with the wind this strong. But what was even more disturbing was the dull sheen spreading across the top of the water. It wasn't a cat's-paw. It was like breath darkening a mirror. The clouds in the sky were racing with the breeze, yet the sea did not move. It seemed to be waiting. But for what he could not tell.

He reached the summit of the hill and looked down. There was the dying mere over to the left. There were the enclosures, the mangy animals, the failing crops, the cottages. There was the harbor with the long black boats. There was the sea, silent and still. But there were no people. It was like a ghost village. He started to walk down past the enclosures. This emptiness didn't reassure him. The village had looked exactly the same when he first came here with Mum and Dad.

And then Brand had appeared, and all the others.

But this time no one appeared.

He looked about him. He had already decided he was going to make for the cottage he'd seen Torin come out of. The old man had been anything but friendly, but he had at least stopped them being beaten to death by the other islanders. It was just possible he might offer some help, though the prospect seemed unlikely. Here was Brand's cottage. Its door was open and no sound came from within. Kit hesitated, then stole closer and peeped in. There was no one there. He looked over his shoulder to check no one was watching him, then stepped inside.

The cottage consisted of a single room, and it was spartan in the extreme. There was a hide spread over the floor, presumably for a bed, with a woolen blanket thrown over it and a rough pillow, also made of wool. At the lower end of the room was an empty fireplace. In one corner was a pair of oars with some netting and other fishing gear; in another was the heavy club the man had brandished at them. A small wooden stool stood on its own by the far wall.

There was nothing else. No crockery, cutlery, books, mirrors, ornaments, musical instruments. No table, toilet, stove, sink, or bathtub. And no sense at all that this was a person's home. It was just a place to sleep in. Brand would have been just as comfortable in Ula's cave. He thought of the ruins in the cove. They were the same sort of size and shape as this cottage. And looking around him now, they didn't seem much worse. This place was simply a ruin in waiting.

He edged back to the door and glanced out. There was still no sign of anyone. He stepped out again and set off down toward Torin's place. The doors of the other cottages were all open. He looked through each one, half hoping to find Mum and Dad, but they were not there. The cottages were as spartan as Brand's, though some had tools and farming implements inside them, and others had more fishing gear.

He reached Torin's cottage and found the door shut. He leaned closer and listened. All was quiet within. He pushed the door cautiously open and peered round it. But the place was deserted too, and there was nothing inside that he hadn't already seen in the other cottages.

This was getting creepy. The absence of people was almost as frightening as the possibility that they might appear at any moment. He went from cottage to cottage, determined, now that he had the chance, to look everywhere for Mum and Dad. But all the cottages were the same: spartan and deserted, and no food or water in any of them. They had to have some kind of communal dining hall somewhere.

He found it a few yards farther down the slope, one of the larger buildings just up from the harbor. It had a long table with stools down each side and simple bowls and cutlery. Behind it was another large building with a simple kitchen area and a cold room that was clearly used for the storage of food.

Except that there was no food. And the water butts were almost empty.

He wandered on from place to place. He found a cottage with a weaving loom, a cottage for washing clothes, a primitive kind of washroom for the islanders, a workshop with tools, a cottage full of fishing gear and boat equipment, and over on the southwestern point, set apart from the other buildings, a latrine.

But still no people anywhere.

From the sea came a slow, heaving sound.

He looked around him. The wind was now rushing down the slopes from the little peak. He felt his skin prickle as it ran over his bare arms. He looked down at himself. He had taken so little heed of his appearance in all that had happened that the sight of himself suddenly shocked him. He was filthy. His T-shirt was torn from all his scrambling about. His shorts were ripped in several places. His sailing shoes were coming apart round the edges. His arms and legs were dirty and bruised. He imagined his face was the same.

Again he heard the heaving of the sea. Again he felt the prickle of wind over his skin. He twitched and looked over the water again. It was as unnaturally still as before. Then he heard a sound from the southeastern point of the island. A murmur of voices, followed by silence.

He stared in that direction. There were two buildings there, the only two he had yet to look in. One was a tiny cottage a short way in from the shore, the other an imposing building, the largest by far in the village, set apart from all the others and raised on a knoll that overlooked the sea. They had to be in there.

He stared at the building for several minutes, then slowly set off toward it. Over to his right he could see the water in the harbor glistening. It was so still it frightened him, yet he sensed a moving presence too. It wasn't coming from the harbor. It was coming from the sea outside. He looked beyond the breakwater, but the water there was just as still as it was within the harbor wall. He stared as far as the horizon and saw the same disquieting stillness. The sun had vanished and the sky looked like a parched face. He heard another murmur of voices from the building on the knoll, then silence again.

And this time he understood.

They were saying prayers.

He didn't catch the words, but there was no mistaking what was happening. He walked on toward the building, squeezing his fists into tight little balls. So this was their chapel, he thought bitterly, the place where Brand and Uddi and Zak and all these other nice holy people came to worship and give themselves up to the glory of God. He felt a mix of emotions welling up inside him.

He reached the knoll and climbed up it to the building. From inside came another murmur of voices, followed by silence. He looked over the chapel. Like the other buildings it was made of stone, but whereas the cottages had thatch roofs, this had tiles and timber gables, one at the inshore end where the door was, the other on the side facing the sea. There were no windows.

He walked slowly round the building. At the seaward side he stopped and looked down at the water. This end of the island consisted of large slabs of rock rising twenty or thirty feet from the sea, but the knoll raised the chapel to nearly twice that height. And as he looked, he saw strange movements below him.

The water was pushing itself against the shore with small, insistent stabs that were at odds with the calmness farther out. The wind had dropped again, and the air was heavy and still. There was another murmur of voices, this time in a long, throaty unison. He didn't catch what was said, but the gravity of the sound told him something had ended.

Yet he sensed too that something was about to begin.

He heard a sound of movement inside the chapel and ran back to the inshore side of the building. The door was still closed. He looked about him, unsure what to do. He felt he should stand here and confront them, demand to know what had happened to Mum and Dad; but he knew he wasn't ready to show himself. He raced down off the knoll and over to the tiny cottage nearby. As he reached for the door, he felt a mad hope that maybe—just maybe—they'd be in here.

But it was just a timber store. He closed the door behind him but left it ajar so that he could see out. There was very little room inside. The store was packed with timber, practically all of it dried driftwood from the sea. He made some space for himself among it and peered through the gap.

The door of the chapel opened and the islanders came out. He ran his eye quickly over them. They were all there. He felt his muscles tighten at the sight of Uddi and Zak. They were standing next to two of the other men, talking in low voices. The ancient woman who Ula said was called Wyn walked up to them and said something to them in a sharp voice. It seemed to be a rebuke, perhaps for talking after prayers. Kit couldn't tell. Whatever it was, the men broke apart and started to move off down the knoll. Torin was the last one out of the chapel. He looked stern and withdrawn.

There was no sign of Mum and Dad.

He heard the long, eerie cry over the sea. He took his eyes from the islanders and stared out over the water. Something was moving on the horizon: a thin white line that stretched all the way across his field of vision. He saw Torin watching it too from the foot of the knoll, then the others, drawn back to join him, presumably by the sound. They all stared out together. But Kit could see now what the white line was.

A wave.

It was moving fast, and it was big—not big enough to engulf this part of the island, but big enough to send spray over the rocks, maybe even up as far as the chapel. He didn't think it would do more than that. He saw that the faces of the islanders were tense and drawn. The wave drew closer. He crouched and braced himself in case any of it came this far.

The wave crashed against the shore. Spray flew up in a cloud that reached halfway up the knoll and doused some of the islanders nearest to the sea. But it did no more. The sea soon calmed again and gave no hint that a wave this size had just passed. But the water close to the shore retained its restless energy. He looked back at the islanders. They were staring out to sea again—and to his horror he saw a second white line along the horizon.

This wave was bigger than the last one and far more ominous. Once again it had risen from a calm sea. He found himself sweating with fear. This wasn't normal. This wasn't possible. The reaction of the islanders told him they were as frightened as he was. Yet though some were stepping back from the shore, others were squaring up to it. Some of the men—Brand, Uddi, and Zak among them—had even taken a few steps toward the sea as though to defy the wave. Torin, too, had joined them and appeared to be uttering some kind of prayer.

The wave rushed in and the nearer it came, the greater it appeared to be. Kit had no idea how high it was. But it seemed as it drew closer to be rising like a cobra's hood out of the stillness of the sea. He watched in terror. He didn't know whether this one would reach him in the timber store after it broke. Fearsome though it was, it didn't seem possible that the green wall could come this far.

He was wrong. The wave shattered against the land and burst right over the top. Spray flew over the islanders, followed by a surging body of water, though it was only enough to drench their legs, not sweep them away. It raced on toward the timber store and broke against the outside. A stream of water came rushing through the gap. He held on to the door as the water whooshed and gurgled around his ankles, knocking pieces of driftwood from the lower shelves. Finally it settled about him and started to trickle out again.

He stared out through the gap once more. Part of the

wave had clearly burst over into the harbor as the boats were still rocking at their moorings, and farther out he could see the unchecked extremity of the wave still rumbling across the sea. A moment later it was lost from view round the southwestern point.

He stared down at his feet and saw foam still fizzing there. He put his eye to the gap again. The islanders had moved closer together and were now mumbling to each other. Below them the once-still water now writhed in an angry swell. Suddenly Brand pointed out to sea.

"There!" he bellowed.

And Kit saw another white line on the horizon. A third wave was forming, and this was the biggest of them all. He couldn't stay in the timber store any longer. The wave would engulf this whole section of the island. Whatever dangers awaited him outside, they couldn't be worse than staying in here. He had to make for the higher ground. He pushed open the door and ran out.

The islanders were already hurrying ahead of him, but some heard the sound of the door and looked back. He saw startled faces and angry stares, especially from Uddi and Zak, but none of them stopped running. He raced after them up the slope. Behind him came the crash of breaking water. He knew he shouldn't turn and look back, but he couldn't help himself. Even as he ran up the hill, he saw the wave rear up, its white mouth spitting fume. Then it plunged down over the chapel, swallowing it roof and all, and rushed on, sucking up the land and all the cottages in its path, including the timber store.

Kit stopped on the slope. Out of the corner of his eye he could see the islanders continuing to climb. But he could go no farther. He was mesmerized by the terror of the thing, and the part of him that believed Mum and Dad were dead and wanted to join them reached out to this awesome executioner.

The water rushed on toward him. Surely it would take him. He wanted it to take him. He wanted it to sweep him away and swallow him forever. But it was losing power. The gradient was biting off its life. It moved on, licking over the dry grass like a snake. And then it died at his feet.

He shivered and breathed out. Below him the island glistened like a serpent's skin. Some of the stones from the smaller cottages had been knocked out, but all were standing, and the chapel appeared to be undamaged. He looked over the sea and saw no more waves at all, just the familiar dark shape moving beneath the surface close to the breakwater. A moment later it vanished from view. And now there was only one danger left. But it was great enough. He turned to face it.

They were coming back down the slope, and there was no mistaking their intent. This time he knew Torin would not be able to stop them, even if he wanted to. Their faces were fixed and unyielding. Kit shouted up the slope at them, determined at least to get some words in first.

"Where are my mum and dad?"

There was no answer.

"Eh?" he yelled. "Where are they?"

He stared at them in dread. They weren't just going to kill him. They were going to tear him apart. He could see it in their eyes. They were close now and the men were spreading out on either side of the group to cut off any escape. He turned and started to run toward the harbor. Then he heard a scream from one of the women. He stopped and looked back. The islanders were no longer coming for him. They were staring up the slope to where old Wyn was pointing.

He followed their gaze. And there, standing on top of the

small peak that overlooked the village, was a figure, a figure he recognized at once: an ugly, naked man with long black hair and a birthmark on his neck and cheek. A man with his arms stretched out to the sides and his hands raised to a level just above his head, as though holding a vast, invisible globe up to the sky.

A man he didn't know.

Yet felt he had known for all time.

11

His confusion was nothing compared with that of the islanders. They looked at the man, then at him, then at each other. They drew together in a huddle. They seemed both vulnerable and yet more dangerous than ever. They were talking in low voices, shooting glances up the slope and back at him.

But Kit's eyes were mostly on the figure. He could not believe this appearance of someone who should be dead. It had momentarily stopped the attack of the islanders, yet it gave him little comfort. This man was terrifying, and who he was, what he was, why he was here, how he had come—these things were more terrifying still.

The figure remained motionless at the top of the slope.

But the islanders were moving. They had broken apart and were now hurrying into their cottages. Kit could guess what was going to happen next and he was right. They soon reappeared with clubs in their hands. He threw another glance up at the figure on the slope.

Still it did not move.

The islanders re-formed, then suddenly split, with about two-thirds heading up the slope toward the man, and the other third coming straight for him. There were men in both groups, but Uddi and Zak were in the smaller one. Only Torin stayed apart. He had joined neither group and remained alone halfway up the slope. He seemed to be against what was happening and had clearly been overruled. But there was no time to think of that now. The islanders were close.

A great shout came from the top of the slope.

"Waargh!"

He stared up at the summit. It was the man. He was still stretching his arms out to the side in that strange dramatic gesture, and now he was bellowing down at them.

"Waargh!"

It was a wild, almost animal roar, and it carried effortlessly down the slope.

"Waargh!"

It checked both groups of islanders for a moment, but then they pushed on. Kit ran farther back toward the harbor. There was no escape here, but he couldn't stay where he was. The islanders were spreading out on either side like a fan. He stopped by the edge of the quay and turned to face the oncoming group.

There were seven of them, four men, three women, Uddi and Zak on each flank. The other men were older, but they looked lean and strong. The women, too, seemed fiercely determined. He glanced beyond them and saw the larger group of islanders surging up toward the top of the hill.

But the figure was now gone from the summit.

He looked quickly back at the advancing group. He could see them watching his face as though they were trying to guess which way he would run. He tried to find a weak point in the line. It had to be one of the women. He ran his eye over them. The oldest of the three was just left of center, and she had another woman to her right. If he was going to try to break through, the best place would be between those two. It was also the nearest point to where he was now.

He made up his mind and charged.

They saw what he was doing and quickly closed to narrow the space. But he had made the right choice. One of the women grabbed at him and for a moment held him fast, but the other swung her club at the same moment and though the impact of the blow on his back made him wince, it also knocked him forward, and this, coupled with the impetus of his charge, pushed him free again.

He stumbled up the slope, but the whole group was hard in pursuit. He could hear the pounding feet, the panting breaths. He felt tired and weak already and was sure he wouldn't outrun them. One of the men was bound to get him. And now, to make matters worse, he could see the bigger group racing back down from the summit of the hill. They had spread out along the top and were hurtling down toward him. Where the naked man was, he did not know. Perhaps they had killed him already and were now coming back for more blood.

They were fanning out across the island. He was caught like a fox. Hounds behind, hounds in front. Only Torin was not part of the hunt. He had not moved from the middle of the slope. His face showed no expression, and he made no effort to catch Kit as he sped past. But Kit could not think of him. One of the islanders was now close behind, and he had to decide which way to run.

He glanced over his shoulder. It was Zak. The rat-faced man was the fastest of the chasing group and had nearly caught him before. But here, too, only yards away, were the faster runners from the bigger group: two men sprinting straight for him and Brand just behind them, wielding his club like a berserker. Kit looked quickly about him. He couldn't go forward or back, nor could he go right. There were three more islanders racing round from that side. There was only one way to go. He darted left and vaulted over the gate into the nearest of the enclosures.

Geese scattered this way and that as he tore over the grass toward the western shore. Behind him he heard Zak's ever-present breathing. It was harsh and violent and deliberately loud. He sensed the man's hatred in those heavy breaths. Each one seemed to stab him in the back like a curse. But then another sound split the air, another great roar from the top of the hill.

"Waargh!"

He glanced up again toward the summit. The man had reappeared, his arms stretched out to the side as before. The islanders hesitated and seemed unsure which way to run, but Kit carried on. He knew Zak wouldn't stop, and a glance over his shoulder told him he was right. The man was closer than ever.

But many in the chasing group seemed confused. Most had climbed over the gate and were still in pursuit, though Uddi had sped off round the top of the enclosure in an attempt to cut him off that way, but some had joined the larger group, which was now charging back up the slope toward the strange man. Kit put all his efforts into reaching the far gate of the enclosure. If he could just get over that quickly enough, he might be able to run up the western side of the slope before Uddi cut him off.

But he quickly saw this wasn't going to work. He made it to the gate, vaulted over, and started to race up the slope, but Uddi was already blocking the way ahead. Kit stopped in his tracks, breathing hard. From behind him came a light bump as Zak leaped over the gate and blocked his other means of escape.

"Waargh!" roared the man up on the summit. His arms were still stretched out to the side. He was like a creature from another world, a wild, untameable creature. And yet he was a man. "Waargh!" he roared. "Waargh!"

And suddenly, without knowing why, Kit stretched out his own arms and shouted back at him.

"Waargh!"

It was the puniest sound imaginable after the man's great bellow, but the islanders all heard it and the effect was immediate. They turned as one toward him, even those on the upper slopes who were now close to the man. And for a strange, surreal moment there was stillness everywhere. The sea turned without a sigh. Then the islanders charged again, some for the man, some for him.

He raced forward. There was nowhere else to go, and he had a better chance of evading the more clumsy Uddi than his wiry companion coming up behind. The big man watched him approach, then drew back his club ready to strike. Kit screamed at him as he drew close.

"What have you done to my mum and dad?"

He saw Uddi's grip tighten round the club.

"What have you done to them?" he yelled.

Uddi swung the club. Kit ducked and felt the top of it skim his shoulder blades. He squirmed to the right in an effort to squeeze past, but a hand seized him by the scruff of the neck.

"Get off me!" he screamed, struggling to break free. "Get off me!"

Somehow he knocked the club to the ground, but Uddi's grip was still firm and the man then struck him hard in the face. Kit felt his legs wobble but somehow stayed on his feet. He saw Zak closing in, followed by three others from the chasing group. He kicked out at Uddi again, then, remembering what Ula had done, twisted his head round and bit hard into the man's hand.

Uddi roared with pain and let go. Zak dived forward, hands outstretched, but Kit broke clear and plunged on up the slope. Now more islanders were surging down to block the way. He looked quickly up to the top of the hill. The naked man had vanished again, and a party of islanders was racing over the summit in the direction of the valley. But others had clearly been sent back this way to deal with the troublesome boy.

He ran on up the western slope, aware of Uddi and Zak and the others behind him and now this new body of islanders ahead. His mind was racing as fast as his feet. He glanced to either side of him, searching for a means of escape. To his left was a cliff, lower than the one Ula had jumped from but peppered at the base with rocks. To his right was the long stone wall that bordered the next enclosure. But it was too high to vault over, and if he tried to climb it, they'd catch him well before he had time to get over.

Suddenly he saw a low gate in the wall. He vaulted straight over it and tore across the enclosure. Three bedraggled sheep looked passively up at him as he raced across. He heard shouts from Uddi and Zak urging the islanders on the other side of the enclosure to cut him off. Torin was nearest. He hadn't moved from his original spot and he didn't move now, but another group of islanders heard the call and started to charge toward the far gate.

It was hopeless. With Uddi, Zak, and the others pounding up behind, he was cut off at both ends. If he could get to the far gate first, he might have a chance, but if not, he was finished. They'd climb into the enclosure, block both gates, and club him to death. He pelted on across the grass, aware of Uddi and Zak close behind him, aware of the others racing toward the far gate, and aware now of something else down to his right, something huge and white and terrifying.

He had not seen the wave coming. No one, it seemed, had seen it coming. It had raced in unnoticed across the still gray sea. But now it broke. There was a thunder of spray that rose high above the chapel, then a deluge of water that poured over the lower slopes. The islanders stopped running but Kit tore on. He could see the water foaming across the bottom of the island, but he knew it wouldn't come up this far. It was losing force already. The islanders started running again but the tiny delay had made the difference. Kit reached the gate first and vaulted over.

But still his path was blocked. Some of the islanders had returned from the valley and were now between him and the top of the hill. He bolted diagonally across the slope toward the eastern shore. There was no other way to go. He couldn't run through the group coming down from the summit, but he might just be able to skirt round them. They saw what he was doing and started to spread out to cut him off. He saw the mere just ahead and put on speed.

There was another crash below him as a new wave struck the shore. He glanced quickly toward it and saw spray flying over the chapel. But the building remained undamaged. He gave it no further attention. He was close to the mere now and the nearest of the islanders, an ungainly man with gray hair and fixed eyes, was only yards away. Kit swerved inside him and cut past, his feet splashing through the marshy perimeter of the mere, and struggled up the eastern section of the slope.

The summit was almost within reach now, but to get there he had to run through the straggling streams that fed down into the mere; and the islanders he had just broken past were already hurrying back up the slope to catch him at the top. He splattered his way up through the streams, water flicking over his legs, and drove himself on toward the top.

From below came the sound of another breaking wave. He didn't even look at it. His eyes were on the summit and on the converging islanders. Uddi and Zak had caught up now and were overtaking the others. He could see their faces fixed on him as they rushed up the slope. They were going to meet him at the top at exactly the same moment unless they slipped or something else happened.

Suddenly a new figure appeared on the summit.

It was Ula.

"Quick!" she shouted.

And as he scrambled up toward her, his feet skidding on the marshy ground, she whipped out a sling and whirled it about her head. The next moment a stone flew down toward the approaching islanders. It missed, but it was enough to check them for one or two precious seconds. Kit pushed himself desperately on. More stones were now flying from Ula's sling, and this time with greater success. Uddi took one on the cheek, Zak one on the arm. Two of the women were hit about the body.

"Quick!" shouted Ula.

He was nearly there now, but it was going to be close. For all the danger of the flying stones the islanders were still surging on. He scrambled over the last few yards and joined Ula on the top. She grabbed him by the arm.

"Come on!" she said.

And she tugged him toward the valley. They raced down the other side of the hill, heading for the nearest trees. He took no heed of the slope. He knew he could trip or slip at any moment, but he had to get away. Ula was flying ahead with her usual reckless confidence, and he followed as best he could. He didn't look back. He knew the others would be close behind. And now there were new dangers in front of him.

More islanders.

Many of those who had gone chasing after the strange man were still on this side of the hill. He could see them at the bottom of the slope where the valley floor began. But it was clear that their quarry had eluded them. They were standing motionless and staring toward the northern end of the island. And in spite of the risk of slipping Kit took his eyes from the ground and stared with them.

A fire was burning on the summit of the great peak, and a strange mound that had not been there before had suddenly appeared. It was hard to tell from this distance what it was. But what was stranger still was the figure standing beside it, a figure unmistakable even from here, with his arms stretched out to the sides and the same wild defiance.

Kit shuddered even as he ran down the slope. It was impossible to get from this hilltop to that in such a short time. There was no man on earth with that much speed. But the sound of shouts behind him broke him from these thoughts. Uddi and the others were past the summit now and thundering after them, calling as they ran to those in the valley; and this group now turned to look up. He saw hands pointing toward him, and then a bustle of activity as the islanders below came rushing up the slope.

"Stay with me!" Ula shouted to him.

She turned to the right and raced toward a small patch of trees. He followed breathlessly, his body aching with the strain. But there seemed no escape. The islanders below were spreading out to catch them, and Uddi and Zak and the others were still hurtling down from the top.

"Ula!" he shouted. "We won't get round them that way!"

"Keep running!" she called over her shoulder. "Do what I do!"

He drove himself on, but it seemed there was no hope.

From the top of the great peak came the wild roar again.

"Waargh!"

It seemed to echo all round the valley. It did not seem possible that a man could roar this loud. But Kit no longer knew whether this was a man at all, nor could he escape the uneasy feeling that this call was somehow intended for him. Whatever it was for, it checked the islanders again, just for a second.

But Ula did not stop. And as he followed, he saw that if they kept their present speed up, they might just be able to get round the group and dive in among the trees by the edge of the valley. Ula dashed on, light and swift, leaping over mounds and rocks, and he raced after her, desperate to escape the islanders before his strength left him. The slope flattened out at last and there were the trees just ahead. But the islanders were close too.

"Hurry!" shouted Ula.

They dived in among the trees, Ula just ahead of him.

"Come with me," she said.

He did as he was told. She clearly knew exactly where she was going. She took him this way, that way, down tracks, through clearings. At one point she seemed to be leading them in a circle. He soon lost all sense of direction. But all the time he could hear the footsteps and mutterings of their pursuers, often just a few feet away.

Ula ran on, as nimble as ever. She seemed unaffected by tiredness. He did not even hear her breathe. His own breaths were heavy and labored, and he was sure the islanders must hear them. But there was nothing he could do about that. He was running as quietly as he could.

They entered a small glade bordered by cairns. Ula looked at him and put a finger to her lips. He nodded and looked about him. She surely wasn't going to stay here. The glade had nowhere in it to hide, and sooner or later the islanders would pass this way. He could already hear some of them moving among the trees over to the left.

But Ula had now run over to the biggest of the cairns and was kneeling at its base. He hurried over and joined her. The cairn was about four feet high by four feet across. He looked down at Ula. She was pulling some of the larger stones out from the base, her hands moving quickly and silently.

He stared. This seemed the craziest thing to be doing right now. He supposed she must have some weapon hidden behind one of the stones, but it seemed stupid to be wasting time with this now. And if she took out any more of the big stones, the cairn would come crashing down and the islanders would hear it.

But the cairn didn't come crashing down. It stayed firm even though she took out several more of the big stones. And now he could see that there was a large hole at the base. She looked quickly up at him.

"Get in," she whispered.

He bent down and looked through the hole. To his surprise he saw that the cairn had been hollowed out, and there were some rough supports around the sides and across the top to keep the outer stones in place. They looked like pieces of driftwood bound together with a fishing net. He stared at the gap. It wasn't very wide, but he could just about make it.

He squeezed through into the cairn and sat there in the darkness, his knees pulled into his chest. Ula slipped through, then reached out to the stones she had removed and started to replace them from the inside. With each stone the light faded further, and then suddenly it was gone. They sat there in the darkness, their bodies pressed tightly together.

From outside came the sound of footsteps.

12

He felt Ula touch his arm. But he needed no warning to be quiet. He nodded and felt her hand leave him. He closed his mouth tight in an effort to block off the heavy sound of his breathing. Ula was silent, but he could feel her body quivering against his.

The islanders were close, and they were all around. None were talking, but he could hear them moving about. He looked at Ula. Her face was only inches from his, yet he could barely see her features in the darkness. All that was clear was the steely brightness of her eyes. She was watching him with that fixed, catlike intensity he had seen before.

He turned his head away. Darkness pressed upon his eyes. It was like a black veil, as black as his life had now become. The sounds of movement went on around them, then suddenly he heard feet tramping away out of the glade, and then silence.

He looked round and saw Ula still watching him. His eyes were growing accustomed to the darkness now, and he could see her more clearly. She put a finger to her lips and he nodded again. They sat there in silence for what seemed a long time. Her body was still quivering.

Then slowly it relaxed.

"I think they've gone," she said.

But he had ceased to care. Constant danger had kept his grief at bay, but now in this dark, still place it rushed upon him. Before he could stop them, tears were flooding down his face. He felt his body shudder, then Ula's hand closed round his arm. Somehow he managed to speak.

"Mum and Dad . . . they're . . ."

Ula did not answer. He blundered on, still crying as he blurted out the words.

"I got back to the boat . . . after I left you . . . and I found the tents ripped to shreds . . . and Mum and Dad were gone."

He looked at her through the tears.

"They're dead, aren't they?"

"I don't know."

"But you think they're dead?"

He caught the slight nod of her head.

He pushed his face into his hands and went on crying. It was some time before the tears dried up. He sat there in the darkness, his knees drawn in to his chest. He felt nothing but numbness. Ula spoke, her hand still round his arm.

"I will look for them."

He hardly heard her. She squeezed his arm.

"I will look for them."

"But you think they're dead."

"I don't know they're dead."

"But you think they are."

"Yes."

"Then what's the stupid point of looking for them?" he snapped. He dropped his head. "I'm sorry. I didn't mean to . . . bite your head off." He screwed his eyes tight, lost in dark visions.

"We don't know for certain," said Ula. "So I will look for them."

He said nothing. It was an effort to speak, an effort even to think.

"You must hope," she said.

But he felt no hope. Even Ula's promise to look for them could raise no hope in him. He murmured into the darkness.

"Why do the islanders hate us?"

"They hate evil."

"But I'm not evil. Mum and Dad aren't evil." He scowled. "Weren't evil."

"The Skaerlanders believe everyone from the outside world is evil."

"But that's wrong. That's just plain bloody wrong."

"They have their reasons for seeing it that way."

"What the hell does that mean?" he growled.

He felt her hand leave his arm. He reached out at once and caught it.

"I'm sorry. Please, I . . ." He squeezed her hand tight. "I just . . ."

"It's all right."

"I just . . . can't think straight right now." He let go of her hand and wiped his eyes with the back of his arm. "Please . . . tell me about the Skaerlanders."

She was silent for a moment. Then she spoke.

"They've been persecuted for centuries by those from the outside world. They've been ridiculed, abused, tortured, and killed."

"But why?"

"Because of their beliefs."

"What beliefs?"

She looked at him.

"This is a religious community. The first settlers came to

Skaer hundreds of years ago. The people here now are descended from them. They call themselves the torchbearers of the one true God. And they believe exactly what their ancestors believed."

"And what's that?"

"That they alone will be saved. And that all other faiths but theirs are an invention of the Devil."

"Lots of people believe that."

"The Skaerlanders are prepared to die for it."

"And kill," he muttered.

"Yes," she said. "And kill. They believe they've been chosen by God to build a sanctuary here on Skaer. A kind of heaven. And that it's their duty to preserve the purity of this place at all costs."

"By killing!"

"They don't see that as wrong. They believe the Devil's influence on the world is now so great that the human race is beyond redemption. So people from the outside world who come here are destroyed to keep this place pure. So are members of the community who go against island laws. It has always been this way. The Skaerlanders see all outsiders and rebels as enemies of God sent by the Devil. And they believe it's holy to kill them."

Kit glared at her.

"This isn't heaven. This is hell."

"It was meant to be heaven," said Ula. "A place where God could visit his children."

Kit felt more tears well up. He forced them angrily back.

"I've never believed in God," he said darkly. "And I never will now."

Something cold pressed against his hand. He looked down and saw Ula offering him a small bowl with a lid on it.

"What's that?" he said.

"Water. Drink it."

He took the bowl from her and removed the lid. There wasn't much water in there.

"Is it fresh?" he said.

"It's been in the cairn for two days."

He put his nose to it. It smelled all right. He tipped the bowl and sipped some of the water, then held it out to Ula.

"No," she said. "You."

"You must have some."

"I don't want any. You must drink."

He drank a little more.

"Drink all of it," she said.

She clearly wanted him to, and he found he was too thirsty to resist. He drank the rest of the water, then gave her back the bowl.

"Thank you," he said.

"I don't have any food here. There is very little food on Skaer now."

"How do you stay alive?"

"I scavenge what I can. But everyone here is hungry."

"There's food on the boat," he said. "We could–"

But she shook her head.

"You can't go there. They'll be watching for you."

She looked away suddenly.

"What is it?" he said.

"I'm thinking where to take you."

"You don't have to look after me."

"You'll die without my help."

"I don't much care."

She looked sharply back at him.

"You must care," she said. "You mustn't give up."

"Why?" He stared dully back at her. "Why shouldn't I give up? I've got nothing to live for. I don't even deserve to live. I ran the boat onto the rock. I got us stuck on this island. I didn't warn Mum and Dad when I should have done. I left them sleeping. And now they're probably dead. I don't deserve to live. It's all my fault."

"Maybe it's not your fault."

"Of course it's my fault!" he snarled. "If it hadn't been for me, we'd have sailed past the island and never even known it existed!"

"Maybe you were meant to come," she said quietly.

"What's that supposed to mean?"

She didn't answer.

"Eh?" he said. "What's that supposed to mean?"

"Maybe God brought you here."

"Maybe the Devil brought me here."

"Maybe he did."

They looked at each other defiantly. Then he shrugged.

"I don't believe in God. I just told you."

"But you believe in the Devil?"

"I don't know what I believe in."

He could feel anger rising inside him, deep, powerful anger. It wasn't directed at Ula, and he hoped she understood that. But he knew it showed in his eyes. He looked into hers and saw the same steely gaze as before. For some reason he found himself thinking of the man's eyes staring up at him through the water.

"We must go," she said.

He knew she was right. They couldn't stay long in this place. It was too cramped, and he was now desperate to stretch his limbs. Ula put the bowl down behind her, then crawled over to the loose stones and tipped one back enough to open up a small gap.

"I think it's safe," she said, peering through.

"Where are we going to go?"

She looked round at him.

"I'll take you to a place where you'll be safe for a while. But you must stay close to me all the way."

"All right."

She made to turn back to the stones, but he caught her by the arm.

"Ula?"

She looked round at him again.

"Thank you for helping me," he said.

"You helped me with Uddi and Zak."

"Is that why you think I was meant to come to the island?"

"No."

"There's another reason?"

"Yes."

He studied her face in the darkness.

"But you're not going to tell me what it is?" he said.

"No."

"Is that because you still don't trust me?"

"Yes."

Again he saw the steel in her eyes.

"You can trust me," he said. "I'm no more evil than you are."

She watched him for a few seconds, then answered in a low voice.

"But I am evil. I've done more evil than you can possibly know. I've broken every rule of this community. I've even killed. That's why I'm an outcast. As for you . . ." She looked him over. "You must decide for yourself what you are."

"I already know what I am."

"And what is that?"

"I'm an outcast too."

She watched him a moment longer, then turned away.

"We must go."

She removed the stones one by one and crawled out of the cairn. He followed and stood up, grateful for the chance to stretch himself. Ula was already busy replacing the stones. He stood there and watched her. He had been wrong about this girl. She wasn't just wild. She was also bright and articulate—and dangerous. He hoped he would never make an enemy of her.

She jumped to her feet.

"Come on. And keep close to me."

They set off across the glade and into the trees. Ula didn't move with her usual quickness. He sensed this was for his benefit, but even at this slower pace he found himself struggling to keep up. He kept as close to her as he could, watching her at all times for any sudden change of direction. She was keeping her body low and he did the same, and in this manner they made their way across the valley.

She was taking him toward the western shore, keeping wherever possible to the trees and scrub. Only occasionally did they break cover, usually to cross a small hollow or clearing, and then they were buried again in foliage. She seemed to know every rock, every tree stump, every nuance of the land.

Suddenly she stopped and held out a hand. He stopped too, watching her. She was looking quickly about her, like an animal sensing danger. They were in a small copse of stunted trees with rocks scattered among them. He saw no one, heard no one, but clearly Ula had picked something up. Suddenly she pointed to a rock.

"Get behind that!" she hissed.

He ran over and crouched behind it. Ula was close beside him. He felt her hand press down on the top of his head. He lowered it further and waited, trembling. Still he heard nothing.

Ula's hand continued to press down on his head. He heard a light padding sound a few yards away, then silence. Ula waited for a moment, then took her hand away and stood up.

"Did you see who it was?" he said, still crouching behind the rock.

"Brand's parents."

Kit felt despair roll over him again.

"At least his parents are still alive," he said bitterly. A thought occurred to him. "What about your parents?"

"What about them?"

"Are they still . . . I mean, I just wondered . . . which of the islanders . . ."

He stopped. It was clear from her expression that this was not a subject he should pursue.

"Sorry," he said quickly. "It's none of my business." He stood up. "Was Brand with his parents?"

"No, he'll be with the others. Searching the island."

"For the weird man?"

Ula said nothing. Kit looked at her.

"You're not going to tell me about the man, are you?"

She turned away.

"We must hurry."

And she set off out of the copse.

"Come on," she said.

"All right, all right," he muttered, and hurried after her.

But now things were getting really dangerous. He hadn't felt exposed so far but the trees were coming to an end, and he could see that the land beyond them, which dipped away toward the cliffs, was in clear view from either of the two peaks. Ula stopped by the last tree and held out a hand to check him.

"Listen," she said. "You must follow me closely and you must be quick." She pointed down the slope. "You see those rocks over there?"

He looked and saw three great slabs atop a large grassy mound.

"Yes."

"We need to get behind them as quickly as we can. From below the mound it's easy to reach the place where we're going. But you mustn't run until I say."

"Okay."

She was already looking about her. He saw and heard no one, but he trusted her senses much more than his own.

"Now," she said.

She set off across the open ground. This time she didn't slow down for him. She raced ahead like a gazelle. He tore after her, puffing hard, but he was well behind by the time he reached the rocks. She was already hidden under the shelter of the big mound.

"Do you think anyone saw us?" he asked breathlessly.

"Ssssh!"

He saw her eyes darting about again. Suddenly she pushed him back against the mound and threw herself over him. He stared at her for a moment, then caught a movement in the corner of his eye. He turned his head in that direction. Farther down the slope two men were wandering along the top of the cliff, both carrying clubs. Ula was watching them too, even as she kept him pressed back against the mound.

"Don't move," she whispered.

He had no intention of moving. The men only needed to glance to the left to spot them here by the rocks. But the islanders continued along the top of the cliff and eventually disappeared from view. Ula stepped back and released him.

"Now," she said. "Be quick."

And she scrambled down the slope toward the cliff top where the two men had been. Kit followed warily. He had no liking for cliffs, and this was higher than the one on the eastern shore.

"Quick," she said.

She led the way along the top, moving in the opposite direction to that of the two men, and after a while came to a section of clear ground that rose to a stony lip at the cliff edge.

"Look over," she said.

He did so and saw a ledge about ten feet below running horizontally along the cliff face. It extended all the way round this section of the shore. He looked nervously back at her.

"I'm not climbing down to that."

"It's easy. Look. The rock is full of places for your hands and feet."

It was true, but he still didn't like it. One slip and he would fall to his death.

"I'll go first," she said. "Watch what I do."

And before he could argue further, she was over the edge. He watched her with a sinking heart. She made the climb look easy, and in truth he could see that it was. But the distance he would fall in the event of a mistake put a different complexion on the matter.

She reached the ledge and looked up at him. He took a step back. This was madness. What was he doing here? He should be looking for Mum and Dad. He should be running about the island, searching every hollow, every nook. He stared up at the sky. It was darkening. The clouds had closed into black fists and were now racing down with the wind. He looked up at the big hill. There was no sign of the strange man at the top. But the fire was still burning there. And that mysterious mound seemed to have grown.

"Come on," said Ula.

He turned back to the cliff edge. There was Ula's face

staring up at him, and below her, the sea, darkening like the sky.

"Hurry," said Ula.

He climbed over the edge and searched with his foot for one of the cracks he had seen Ula use.

"Wait," she said. "I'll climb up and help you."

He waited, clinging uneasily to the lip, and a moment later he felt Ula's hand close round his ankle and guide his foot to the crack. He dug his toe gratefully into it. She guided his other foot to the next crack and somehow, with her help, he made his way down to the ledge.

But this proved even more frightening than the climb itself. It had looked fairly wide from above, but now that he was down here he felt the terrifying proximity of the edge. Ula, however, seemed unconcerned that there was a sheer drop only two feet to her left and set off down the ledge as though she were taking a stroll. He followed awkwardly.

This was horrible. It was like stumbling along a plank. It wouldn't have been so bad if the side of the cliff had had things to hold on to, but unlike the place where they had climbed down, the rock face at this point was mostly smooth. There was also a slight overhang from above so that the top of the cliff loomed over him as though it wanted to force him into the sea.

He made himself walk on, keeping his body low for fear of brushing his shoulder against the overhang and tipping himself off balance. Ula was some way ahead, but now he saw that she had stopped and was waiting for him. He caught her up and stopped too, his hands tight round a jutting rock.

"I have to leave you now," she said.

"But—"

"I'm going to look for your parents."

"But I must come with you."

"No, the Skaerlanders will catch you. You're too easy to see. And you don't know the island. I'm best on my own."

"Ula—"

"You'll be safe on the ledge. No one will find you if you keep out of sight."

"But I can't stay here."

"I don't mean here. Come with me."

And she led him a few feet farther to a curved section of the cliff where the ledge widened to form a kind of balcony under the overhang of rock.

"This is a safe place," she said. "You can even sleep here if you want to. It's a good place when the weather is dry. And there's a little food here."

"Food?" said Kit, looking about him.

"Yes. Not much but a little."

And she knelt down inside the overhang and started to pry at the edges of a large, heavy stone in the corner. After something of an effort she managed to move it to the side, and he saw a small, dry hollow underneath containing two lidded bowls.

"There's not very much," she said. "But you can have what there is."

She pulled one of the bowls out and took off the lid. Inside were some loose berries of a type he didn't recognize. They looked dry and withered and unappetizing. She bent down and smelled them.

"They're still all right to eat."

She pulled out the second bowl and removed the lid. Inside was a small fish and what looked like the cooked remains of some kind of rodent. There was also a small amount of loose meat that appeared to be from a bird.

Ula sniffed inside the bowl, then tipped the contents over the edge.

"It's all gone bad," she said.

"Why didn't you eat it when it was fresh?"

"I have to save food as well as eat it. I can only stay alive by moving about. I have lots of hiding places on the island. And I try to keep food in as many of them as possible. I thought the vole and the fish might be bad, but I expected the gannet to be all right to eat."

"Gannet? Was that gannet meat you just threw away?"

"Yes."

He shook his head.

"How on earth did you catch a gannet?"

"With a stone from my sling. When they land on the island, I'm sometimes lucky."

She frowned suddenly.

"I must go now."

He looked at her. There was something in her gaze that he found disconcerting. She went on in a pensive voice.

"It would be best if you could wait here till I come back. But . . ."

She fell silent.

"But what?" he said.

"I don't think you will wait here."

"What do you mean?"

"I think you've come to this island for a purpose. And that purpose will make you do things you cannot predict."

He said nothing.

"I'll look for you here," she said. "If you're not here, I'll look inside the cairn. And if you're not there . . ." She paused. "Then I'll find you. Somehow."

"Thank you," said Kit.

"Stay away from the Skaerlanders," she said. "And stay away from the man."

He looked hard at her.

144

"You know who he is, don't you?"

"I know who I think he is."

"And who do you think he is?"

"I don't want to say."

"Why not?"

"Because I'm confused."

"About him?"

"About him, about you, about everything." She looked away over the sea. "I've been close to despair for so long. I'm not like the Skaerlanders. I don't believe in their God."

"Then we're the same."

"No, we're not." She went on staring over the sea. "You don't believe in God at all. But I do. It's just not the same God that the Skaerlanders believe in."

"What's your God like?"

"I don't know," she said. "I haven't seen him face-to-face. But I feel him. Sometimes I feel him very strongly." She dropped her voice. "And I've sent him a message."

"A message?"

"Yes. I made a boat. A tiny model boat. I carved it out of driftwood and weighted the keel down with stones. I told God it was a prayer boat, and it was carrying my heart's desire to him. Then I launched it into the sea. I don't know what happened to it."

Kit opened his mouth to tell her, then closed it again. He didn't know why.

"And now I'm frightened," she said. "Frightened that God never received it. And that the Devil took it instead."

"Why do you think that?"

"Because of what's happened since."

She continued to stare over the sea. He hesitated.

"What was the prayer your boat was carrying?"

"It was a prayer asking God to send me help."

"And did help arrive?"

She looked round at him.

"You arrived. But you brought the man back too."

"Back? He's been here before?"

"Yes. Once."

"When?"

"A long time ago. Back in the very beginning. The island stories tell us about him." She ran her eye uneasily over Kit's birthmark. "But they tell us nothing about you."

"Why should they?" he said. "I'm not part of your island history. I'm just a boy."

"A boy who looks like the man. So like him, you could be father and son."

"But I'm not his son!" Kit felt his anger rising again. "I'm somebody else's son! I'm . . . I'm Dad's son . . . and Mum's son! I'm nothing to do with this man! Nothing at all, okay?"

But his words sounded hollow even to himself.

"I must go," said Ula.

And before he could speak again, she reached up to the overhanging rock and started to haul herself toward the cliff top. He stared, dumbfounded. He had expected her to retrace her steps to the place where they had come down, but she was climbing straight up from here. Yet this was far more dangerous. The climb took her well beyond the extremity of the ledge so that at one point she was actually suspended over the sea. Then suddenly she was past the outermost tip and out of sight.

"Ula!" he shouted.

But she was gone.

13

You must hope.

Ula's words came back to him. And then his own.

This isn't heaven. This is hell.

He slumped down on the ledge, his back against the rock face, and made himself eat the berries. They were sharp and he didn't like them, but he knew he had to force them down. There was no telling when he would eat again.

"Hope," he murmured. "Hope."

She was right. He had to keep hoping. He had to keep telling himself they might still be alive. He finished the berries and stared out over the ledge.

She was right about that, too. It was safe here. He could stretch his legs right out without his feet dangling over the edge. The floor even sloped in a little toward the cliff, so he was in no danger of rolling off into the sea if he fell asleep. And he wanted desperately to sleep.

But this was nothing compared with his ache to find Mum and Dad.

"Where are you?" he called. "Where are you?"

The sea heaved and rolled but gave no answer.

"There's got to be hope," he said aloud. "There's got to be hope. Ula wouldn't have gone looking if there was no chance of finding them."

But the goblin of doubt would not be shaken off so easily.

Ula nodded, it said to him. *Remember? She nodded when you asked her if she thought they were dead.*

"No!" he shouted at it.

His voice sounded pathetic.

"No! No! No!"

It still sounded pathetic—as pathetic as he was, slumped here like this. He scrambled to his feet. He should do something. He should go and look for them. He should—

"No!" he snapped. He drummed his hands against the rock face. "They'll catch you if you wander off. Ula said so. You'll only make things worse by running about." He tried to calm himself. "She knows the island. If anyone can find them, she can."

He stared up at the sky again. The clouds that had looked like fists were now merging into a huge black face. At least, it looked to him like a face. He could see the nose, the ears, the hair, the brow, the neck, and three gaping holes for the eyes and mouth.

A face worthy of his despair.

"You don't frighten me," he snarled at it. "You're just a cloud. A big, black blob of vapor. You're just—"

He heard the eerie moan below him.

He gave a start and looked down, and there in the water was the dark shape slipping beneath the waves.

"What are you?" he murmured. "What the hell are you?"

He stared at the moving form, trying as before to get a proper glimpse of it. But it was as elusive as ever. It plowed on through the choppy waters close to the cliff, never quite breaking the surface, and then slid away toward the sea and disappeared.

A few moments later it broke into view again, this time over to the left. He went on staring. All he could see from here was a glistening fragment of the creature. It was clearly immense, but exactly how big he could not tell. It dived again and vanished from view. He slumped back on the ledge and stared up at the overhang of rock.

Another cry came from below. He jumped to his feet again and peered over once more. This time there was no sign of the creature. Only a wave rolling in.

But it was huge.

He watched as it crashed against the base of the cliff. Another wave followed, then another, and another, each one smashing into the rock with venomous power. He watched with dread. There was something so deliberate about these waves. They did not seem random at all. More waves rolled in, each one larger than the one before.

He went on watching from the ledge. He felt in no danger here. Not even the biggest of the waves could reach up this high. Yet the sight of them pounding the shore still frightened him. He pulled back from the edge and slumped against the rock again. The sound of the waves went on below him, *crash, crash, crash,* as though they wanted to batter the island to pieces. He closed his eyes, determined to ignore the relentless onslaught of the sea.

"Sleep," he muttered. "Please let me sleep."

And somehow he did, for several hours. He remembered none of it. All he knew when he woke was that he was frightened. Dusk had fallen. He stared up at the overhang and for a moment forgot where he was. Then the memory came back, and with it the pain.

The cry came again, far out to sea. He crawled to the

edge and looked over. The sea was fizzing with energy. It was almost completely black. There were no more big waves, just these smaller seas snapping at each other and at the cliff. He looked up at the sky. It was a dull gray, yet the cloudy face was still there. It had stretched during his hours asleep and now looked like a face elongated in a hall of mirrors.

He heard the sound of voices and froze.

They were coming from directly above him. He stared up at the overhang of rock. If only he could see past it to the top of the cliff. He had no idea who was up there. It certainly wasn't Mum or Dad or Ula. It was a kind of weird murmur and sounded like lots of people whispering together. He couldn't pick out any words.

The only people who could be up there were islanders, so this might well be a trick to lure him up to the cliff top. Yet this explanation didn't feel right. The islanders would hardly whisper at him. If they knew he was here, they'd either keep quiet and lie in wait for him or come down and get him. And if they didn't know he was here, why would they whisper to each other?

The voices went on, still from directly above him. And as he listened, he had the strangest sensation that they were somehow speaking to him. He looked up and saw the ugly cloud leering over him. In its exaggerated state the mouth and eyes seemed more grotesque than ever. He ran his hand over the rock face above him.

No, he told himself. It's too dangerous.

The voices went on, whispering, whispering.

In spite of himself he started to climb up the rock. He knew this was stupid. He couldn't climb like Ula. He didn't even know who was up there. But he had to find out who was making this sound. He tried to focus on the rock face. At least the first part was easy. Even with dusk falling he could see the handholds that Ula had used. Perhaps this wouldn't be so bad after all.

But he was wrong. As he moved toward the extremity of the overhang where there was nothing beneath him but sea, he felt the pull of gravity. His body sagged. The pressure on his hands increased. Even worse were his feet, which could not grip the way his hands did and were now threatening to slip out of the cracks. If they came out completely, he would be dangling there by his hands alone.

He dug his toes into the cracks, squeezing his feet hard against the sides. But now fear had mastered him. He had frozen. He tried to make himself move, but it was no good. He couldn't go forward and he couldn't go back. He was just clinging there, willing himself to move but unable to do so.

The whispering grew louder above him.

"Do it," he told himself. "Do it."

He forced his left hand up the rock face, feeling for the next handhold. His fingers caught a small fissure and gripped tight. He hauled himself up a few more inches. He was still below the outer point of the overhang, and the downward pull of his body was almost unbearable. He wouldn't be able to hold on for much longer, and he still couldn't see over the jutting edge of the overhang to search for the next thing to grasp. He swallowed hard and eased his right hand over the top.

"Please don't be smooth," he begged.

But the rock was smooth. There was hardly anything to grip. He felt a rush of panic. His left hand was losing its grip. His feet were sliding in the cracks. He fumbled about with his right hand. To his relief it brushed over a small crevice. He dug his fingers into it, searching for a hard edge. A trickle of small stones ran down from above and scattered over his face.

He closed his eyes but went on scrabbling with his right

hand for a firmer grip. More stones trickled down, but at last he found an edge. He pulled himself farther up, his feet shifting from crack to crack as he went, and at last his head drew level with the outermost point of the overhang.

There above him was the cliff top and with it the welcome sight of cracks and stumps that he could use to climb farther. He clambered up the last part of the cliff and stopped at the top, breathing hard, his body shaking. Before him was a clearing bordered by rocks and bushes. There was no sign of anyone here.

The whispering had stopped.

Darkness was falling quickly, but he could still make out the small hill at the southern end of the island where the village lay. Fires were burning along its top. He looked to the left and saw the great peak at the opposite end of the island frowning down at him. The solitary fire that he had seen on the summit earlier was still there, as was the strange mound that had so mysteriously appeared.

Beside it was a figure.

The whispering started again.

He looked uneasily around him. It couldn't be the figure on the summit. There were too many voices for that. And though they were loudest when he turned toward the hill, they seemed to come from the air itself.

"Who is it?" he murmured. "Who's whispering?"

There was no answer.

He started walking toward the great peak.

"Hope," he said mechanically. "You must hope."

But his words sounded like those of a speaking toy.

"Hope," they squeaked back at him. "You must hope."

He kept on walking, his eyes fixed on the top of the great peak. But he no longer knew what he was seeing there. One moment there was a figure, then there wasn't. Sometimes the mound was gone, then it was there again. He even doubted the fire. He would see it and suddenly, in the next instant, it was an illusion, a piece of trickery from his burning mind.

He stopped at the base of the hill.

"Hope," he murmured. "You must hope."

He started to climb.

"You must hope."

The voice was mimicking him now. And that wasn't all. He didn't just speak like a toy; he even felt like a toy. His feet stamped, his arms swung, his head turned, his eyes moved, yet he had no command over any of them. It was as though someone else had the remote control; but that someone else had now got bored and put it down, so the clever-speaking toy was just meandering about wherever the mood took it. And the mood was taking it up the great hill.

He could see the fire more clearly now, and he was starting to believe in it again. Of all the illusions confronting him this one worried him the least. The figure and the mound might turn out to be nothing, but he could smell the fire. It felt real. And his wits weren't so completely lost that he hadn't taken in the fact that for the smell to reach him, the wind must have changed direction. It was now coming from the northeast.

"You see?" he said defiantly, to nothing in particular. "I'm not completely off my head."

But he was no longer sure about that.

He stared up the hill again. He had been climbing for some time, yet he still seemed a long way from the top. He stopped and looked across at the smaller hill on the far side of the valley. And now it became obvious just how far he had climbed. From this vantage point he could see the other summit clearly, the fires dotted along it like a defensive wall. He saw figures gathered by each blaze.

It was impossible to count the people in the darkness, but

it looked as though all the islanders were there. He turned and stared back up the great hill and saw in the glow of the fire the outline of the man standing by the mound, his arms stretched out to the sides.

And far above him, the cloud face, now yanked almost beyond recognition, its mouth so wide it seemed to swallow the island. Kit stared at it and then shuddered. How had he not seen the likeness before? Did the face have to be so distorted before he could recognize who it was?

The wind increased. The whispering died away.

He shuddered again and trudged on up the slope.

"Hope," he panted. "Bloody, bloody hope."

He drew closer to the top. He caught the smell of the fire again. He saw the angry splutter of the flames. He saw the mound and suddenly realized what it was made of.

Stones.

He pushed on to the top. There was no sign of the man. It was just him and the fire and the stones. He wandered over to them. They were flickering as the flame light caught them. On the small peak at the other end of the valley he saw the figures gathered there. He felt sure they could see him now. He moved closer to the blaze and then, on an impulse, stretched out his arms to the side as the man had done.

From across the valley came a furious roar.

"So you can see me," he sneered. "Murdering cowards!"

He saw the figures hurrying this way and that like ants. But none of them came in this direction.

"You're waiting for daylight, aren't you?" He lowered his arms. "And then you'll attack."

He looked up at the cloud face and saw the mouth gaping over him.

"Swallow me," he whispered. "Why don't you?"

He turned and stared down into the cove. Moonlight was

falling upon the water, and he could see *Windflower* shimmering like a ghost ship. There, too, was *Splinters,* another, smaller ghost ship, and there, moving among the ruins along the shore, was the strange, naked man.

He seemed uninterested in everything but his own activity, which consisted of selecting stones from the ruined cottages, carrying them to a pile which he had built on the spot where the tents had been, and then returning to the ruins for more stones.

But he was not alone.

Shadows were moving around him as he walked back and forth. Suddenly he stopped at the pile, placed the stones he had been carrying, and looked up the hill. Kit stared back down at him.

"Hope," he heard himself say.

He looked up at the sky and saw the cloud face was gone.

"This isn't heaven," he murmured. "This is hell."

And he set off down the hill toward the man.

14

Coldness hit him at once. It was those same icy patches of air that seemed to float through him and around him. And suddenly it felt as though he, too, were floating, adrift from all he knew. He watched his feet as they tramped down the slope. He watched them rise; he watched them fall. Yet there was no feeling in them. He had become a creature without substance, a piece of flotsam in a sea of shadows. A memory of a boy, no more.

"I'm Kit," he said firmly. "I'm Kit Warren."

His feet went up and down.

"My mum's called Sarah. My dad's called Jim."

Up and down went the feet.

"I'm . . . I'm . . ."

Up and down, up and down.

"I'm fifteen. I like soccer. I like sailing."

He pushed his feet down harder, determined to feel something in them. He heard the sound they made, but that was all. They seemed to be stamping on air.

"I . . . I go to a school called . . ."

But he couldn't remember.

"My dad's a builder," he spluttered. That was better. He remembered this. "His . . . his business has just gone bust. Only it wasn't his fault. He was let down by people. And the bank called in the loan. And then . . ."

Stamp went the feet. *Stamp, stamp, stamp.*

"My mum, she's . . ."

Stamp, stamp, stamp.

"She's . . ."

Stamp, stamp, stamp.

"She's a nurse," he said, driving the words out of himself. "She's a nurse. She likes doing yoga and she's good at painting. And she keeps telling me I'm not ugly. She says I–"

He bit off the words, midsentence. What was he doing, burbling like this? His feet went on stamping down the hill. He fixed his attention on them, unwilling to let his eyes stray farther down the slope. But they moved in spite of him, searching for the man.

They soon found him. He was doing what he'd been doing before: fetching stones from the ruins, carrying them to the pile, then turning back for more. Kit watched with uneasy fascination. It was hard to see the point of demolishing the old buildings like this. It even seemed slightly disrespectful, like stripping the bones from a corpse.

But he had other things to think about now. More chilly patches were passing through him, and as he moved farther down he saw shadows gathering around him. They were everywhere–on the slopes, along the shore, over the water. But they were clustered most thickly around the man himself.

"I'm Kit," he growled. "I'm Kit, I'm Kit, I'm Kit."

He clenched his jaw.

"I like rugby. I like basketball."

More shadows swirled around him.

"I'm good at French. I like animals. I can tie a running bowline."

He was burbling again, but he couldn't stop.

"I used to have a guinea pig. He was called Sammy. He was a tortoiseshell."

The whispering started again.

He stopped and listened. From below came the ripple of waves on the shingle and, farther out, the breathing of the sea. It was calmer now, much calmer, and the wind had eased again, though it was still blowing fairly strongly from the northeast.

"Who is it?" he said. "Who's whispering?"

There was no answer. He made himself walk on down the slope. The pile was close now and he could see the man striding toward it from below, his arms full of stones. They would meet there at about the same time. He stared at the approaching figure and the dusky clouds that encircled him.

"You're a king of shadows," he said under his breath. "That's what you are. A king of darkness." He glanced at the clouds around his own body. "Maybe that's what I am too."

They stopped on opposite sides of the pile.

"Who are you?" said Kit.

The man bent down, placed the stones on the pile, then straightened up and looked him in the face. Kit took a step back. He had seen the man's eyes before, but not like this. Energy flowed through them like a river. What kind of energy it was, he didn't know. He only knew that this man terrified him.

"You don't scare me," he said.

The eyes went on watching him. Kit shifted on his feet. There was something about this naked man that made him feel naked too, as though he had no clothes, no skin, no bones, no breath, no essence of any kind. He felt his hands move over his body in a feeble attempt to pull what clothes he had more tightly around him.

The man turned away suddenly and set off back toward the ruins. Kit watched, unsure what to do. He was now shivering with the cold. He stood there for several minutes, looking about him, yearning to see Mum and Dad running toward him.

But he was alone. Even the whispering had stopped again.

"Hope," he muttered. "Hope, hope, hope."

His words faded into the air.

Without knowing why he set off after the man. But the strange figure was already coming back, laden with more stones. They approached each other in silence, Kit watching to see what the man would do and whether their eyes would meet.

They did not. The man simply walked past and continued up the slope. Kit carried on toward the ruins and did not stop until he'd reached the wall from which the stones were being taken. He looked down at it, trying to understand what the man's purpose was here, but it seemed unfathomable.

He saw the figure returning and drew back a few yards, unwilling to be too close. The man bent down at the wall and picked up more stones. Then he turned, walked over to Kit, and passed them to him without a word. Kit stared back, half in surprise, half in fear.

But he took the stones. And the man turned back to the wall, gathered some more for himself, and headed for the pile again. Kit watched him go, then, after some hesitation, set off after him.

He had no idea why he was doing this. He knew it made no sense. But nothing made sense right now. The stones were heavier than he'd expected, but he stumbled on. Before long he saw the man coming back empty-handed, and he watched again to see if there would be some acknowledgment of him.

There was none. The man passed without a glance in his direction. Kit frowned. Somehow they had to talk. Somehow he had to find out who this man was and why he was here. He reached the pile and placed the stones on top, just as the man had done. Then he straightened up and stared toward the summit of the hill.

But there was no summit to see.

It had vanished behind a screen of shadow. He could make out the immediate foothills and some of the ground on the eastern and western shores, but all else was cut off. Far above the veil the sky was still visible, yet the moon, which continued to illuminate the water in the cove, did nothing to penetrate this strange black wall.

It was moving, too, shifting and swirling like fog. He thought of the mist that had surrounded them in *Windflower*. It had had the same malevolent intensity. He turned and set off back toward the ruins only to see more black approaching. It was the shadows that whirled about the man, and there he was in their midst, carrying more stones. Kit clenched his fists. They had to talk. They had to.

"Stop!" he shouted as the figure drew near. "You must talk to me!"

But the man walked straight past again and continued toward the pile.

"All right," said Kit. "We'll do it another way."

He had to be bold, even if he didn't feel bold. He waited for the man to deposit his stones and return, then stepped out and walked alongside him.

"I'm coming with you," he said, trying desperately to

sound confident. "If that's the only way to get you to talk."

He soon regretted this decision. It was obvious within seconds that there would be no conversation between them. But that wasn't the worst thing. Just walking next to the man was difficult. It wasn't only the chill. Something played off him, something powerful, something unearthly.

The man stopped suddenly and turned toward him. Kit stopped too and stared back as best he could. But it was hard. His body was quivering uncontrollably. He felt as though something were coiling itself round his spine. The eyes that watched him were as dark as the shadows around them. Kit took a slow juddering breath.

"Tell me who you are," he said.

The eyes did not move.

"Tell me." Kit was pleading now. "Please tell me."

The eyes remained still. Yet they were endlessly changing. In the water they had been a misty gray. Now they were black. And as Kit watched, they seemed to widen and merge into a single eye, a vast liquid mirror in which he saw nothing but himself. Then suddenly they looked away.

And the man walked on.

Kit followed, keeping back. He did not speak again. He knew now that words were not the language of this man. Yet he sensed too that in some strange way something was being said to him, something he couldn't grasp, something he wasn't sure he wanted to grasp.

He studied the man in front of him. The naked body moved with a light, springy step. The muscles were sinewy, the hair unkempt, the hands strong and capable. Even without the birthmark and ugly face the man would look just like him.

"But you're not me," he whispered. "You can't be."

The man reached the wall and bent down. Kit stopped a

few yards back and watched, unsure what to do. The man gathered some stones in his arms, straightened up, and set off with them. Kit stood aside to let him pass, but the man came straight up to him and pushed the stones into his chest. Kit stared into the black eyes, then stretched out his arms and took the stones.

"Okay," he said. "I'll carry them."

There was no change of expression from the man. He simply turned back to the wall and bent down again. Kit set off toward the head of the cove. All right, he thought, I'll carry the stones. At least I know what he wants me to do. Even if I don't know why.

But an even greater mystery was waiting for him at the top of the cove.

The pile was smaller than it had been.

He stopped a few feet from it. There was no doubt about it. There were fewer stones here than there were the last time he saw it. He walked slowly forward, his eyes running over the pile. This was too spooky for words. There were several particular stones he remembered the man putting down that were no longer here.

He looked uneasily around him. Nothing was moving but the shadowy veil just up the slope. It swirled and billowed in front of him, and still blocked any view of the top of the hill. This wasn't natural. The stones couldn't have moved by themselves. Something or someone must have taken them.

He placed the stones he was carrying on the pile, then stepped back, watching them closely. They sat there, heavy and inert. For a moment he thought of staying and keeping them in view, but that seemed pointless. He turned and set off back toward the ruins. He said nothing to the man as they passed, and the man, as expected, said nothing to him.

They went on carrying stones. Yet with every trip Kit found that the pile had decreased in size. Sometimes it was the stones he had just put down that were taken; sometimes it was other stones. Always some were missing when he went back to the pile. Where they were going and who was taking them he could not imagine. No doubt the man knew. But Kit was resolved not to ask him about it, not just because he knew he wouldn't get an answer, but because by now another thing had become clear.

The man was in a serious hurry.

He had come to move the stones and he was focused only on that.

So, like a sleepwalker, Kit went on picking up, carrying, putting down, picking up, carrying, putting down. He supposed he should be doing something else. But he could think of nothing that would make him less unhappy than he already was. So he went on shifting stones with the man, moving from ruin to ruin.

And as he moved, the night moved too, through its slow, almost imperceptible, cycle. He soon lost all sense of time, but in what he took to be the small hours he felt the shadows increase in number and the chilly patches deepen around him. His teeth started to chatter as he moved among the ruins clutching the stones tightly to him.

"Drop them," he told himself. "Just drop the bloody things and run."

But he had no will to run. And besides, he wondered, where would he go? Ula's cairn? The ledge on the cliff? One of the caves? He knew there was nowhere to go. He might be able to escape this man, he might be able to escape the islanders, but he'd never be able to escape the pain. Better to stay here and work himself into the ground. So he worked on through the night, yearning for it to pass and for his life to pass with it.

A gray light appeared in the folds of the sky, then slowly strengthened and spread. The black veil lifted and the shadows flitted away. But the cold patches remained, unaffected by the trickling warmth that came with the dawn. He was spent now, and plagued by hunger and thirst and sleeplessness. The work of the night had somehow numbed his mind, but despair had returned as weariness set in, and for the last few hours he had thought of nothing but Mum and Dad.

He heard the eerie cry over the sea and looked at the man. Though free now from shadow, the figure seemed more frightening than ever. The time they had spent together moving stones had done nothing to ease Kit's mind over his strange companion, who even now was busy among the ruins. He seemed tireless and unaffected by cold or hunger.

He wasn't human. He couldn't be.

Kit stopped by the pile with what he knew would be his last load. He had no intention of carrying any more. He needed to rest. He needed to prepare himself for the things that would come today. What those things were he did not know. But he feared them, and he knew he couldn't avoid them.

He placed the stones carefully down and stood back, looking at the pile. It was now about shoulder height, and no more stones appeared to have been taken since daylight came. The man was still down among the ruins, examining the shell of one of the old cottages.

Kit watched, still confused about the man's purpose here. If the aim was to clear the whole area, it was going to be a huge task. They had made inroads during the night, but there was still a long way to go. He looked over the pile again, then let his eyes wander up the slope toward the top of the hill, now visible again in the morning light. And he gave a start.

The pile of stones on the summit had grown.

He stared at it. The base was thicker, the peak higher. Even from down here the difference was obvious. He looked warily from one pile to the other, then felt a whisper of wind on his neck. He turned toward the cove.

The breeze was shifting round to the east. The sea was still calm, but a procession of low waves was rolling in from the great rock half a mile away—long thin combers that seemed to wriggle like serpents. One by one they broke on the shore with a soft, heavy sigh.

Windflower and *Splinters* remained undisturbed.

So, too, did the man, busy as ever with the stones. He was bent over one of the broken-down walls and did not see what Kit saw when he turned back toward the hill.

The throng of islanders lining the summit.

15

They came swarming down the slope, clubs in
hands. Kit stared in horror. They all seemed to be there, even
the old crone called Wyn, hobbling behind the others. She
had a walking stick in one hand and a club in the other. Kit
threw a glance over his shoulder. The man was making his
way back toward the pile with an armful of stones. He must
have seen the islanders now, yet he gave no sign of alarm and
seemed interested only in the stones he was carrying.

Kit looked back up the hill. The islanders were moving
fast, but the slope was awkward and the man would certainly
get here first. He tried to think what to do. They couldn't
fight the islanders—that was for sure. Their only hope was to
run. Yet all his instincts told him the man would not do this.
He seemed completely unafraid. Kit waited for him to reach
the pile, then spoke at once.

"We've got to run."

The man took no notice either of him or the approaching islanders and simply started to unload his stones.

"For God's sake!" said Kit. "We've got to run!"

The man looked at him. His eyes had turned from black

to gray but energy still poured from them. It was clear from this one glance that the man was not going to run. Kit checked on the islanders. They were already halfway down the slope.

"Listen," he said to the man. "We can't stay here. We—"

But the man merely turned away and set off back to the ruins. Kit watched, trembling. This was crazy. The man must be out of his mind. He couldn't go on carrying stones with his life in danger like this. Yet that was exactly what he was doing. He reached the broken-down wall, gathered more stones, and, in the same unhurried manner, started back toward the pile. Kit looked frantically up the hill again.

The islanders were much closer now and he could see their faces clearly. The leaders had slowed down to let the stragglers catch up, and with the exception of old Wyn, who was well behind, they formed a single body. He noticed for the first time that Torin was not among them.

But everyone else was there. He tried to pick out the most dangerous members of the group. Uddi and Zak, certainly. They were right at the front and were making no attempt to hide their particular hatred for him. Brand, too, looked fierce and ready for trouble, and so did several of the women.

The man arrived at last with his new load of stones. Kit turned quickly to him.

"Please," he begged. "Don't go back to the ruins."

The man placed his stones on the pile, then straightened up and stared toward the islanders. His face showed no emotion.

"Don't leave me," said Kit.

He turned to face the islanders. They were barely thirty yards away now but had stopped and formed into a line. Brand raised his club and bellowed down the slope.

"Go back to your pit!"

There was a growl from the other islanders. Another man raised his club.

"We know who you are!"

There was another growl from the group.

"Go back to your pit!" roared Brand. He took a step forward and brandished his club at the man. "And take your cub with you!"

Kit looked anxiously round at his companion, but as before the face showed no emotion. The man went on watching the islanders, his hands stroking the stones on top of the pile. Brand took another step forward.

"This is a holy place!" he thundered.

Kit could hold back no longer.

"It's not a holy place!" he shouted, flailing his arms at them. "It's an evil place!"

A hiss went round the group.

"It's evil because you're evil!" he yelled.

"You see?" Zak shouted to the others. "He is his master's spawn!"

"And you're murderers and rapists!" Kit ran a few yards up the slope and spat on the ground. "You're evil! All of you!"

A hail of stones came flying down the slope. Kit ducked, but several hit him on the arms and legs. He stumbled back to the pile, wincing with pain. The man had not moved. He was standing exactly as before, stroking the stones with his hands. But he, too, had been hit. Blood was trickling down his cheek. Kit caught him by the arm.

"We've got to run," he urged him. "We can't stay here."

"Look at him!" Uddi shouted. "See how he touches his master!"

Kit glared round at him.

"Like you never touched Ula!"

He felt an icy turbulence in the air, as though all the invisible shadows had suddenly converged around him. He braced himself to run. The islanders were bristling with fury, and he knew they were about to charge. He heard waves rippling onto the shingle behind him, and as they did so, a thought flashed into his mind. He gripped the man more tightly.

"Come to the beach. We can get away in the dinghy."

The man continued stroking the stones.

"Quick!" said Kit. "They'll charge any moment!"

But the man went on stroking the stones.

The coldness deepened further. More waves rippled up the beach. Kit took his hand from the man's arm. He could feel something in the air, a strange, desolate pain that seemed to haunt the cove. He heard the whispering again around his head.

More stones came flying through the air. Kit ducked and somehow avoided injury, but when he straightened up, he saw that the man had taken more hits. Blood was now streaming down his face and neck. Yet still he went on stroking the stones.

"Destroy them!" shouted Brand.

More stones rained down. Kit ducked again, but this time they pounded into his back. He yelped with the pain, but the man had fared worse. His face was now a mess of blood. Yet still he went on stroking the stones.

"Come to the boat!" shouted Kit. "While there's still time!"

And he tried to pull the man from the pile.

But the man did not move toward the boat. Instead, he started to walk up the slope. Most of the islanders drew back in alarm, but Uddi, Brand, and Zak stood firm, their faces defiant. The man took no notice of them. He simply picked up one of the stones that had fallen short, brought it back, and placed it on top of the pile.

At once it caught fire.

Kit gasped. It didn't seem possible. Yet the stones were burning before his eyes. The whole pile was ablaze, stones cracking and splintering, heat fanning over him, charred particles scattering like black dust, and flames leaping up into the air in a sudden, spectacular conflagration. The islanders shrank back, but he knew they were more dangerous than ever now. He tugged at the man's arm again.

"Come to the boat. They'll charge any moment."

He could already see them surging forward again. He looked into the man's face.

"I can't stay. I'm sorry. I can't stay."

He turned and ran. It was no use. He couldn't wait for the man any longer. He scrambled down the embankment and raced across the shingle to *Splinters*. He had no idea whether the man was following. And after seeing what he'd just done to the stones, he hoped he wasn't.

But the man was following. He had jumped down after Kit and was already making his way across the shingle. But the islanders were close behind. They had slipped past the burning stones and were rushing forward, some tearing along the embankments throwing stones as they ran, others led by Uddi and Zak thundering toward the beach.

Kit ripped the painter free and pulled *Splinters* into the shallows. He felt waves rippling against his legs and cold gusts whipping around his body. He saw the man walking toward him, stones flying about his head, and at the far end of the cove, Uddi, Zak, and several others leaping down onto the beach.

"Get in!" he shouted.

The man climbed into the stern and sat down, blood still pouring from his face. *Splinters* dipped under his weight and the keel sank into the shingle. Kit tugged at the boat but she wouldn't move. He saw Uddi and Zak charging toward them, clubs raised. He tugged again and *Splinters* broke free. Stones were now showering upon them but he jumped in, fumbled the oars into the oarlocks, and started furiously rowing. As he did so, Zak and Uddi splashed into the shallows and bounded, screaming, toward the boat.

The man didn't look back. He sat in the stern, ignoring both the men and the falling stones. But from his place at the oars Kit saw the two islanders plunge through the deepening water toward them, straining to land a blow on the man's head. They were only yards away, feet away, inches away.

From behind them came a sudden explosion.

The burning stones shattered in a blaze of yellow and gold. Uddi and Zak froze, just for a second, and looked back, and in that second *Splinters* slipped beyond their reach.

But the dangers were not past. The boat was still in throwing range from both banks and the barrage of stones continued. This time Kit knew he couldn't duck. He had to keep rowing. He kept his head down as best he could and pulled grimly on, but he was taking hits now, painful hits, mostly on the arms and back.

Yet these were nothing compared with the man's. Stones thudded into the naked skin, leaving their marks everywhere. There was no mistaking who the main target was. Yet the man did not wince or flinch. He simply sat in the stern, his eyes fixed on the sea, and let the missiles draw his blood.

Then at last they were out of range.

Kit leaned back and rested his oars. His body was stinging in the places where he had been hit, but he had taken no serious injury. Back on the shore he could see some of the stones still burning, though the pile had mostly been scattered by the blast. The islanders had regrouped and were huddled together on the bank just up from *Windflower*. He looked wearily at the man.

"What now?"

He didn't expect an answer and none came. He took a long, slow breath.

"I still don't know who you are. Or what you are."

The man continued to stare out to sea. Kit frowned and started to row again, though he had no idea where he was going.

"Maybe you're a fish," he went on. "You haven't got a boat. So you must have swum here. And you seem to spend a lot of time in the ocean."

As if in response, the man leaned over the side, brought some seawater to his mouth in cupped hands, and drank it. Kit watched warily. He had thought the man was going to wash some of the blood from his face, but he drank the seawater noisily, then reached over the side, scooped some more, and drank that, too. A third handful of seawater went the same way; and now, only now, did he start to wash the blood from his face.

Kit went on watching, trying as he did so to make sense of this man. But he was an enigma. He'd come from the sea. He was naked. He was ugly. He had a similar birthmark and similar features. He was obsessed with clearing the old ruins. He'd caused stones to catch fire and blow up. He was hated and feared by the islanders, who seemed to know him. Yet he would not speak. He would not say who he was.

The eerie cry sounded over the sea again. Kit studied the man's face but saw no change of expression. He stopped rowing and looked round for the dark shape in the water. But he saw nothing. He turned back to the man.

"I don't know what you are," he said slowly. "I don't know if you're good or evil. You certainly look evil. So I suppose that means I must look evil as well." He paused. "Maybe I am evil. Maybe we're both evil. Maybe the islanders are right."

The man's eyes stared into his. Kit dropped his head, unable to look at them.

"I don't really know what good and evil are anymore. They're just words like . . ." He thought for a moment. "Like hope."

Hope.

It seemed a mockery of a word now.

He stared down at the bottom of the boat, the bleakness of his situation heavy upon him. He felt a pressure on his hands and looked up. The man had leaned forward and placed his own hands round Kit's, and he was now squeezing them into the oar handles. Kit looked into the bloodied face. The hands squeezed his again, then started to move them round and round in the motion of pulling the oars. And Kit started to row again, slowly, awkwardly, the man's hands still tight round his.

"Where are we going?" he murmured.

The man went on moving Kit's hands. Kit peered over his shoulder. All that lay beyond the bow was sea and the great rock that had tried to rip the life out of *Windflower*.

"You don't want to go near that thing," he said.

But the man kept moving Kit's hands, forcing them round and round, until finally Kit understood.

"Okay, okay. I've worked out where you want to go."

The man took his hands away and leaned back in the stern again. Kit rowed tiredly on. He didn't want to go to the rock, but it seemed easier to row than to argue. The wind had eased further and the sea was almost still. But he didn't like it. He didn't trust it. There was a heaviness in the swell that didn't feel right.

He saw a smack of jellyfish several feet down, tiny creatures drifting past the boat. He rowed through them into clear water but soon came upon more. They seemed to stare up at him like small squinting eyes. Back on the shore he saw the figures still in the cove, no doubt watching him as he was watching them. He peered over his shoulder again.

The rock was about a quarter of a mile away. He was now aching with weariness, hunger, and thirst. He thought of hoisting the sail but quickly dismissed the idea. He'd have to move the man about the boat, and it wasn't worth the effort. Better just to row and put up with it. He pulled on, fighting the despair that was starting to overwhelm him again.

More jellyfish drifted by, thousands and thousands of them, then suddenly the water darkened and he lost sight of them. He went on jerking at the oars, his strokes clumsy and mechanical, yet as he rowed, he sensed a restless movement just below the surface of the water.

The man sat motionless.

Finally the rock drew near. Kit looked over it with distaste, remembering the mist and the darkness and the panic, and all that had followed. Here in daylight and in a calm sea it was easy to make out the teeth that surrounded the base. The sight of them made him shiver. Some were so long and sharp it was a miracle *Windflower* hadn't impaled herself or gone straight to the bottom.

How the man expected to land here he did not know.

Then he saw a place, a small gap on the southern side of the rock that seemed to lead between two of the teeth into a tiny haven with still water inside. There was also a ledge that started at that point and spiraled round the rock up to the flat summit. He felt the big hands close round his own again to guide the oars.

"It's all right," he said to the man. "I know what you want."

He rowed toward the gap, but his heart was beating fast now. The closer he drew to the rock, the more it frightened him. It was like a mountain rising from the sea. The waves at the base threw themselves against it and then pulled back with a hideous sucking noise. Here was the gap, fringed on either side by foaming eddies. He rowed *Splinters* quickly through into the calm water on the other side, and a moment later her gunwale kissed against the rock.

He caught hold of a fissure and clung to it, *Splinters* lifting and falling with the swell. The man climbed out onto the ledge without a word. Kit stood up with the painter and made to follow him—then heard a terrifying sound.

A massive explosion.

It echoed across the sea like a billow of thunder. It was followed almost immediately by a second explosion, and then a third. Kit turned, shuddering, toward the island. The air above the cove was a livid gold discolored by smoke and flying debris. He knew at once what it was and tears filled his eyes.

They had blown up *Windflower*.

16

He yelled to the man on the ledge.

"Get in! We're going back to the island!"

The man did not move.

"Get in!" Kit waved him toward the boat. "Or I'm going without you!"

Still the man did not move. Kit glared at him.

"Suit yourself!"

He pushed *Splinters* clear of the ledge and started to row back toward the gap. He could barely see for tears, but somehow he drove *Splinters* between the teeth and out into the sea again. He saw the man still standing on the ledge watching him, but he rowed on, his mind screaming with thoughts of *Windflower.*

She'd have had no chance. The islanders must have lobbed burning stones or lighted driftwood through the hatchway. There was plenty of combustible material inside the cabin, and sooner or later the fire would have reached her fuel tanks and stores of cooking gas.

He stopped a hundred yards from the rock. He had no idea what to do. All he knew was that he had to go back and see what—if anything—was left of *Windflower*. There might be something he could salvage. At the very least, he should pay his respects to the boat. Dad would want him to do that.

He stared back at the rock and saw that the man had climbed to the summit and was now standing at the southern end, gazing toward the island. He seemed somehow larger than he really was, and from here he seemed to dominate the rock. But beyond him was something even more strange: a black cloud racing in from the northeast, moving at spectacular speed. Kit watched, and then suddenly realized what it was.

Gulls.

They came screaming in toward the land. There were thousands of them. Most flew on toward the island, but several hundred landed on the rock and started to swarm over it, screeching. The man stood impassively among them, staring as before toward the island.

Kit turned toward it too. Most of the birds had already reached the shore and were flying on toward the eastern cliffs. His eyes moved quickly to the cove. The islanders were still there, moving about the beach and the embankments. He knew they were watching him, waiting for him. There was no more smoke rising, but even from here he could see some of the wreckage from *Windflower* floating about the cove.

He unshipped the oars and hoisted the sail. It flapped and twitched in the breeze. He shipped the rudder, dropped the centerboard, and set off toward the island. His mind was full of darkness. He felt rootless, as though he had nothing and nobody left. All he had was the slender possibility that Mum and Dad might just be alive, that perhaps the islanders were keeping them prisoner in a cave somewhere. If he could only find out where they were, then maybe . . .

Maybe there really was a thing called hope.

But right now he didn't believe in it.

A squall brought his attention back to *Splinters*. He trimmed the boat and sailed on. But the wind was picking up, and picking up fast. The sea, too, so calm just a short while ago, was suddenly moving again. It wasn't rough but it was tricky. The waves flickered and scurried like so many restless animals, snapping at each other and at the boat. He clenched the tiller and kept his eyes on the water to windward, searching for more squalls.

Here was one tearing in from the east. He could see it eating up the sea as it raced toward him. He felt the sail shiver and eased out the sheet, unwilling to take the full force of the gust. *Splinters* shuddered for a moment, then the squall passed and he sailed on.

But the sea still felt wrong. The waves were not just fighting the boat. They were fighting each other. There was a troubled energy somewhere at work, and the surface of the water was distorted with endless movement and a feeling of resistance. He stared over the side and saw jellyfish all around him.

The eerie cry sounded across the sea.

He looked round, searching for the huge dark shape. There was no sign of it, but he caught a turbulence of foam a hundred yards astern of the boat; beyond that, back on the great rock, the man was still standing there, staring toward the island, birds swarming around him.

The island drew close. The rocky scar slipped past to his right, the bluff to his left. He saw the ruins on either side and the charred remains of the pile he had helped the man to build. He saw islanders lining both banks and others, Uddi and Zak among them, waiting on the beach. He sailed on toward the mouth of the cove, keeping just out of throwing range. He could see that the people were ready with stones. Many were shouting and shaking their fists at him, but he took no notice. All he cared about was *Windflower*.

But only pieces of her were left.

He could see them floating about the cove among the jellyfish now drifting in their multitudes toward the beach. Fragments of the hull bobbed together with an assortment of articles that had somehow survived. He saw a life jacket, a biscuit tin, an oar, a plastic mug, a tennis ball. He saw more things than he could bear to look at.

He tried to think what to do. Part of him wanted to sail away to sea. Better to die out there than here. And yet if there was some possibility that Mum and Dad could still be alive . . .

He bit his lip.

If Mum and Dad were alive, then he should stay. He couldn't sail away while there was still hope.

"Hope," he said aloud.

There was that stupid word again.

For some reason it made him look back toward the rock. And there was the man, still standing in the same spot, staring toward the island. Despite the distance he seemed somehow larger than ever, and his arms were now stretched out to the side just as they had been up on the summit of the hill. He looked a strange and terrifying figure.

The sound of jeering brought his attention back to the cove. He looked round and saw the islanders mocking him. He stared at them bitterly. There was no point in hanging around here. There was nothing to salvage. Then he saw something among the floating wreckage.

The little carved model. Ula's prayer boat.

The thing that had started all this.

He headed straight for it.

He knew this was crazy. He should be sailing away from

the cove, not back into it. The prayer boat was close to the beach and to pick it up he would put himself in danger again, not just from flying stones but from Uddi and Zak and the others rushing out through the shallows, though he was pretty sure the water was too deep there for them to reach him.

But he had to have that prayer boat. He didn't know why. He just had to have it. He sailed into the cove, checking the wind as he did so. It was dropping as the eastern shoulder of the island blanketed it from the sail, but he felt confident there was enough of a breeze to carry him in and out again as long as he was quick and didn't give away his intentions too clearly.

He sailed on, watching the sides of the cove and the luff of the sail. A roar went up all around him, and once again he saw islanders shaking their fists. There was Brand stirring them up, his bright red hair tossing like fire. The first of the stones came hurtling at him.

He covered his face with his arm. None of the stones struck him, but some bounced off the sail into the water with little spurts of spray. More stones followed. He ducked again, but this time one caught him in the side of the face.

"Ah!" he gasped. He put a hand to his cheek and felt a bloody gash.

A cheer went up from the shore.

More stones came flying. He ducked again. All missed, but several pounded into the hull. He checked under the boom. The prayer boat was dead ahead, but so too were Uddi and Zak wading out from the shore toward him.

He sailed on, praying that the water would be too deep for them to reach him. But they kept on coming, wading strongly toward him, the prayer boat now equidistant between them. He stared at it, and at them, and at the water level around them. He had hoped it would be deeper by now, but it was only up to their waists.

More stones flew at him. One caught the top of his head, another his leg. He ignored the pain and sailed on. A cloud of gulls screamed past. Another stone struck him on the head. He forced it from his mind and carried on, his eyes fixed on the prayer boat and on Uddi and Zak. The water was up to their chests now. And there was the prayer boat, still out of reach. Another few seconds and he would have to go about and make his escape, with or without the prayer boat.

More stones thudded down. One grazed his hand, another his arm. He stared ahead. Uddi and Zak were only yards away, the water now up to their necks. They were sweeping with their arms, breaststroke-style, pushing the water aside in an effort to reach him.

But here, at last, was the prayer boat. He pushed the helm down. *Splinters* spun round into the wind and onto the other tack. As she slid round, he reached over the side and plucked the prayer boat from the water.

Uddi lunged at the same moment. His hand caught the gunwale and pulled *Splinters* off course. Kit thumped his fist down on the man's fingers. Still they held on. Zak threw himself forward, half-swimming, and gripped hold of the rudder. Both men glared up at him, their faces fierce with triumph.

Splinters rocked from side to side, losing way, her sail out of trim. They had her now, and he would not get away unless he did something quickly. He dropped the prayer boat onto the bottom-boards, seized one of the oars, and stabbed it into Uddi's chest.

The man gave a groan but held on somehow. Zak yanked at the rudder, trying to pull it off its pintles. Kit stood up and stabbed with the oar again, this time at Uddi's face. It struck him on the cheek and jerked his head back. With a shout of pain he let go of the boat and fell back into the water. But Zak still clung to the rudder and was now trying to climb into the hull.

"Get off!" shouted Kit.

He struck out with the oar again. It hit Zak in the chest and pushed him back but still he clung on. More stones came flying. Kit covered his face but three struck him hard in the side of the head. He staggered, and for a moment his vision blurred and he thought he was going to fall over the side.

He kept his balance somehow and stabbed at Zak again. This time he missed altogether. Zak caught the end of the oar and with a savage roar tried to wrench it from him. And now Uddi was swimming forward again, reaching for the side of the boat.

"Get off!" Kit shouted. "Get off! Get off!"

With an effort he pulled the oar from Zak's grasp and drove the end into the man's face. It struck him in the mouth, and he fell with a bellow of pain into the water. When he came to the surface again, Kit saw that most of his front teeth were gone.

But now Uddi's hands were on the gunwale again. Kit raised the oar high, then brought the blade sharply down on the man's fingers. Uddi gave a scream of pain and fell back into the water.

Kit saw his chance, but it would only last a second before the men rallied. *Splinters* was floundering head to wind and had no way on her. He frantically shipped the oars and started to row out toward the deeper water, stones still falling around him. The two men recovered quickly but did not try to follow. He was beyond their reach now. But Uddi roared after him.

"You won't escape retribution!"

"Go to hell!" shouted Kit.

"You'll die!" shouted Zak, his bloody mouth mangling his words. "Just like your mother and father!"

Kit stopped rowing.

"What about my mother and father?"

The two men only laughed. Kit stood up.

"What did you do to them?" he screamed.

But another voice answered. It was Brand, standing on the western bank next to old Wyn.

"What do you think we did to them?" he bellowed. "We cleansed the world of their evil filth!"

"You . . ." Kit stared at him, and at the others standing all around the cove.

"You have no place here!" shouted Brand. "You and your master will both die!"

The islanders started to roar again. More stones came whistling through the air. One hit him on the neck, another on the cheek, three or four about the body. He slumped on the thwart, grunting with the pain. More stones cascaded down on him. It was like an endless torrent. He put his hands over his head. He couldn't think. He couldn't do anything. He just wanted to die. The stones went on pounding into him and into the boat.

He heard the sail clap. He braced himself, took his hands from his head and unshipped the oars, then seized the helm and pulled in the sheet. *Splinters* started to move again, slowly at first, then with greater speed as she drew clear of the land, and somehow, with the stones still tearing about his head, he sailed out of the cove and into the open sea.

He was shaking uncontrollably now, shaking and sobbing, unable to stop. Somehow his hands sailed the boat, but his mind was on Mum and Dad. Hope was truly gone now.

They were dead after all. He had known it all along really. He just hadn't been able to bring himself to believe it.

But he did now.

He looked around him through a mist of tears. He didn't know where he was anymore. He just knew he was in a hell that seemed to have been created specially for him. He stared over toward the great rock. It was now black with birds. There was no sign of the strange man.

Not that he cared. The man could not bring back Mum and Dad.

He could barely sail now. Every part of him throbbed with pain. He had blood all over him. He had stopped sobbing, but he was breathing feverishly. He sailed past the scar and set off down the western shore. He didn't know or care where he was going. He just sailed on, drunk with grief, past the entrance to the great cavern, past the rocks and screes and rising cliffs. There was no sign of any islanders, nor even of birds.

It was a barren shore, devoid of life.

He let the sheet run out through his fingers, then took his hand from the tiller and sat there staring over the side. *Splinters* rocked in the swell. Strange, he thought, how both wind and sea had calmed down again, and how he, too, had suddenly calmed down. He felt almost dangerously still. He gazed at the water. It had that coppery sheen he had noticed once before. There was no restlessness in it now. The waves moved softly against the hull, and there were no jellyfish or other creatures to be seen.

Just sea. Deep, endless sea.

A fitting winding-sheet, he thought.

He stared at the island again. It was barely a quarter of a mile away, yet it seemed somehow more distant than it was, just as the man had seemed larger than he really was when he stood on the rock. Kit looked down over the dinghy, this tiny remnant of the world he had once known, and his eye fell on the prayer boat again. He picked it up from the bottom boards and studied it.

"So what did you bring?" he said to it. "Eh? What did you bring in answer to Ula's prayer?"

He stroked a finger all the way along its keel.

"You brought nothing but trouble. You made me pick you up. And then I ran us on the rock. And now Mum and Dad have . . ." He broke off, his hand clenched round the prayer boat. "I should hate you," he went on, still holding it. "I should hate you for all you've done. But somehow . . ." He wiped his eyes with the back of his hand. "Somehow you're all I've got left." He stared at it. "So I'll take you with me."

He moved closer to the gunwale, clasping the prayer boat tight. This needn't be difficult, he told himself. All he had to do was climb over the side and then slip away. If he didn't struggle, it would be quick. He looked over the gunwale. There was the water, so close, so ready. He thought of Mum and Dad.

And climbed over.

The water enfolded him like an embrace. It felt strangely warm. He relaxed a little. This wasn't going to be difficult after all. He held the prayer boat in one hand, the gunwale in the other. Above him the sail moved from side to side as the breeze played with it.

"Let go," he murmured. "Do it now."

He let go and *Splinters* started to drift away. Still clutching the prayer boat, he watched the dinghy ease from him, a yard, two yards, three yards, a thing of strange beauty in this strangest of moments. Yet in that moment, as *Splinters* drew farther from him, he felt something close round him, something familiar, yet something he couldn't place. Then he remembered. It was like . . .

Like the feeling he'd had when the man's hands had closed round his own and squeezed them into the oars and forced him to move. There were no hands now, none save his own, and those were holding the prayer boat. Yet there was something in the way the sea closed round him; as though it, too, was forcing him to move.

Still holding the prayer boat, he struck out for *Splinters*.

She was still drifting away, and if the wind picked up any further, he would lose her and be lost himself. He felt curiously unconcerned about this, but he struggled on toward her, hampered in his swimming by the prayer boat. Then he saw that *Splinters* had stopped. It almost seemed to him that she was waiting for him.

He reached her and gripped the gunwale, breathing hard; then he dropped the prayer boat over into the dinghy, hauled himself on board again, and sat there on the thwart, water dripping over the bottom boards. He stared about him again. Nothing had changed. The island was still here, and he was still here. He had not drowned after all.

Yet he had died. He knew with absolute certainty that he had died.

Whatever life had been, it was no longer for him.

Then he saw a light moving on the shore.

17

It was Ula. She was carrying a burning torch and waving it from side to side to attract his attention. He watched, too numb to think or move quickly. She went on waving the torch. It looked like a piece of dry driftwood she had set alight.

He looked up at the sky. He had no idea what time of day it was. Close to noon probably. There was no sun to speak of, just smoky clouds almost everywhere. He looked back at Ula, then moved painfully to the helm and started to sail toward the shore.

But he barely took it in. He barely took anything in now. His mind was on the water that had closed around him, the dark oblivion that was still so near. He was dry of tears for the moment, but he could feel them close to the surface, ready to break out again. He didn't know what he should do anymore.

Perhaps Ula would know. Perhaps she would tell him what to do.

He hoped so.

He was acting like a robot, altering course, trimming the

sail, checking the wind, going through all the motions of sailing a boat but with the greater part of him detached. He felt as though his mind and emotions had shut down. It was hard to believe they would ever open up again.

The boat drew near to the shore. It was a part of the coast he had not seen before, with a small pebbly strand bordered on either side by high rocks and a cliff straight above. He couldn't imagine how Ula had found her way there without a boat, but he knew enough of her now to understand that she could do things most other people couldn't. She had probably climbed down the cliff face, though it looked pretty sheer to him.

He saw that she had thrown away the burning torch and was now wading out to meet the boat. He eased off the sheet to stop *Splinters* from going in too fast. Ula caught hold of the bow and brought the dinghy round head to wind. He tried to speak but found he could not. He could only stare. He saw Ula watching him closely. Then suddenly, with typical deftness, she pulled the boat round toward the sea, pushed her off again, and jumped in.

"Take me away from the shore," she said.

He looked at her as she sat there, dripping on the thwart.

"Take me that way," she said, pointing toward the south.

He hauled in the sail and set off. She didn't look back at him. She had twisted round on the thwart and was now facing the bow, so he couldn't see her expression. She didn't seem interested in speaking and he was glad of it. He needed to be silent.

He had no idea where she was taking him. If they sailed far enough in this direction, they would end up at the village, but that was a long way off and he was sure she didn't want to go there of all places. She spoke suddenly.

"I didn't find your parents."

"They're dead," he said bluntly.

She looked round at him.

"How do you know?"

"Brand told me."

"Brand?"

"Yes. He said the islanders have cleansed the world of Mum and Dad's evil filth." He glared at her. "So that's all right, then. The world's going to be a cleaner place. We can all go out and celebrate."

He wanted to shriek. He wanted to strike out.

"What happened?" she said quietly.

"I had a run-in with Uddi and Zak. And all the other holy people who live here." He was struggling to breathe, struggling to stay calm. "They blew up our boat. That was clever of them, wasn't it? I expect you heard the explosion. So I sailed into the cove and spoke to that nice Reverend Brand. And His Grace was kind enough to tell me that Mum and Dad are dead."

She stared at him.

"You should never have sailed into the cove with the Skaerlanders there. It was too dangerous. Why did you do it?"

He looked for the prayer boat and saw it had rolled under the thwart. He reached down and picked it up and held it out to her.

"To collect this," he said.

She took it and held it up, her eyes running over it.

"I found it before I ever met you," he said. "I picked it out of the sea. Then after *Windflower* blew up, I saw it floating in the cove. I just had to go in and get it. I don't know why." He hesitated. "I'm sorry I never told you I had it. I suppose I didn't want to disappoint you. You sent it out in search of help. And all you got was me."

She ran a hand over the little boat.

"Maybe it was you I was praying for," she said.

They sailed on down the coast. The wind was now light and though the cliffs blocked much of the breeze, it remained steady. He was glad of the easy sailing. He had so little energy left now. Ula spoke again.

"You're shaking," she said.

"I can't stop myself."

"Keep going. We're nearly there."

He didn't ask where. He just sailed on, on, on. Then at last Ula pointed to the shore.

"There," she said.

They were approaching some kind of promontory, not a large one, more an elbow of rock that jutted out from the rough, cave-strewn coastline they had been following. He kept well clear, unable to see whether there were any low-lying teeth around the tip.

"It's safe," said Ula, as though she'd read his mind. "You can go much closer to the end."

"How do you know?" he said, still wary of the rock.

"I know the whole coastline of this island. I know all its secrets. That's why I'm still alive."

He still didn't like the look of the rock, but he sailed closer.

"Go round the point and lower the sail," she said. "You can use the oars for the last part."

He rounded the tip, still distrustful of it in spite of Ula's reassurance, but there were no hidden teeth, and *Splinters* slipped round without a single graze. On the other side of the promontory he saw the coastline stretching away again to the south, but immediately to their left was a black hole in the cliff face. Yet another cave, and clearly a large one.

"Drop the sail," she said.

"You'll have to change places with me." His voice was

now dull with fatigue. "I need to get to the halyard. And I'll have to sit where you are to row."

They changed places. He lowered the sail, pulled up the centerboard, and shipped the oars.

"Into the cave?" he said.

"Yes. You don't need to drop the mast. The cave is very high."

She was right. The ceiling was well above the top of the mast. The cave twisted round to the right so that the farthest end received little daylight, but Ula knew her way and directed him toward a plateau of rock in the corner. He brought *Splinters* alongside with a light thud.

He stood up wearily and made to clamber out, but Ula was on the rock before him, her hand held out for the painter. He passed it to her and she ran over to a jagged boulder and made fast. He climbed slowly out, aware from his first step how wet and slippery the rock was. How Ula could skip across it the way she did was a mystery. He felt her hand on his arm and realized that she was guiding him in the darkness.

"Thank you," he said.

She led him across the rock to the far end where he found a large flat slab.

"Climb up on this," she said. "It's dry. Look. Do what I do."

She climbed ahead of him, showing him the places for his hands and feet. He followed her onto the big slab and found, as she had said, a dry surface. The ceiling of the cave arched over them here, but there was still room to stand. Below them the sea washed gently into the cave, moving *Splinters* with it.

"Sit down," she said.

He was happy that she was bossing him about. He seemed to have lost all power to make decisions of his own. He sat down, his back to the wall of the cave, and stared into the darkness. It was a pleasant darkness, a darkness he needed right now. Ula slipped away to the other end of the slab and bent over something he could not see. Then she moved a little to the side, and he saw what she was doing.

She was lighting a fire. She had a pile of driftwood and dry weed already there and she was working the end of a stick into the flat end of another, rubbing vigorously with practiced hands. In what seemed no time at all she had a small fire burning.

"Come and warm yourself here," she called.

He joined her. It was a welcome little blaze. He hadn't realized how cold he was. Somehow, in his despair, he had forgotten his body. Even now as he held his palms out toward the flames, his mind was drifting back toward that threshold of reason he knew he must not cross. He heard Ula speak again.

"You must eat."

He said nothing, did nothing, felt nothing.

"You must eat," she said again.

He looked vaguely at her. For a moment he had forgotten who she was. He had been thinking of Mum. She was always telling him he should eat.

"Eat what?" he mumbled.

"I have some crabs."

And she pulled down three dead crabs from a small ledge just above her head.

"I caught these this morning and left them here in case I found you."

He said nothing. He supposed he should have said thank you, but the words wouldn't come. Ula didn't seem to mind. She simply dropped the crabs onto the fire as they were and turned them with a stick as they cooked.

Kit watched. He could feel tears welling up again. Even this primitive meal was forcing him into painful recollection. He'd eaten crabs by a campfire with Mum and Dad barely two weeks ago. Only Mum had boiled them, not just shoved them among the flames like this. But beggars couldn't be choosers, and the smell of the crabs cooking was making him mad with hunger.

When they were done, Ula lifted them out of the fire with the stick and placed them on the slab. Then she took one, tore off the claws and shell, and passed it to him. He took it from her.

"Thank you," he muttered.

He started to eat. The crab was a little charred and nothing like the one Mum had cooked that day, but it tasted good and he soon finished it. Ula finished hers just as quickly. She passed him the third crab.

"You have this one," she said.

"No, we share it."

She didn't argue. She simply ripped off the claws and shell, and they ate half each. Then they slumped back against the side of the cave.

"I have no water here," she said. "We will have to go and find some later."

"Whatever."

He didn't care. Water or no water, live or die. It made no difference now.

"We can't stay here anyway," she said. "It's not safe."

"They won't come to this place, will they?"

"They might. But the tide will come, even if they don't."

"Will it flood the cave?"

"Not completely. This slab usually stays dry, but I think the water will cover it tonight. The boat will be safe, even at high tide, because the ceiling is so high. But we must spend the night somewhere else."

They sat there in the darkness, watching the fire.

"I'm sorry about your parents," she said.

He didn't answer.

"I looked everywhere for them," she went on. "I looked in every place I could think of."

"But you knew they were dead. You said so."

"I thought they were dead. But I didn't know."

"What will . . ." He clenched his fists. "What will the islanders have done to them?"

"It's best not to talk about this."

"I need to know. I . . . I need to know."

She hesitated.

"I don't know what will have happened. There are many ways people can die. But those who are condemned by the community are usually taken over the horizon in a boat. When the boat comes back, the condemned people are no longer in it. I've never been told what happens to them—only the elders know that—but your parents were probably taken out to sea and thrown over the side."

He shuddered at the pictures flooding his mind.

"You must be strong," said Ula.

He looked down at *Splinters* tugging at her painter. Even in the darkness of the cave he could see the prayer boat on the bottom boards where Ula had left it.

"There's something I didn't tell you," he said.

"What?"

"I didn't just find the prayer boat. That time I first saw it and reached down to pick it up."

"What do you mean?"

He told her everything now, everything that had happened, everything he could remember. He told her about the man, the stones, the cold shadows, the whispering voices, which even now were starting to murmur round his head again. She heard him in silence.

"This man," said Kit. "You must tell me who he is."

"The island stories say he is the Devil."

"The Devil?"

"Yes. In human form. I'm frightened of him. I'm frightened of you."

"Frightened of me?"

"Yes."

"But why? Because I look like him?"

"Because I don't know what part you have to play in all this."

He heard the whispering again around his head. It seemed to be drawing him upward, upward, upward.

"Already you're going," she said. "I can feel it."

"I don't want to go."

"I know. But you can't stop it happening. I told you before. You've come to this island for a purpose. And it will make you do things you cannot predict. Even against your will."

He heard the long, eerie cry. It came from somewhere far off. The water in the cave seemed to tremble for a moment.

"What's making that sound?" he said.

"You've seen it," she answered. "It's the sea creature."

"But what is it?"

"The Skaerlanders say it's the Devil's familiar."

"And that cry is the sound it makes?"

"Yes."

"What about these waves that keep hitting the island?"

"They are the Devil's wrath. So the Skaerlanders believe." She poked the fire with a stick. "And there is one wave they fear more than any other."

"What wave is that?"

"A great wave that was sent once before. The island stories say it was the Devil taking his revenge. They warn that it will come again. Like the Devil himself." She gave a long sigh. "And now the stories are being proved right."

"What do you mean?"

"The Devil came in the beginning. And now he has returned."

Kit leaned his head back against the rock.

"But that can't be true. The man here now . . . whether he's the Devil or not . . . I mean, he can't be the same person as the man who came back in the beginning."

"They're the same being. The island stories describe him exactly. They tell us he's the Devil reincarnated. They say his return will herald the start of the Apocalypse and the end of the world."

Kit heard the whispering around his head again. It was growing louder. And again it was pulling him upward. He tried to push the sounds from his mind.

"These island stories," he said. "What are they? I thought you people didn't write anything down."

"We don't. The Skaerlanders believe the written word is dangerous and can lead minds astray, just as they believe music is dangerous and can lead emotions astray. So both are forbidden on Skaer. The stories are spoken stories. They've been passed down from generation to generation. They say that the world cannot be saved because the Devil's power is too great. They tell us that this island is the last holy place on earth, and it must be kept pure and untainted at all costs. And that those who take care of it will enter paradise and be saved, even when the island is destroyed."

"The island's to be destroyed too?" he said.

"Everything's to be destroyed," she answered. "The stories say that the destruction of the world is irreversible. And only the torchbearers of the one true God will be saved."

He thought of the islanders and frowned.

"And when is this . . . destruction supposed to happen?"

"It's happening now. The stories tell us about the signs of the Apocalypse, the portents that will announce the return of the Devil and the end of creation. Those signs are now with us. The sea creature, the angry waves, the Devil on the rock just as he was before."

"He was on the rock before?"

"Yes. That was where he first appeared all those centuries ago. And that was where he died. So the stories say."

"What happened to him?"

"The Skaerlanders clubbed him to death and threw him into the sea."

They fell silent again. Kit looked down and saw *Splinters* still pulling at the line. He closed his eyes and heard the whispering around him again. He was so weary now. Yet he couldn't sleep. He could only think of Mum and Dad, and that watery oblivion; and the man on the rock. He spoke into the darkness, his eyes still closed.

"But what if he isn't the Devil? What if he never was? What if there's to be no Apocalypse?"

"Do you believe that?"

"I want to believe it."

"But do you?"

"I don't know."

He thought for a moment, then spoke again.

"What of your God? Where is he?"

She did not answer this.

He heard the ripple of water below, the tap of the dinghy against the side of the rock. He heard the whispering voices grow louder.

"Are they speaking to you?" said Ula.

He opened his eyes and looked round at her.

"Can you hear them?" he said.

"No. What are they saying?"

"I can't hear any words. But it's like they're . . . calling to me." He looked away again. "But I don't want to go. I . . ." He stopped, his mind full of pictures too terrifying to behold. "I'm scared, I . . ."

He felt her eyes upon him.

"Come here," she said quietly.

He leaned toward her. She reached out her arm and put it round his shoulders. Her hand was cold; her arm was cold. She pulled him closer to her. He didn't resist. He simply flopped against her. Now he felt her warmth, her strange animal warmth. He lay there against her, darkness surrounding him, filling him, it seemed, from the inside out.

The little fire was dying. All around them were the scattered shells of crabs. He smelled the sea on her, he smelled the crabs on her, he smelled the burning wood. He smelled a faint, salty breeze wafting in through the opening of the cave. He heard the eerie cry far out to sea.

She did not react to it, nor did she speak. He pressed his head into her neck. She did not pull back. She held him tight. He felt himself shudder with tears. They came and went, and then came again. It was some time before he was spent. He closed his eyes and dived into the darkness as deeply as he could go. The whispering voices went on around his head. He ignored them and dived deeper still, into the darkness, into the folds of Ula's skin. He didn't remember sleeping. He remembered only waking.

And finding she was holding him still.

Night had fallen. The fire was dead and he was shivering with cold. The tide had risen to the top of the plateau and was licking its way up the slab toward them. Moonlight was struggling in through the entrance to the cave. The whispering voices were now so loud they seemed to echo all around him.

"Are they still calling to you?" said Ula.

He listened to them. As before, he heard no words, just voices, desperate voices. But they were calling him. He knew it. They were calling him urgently. He looked round at her.

"It's time to go," he said.

18

They stood up.

"Follow me," said Ula. "But be careful. And do exactly what I do."

She set off across the top of the slab. The water was now just a few feet below them. *Splinters* was still pulling at her painter, but she was clearly well secured and quite safe in this protected part of the cave. Ula didn't even glance at the boat. She was picking her way from the end of the slab to a large boulder just below it.

"Watch your feet," she called over her shoulder. "This is slippery."

He didn't like the look of the boulder but managed to step onto it safely. Ula turned, but only for a moment, to check that he was still with her, then she was off again to another boulder, and then another, and so on, moving steadily around the wall of the cave. He kept as close to her as he could, watching where she put her feet, since some of the rocks were barely above the water level; but she knew what she was doing, and bit by bit she led him round to the mouth of the cave.

The sea was calm and the sky dark and overcast. He saw the moon trying to push its beams past the cloud cover, but only a scant light flickered over the promontory. The voices around his head were now louder, more insistent. He saw Ula watching him in the darkness and knew what her question was.

"I don't know what the voices are," he said. "Or why they're calling me up there. I just know I've got to go."

She went on watching him for a moment, then turned abruptly toward the cliff.

"Come with me, then," she said.

And she started to clamber up the rock face. His heart sank at the prospect of another climb, but he set off after her.

"Don't go so fast," he called. "I can't climb like you."

"It's easy," she called back. "There are plenty of holds."

She was right. Even in the darkness, the climb was straightforward. But the whispering was growing louder, and the higher he climbed, the more intense it became. He saw Ula waiting for him halfway up the rock face. He struggled on up the cliff. He was still cold and weary, still hungry, still parched with thirst. His body ached where the stones had thudded into him. He reached Ula and looked across at her.

"What is it?"

"We must be very quiet from now on," she said. "There will be people looking for us. Especially you. If you must speak, keep your voice as low as possible."

"Okay."

They climbed on together up the cliff. He tried to keep his mind on the rock face, but the whispering voices were growing louder than ever. He wished they would stop. They were so full of pain. The top of the cliff drew near. Ula climbed on ahead of him and peered over the edge; then, a few moments later, she called down in a low voice.

"It looks all right, but come up slowly and don't speak."

He climbed on, desperate to be on firm ground again. He reached the top of the cliff and stopped next to her, his hands clasped round the rocky lip. Beyond them was a large hollow with scrub all around it. They were closer to the south end of the island than he had expected. Just down to the right was the smaller of the two hills, and about a mile and a half in the other direction was its larger companion. There were no fires on either peak.

But burning torches were moving about the valley.

"Stay by me," Ula whispered, and eased herself over onto the top of the cliff. He followed, glad to leave the rock face behind him. She didn't move at first but kept low, her face darting this way and that; then suddenly, without a word or a nod, she set off toward the smaller hill.

He felt uneasy about this at once. The whispering voices were clearly pulling him the other way. He glanced toward the great peak. The insipid light from the moon did little to illuminate the hill, but he could see the outline against the sky. It seemed to glower over the valley like a brooding shadow. He had no wish to go there but he knew he had to. The voices demanded it. He touched Ula on the shoulder.

"We're going the wrong way," he whispered. "They're calling me toward the big hill."

"We need water first," she answered. "You must drink. We must both drink."

He knew she was right. Yet he sensed something other than practicality behind her words. He sensed fear—fear of the great hill, of what his voices might be leading them to. He could not blame her for that. He was frightened too. But for the moment he said no more and let her lead him on across the valley. She cut a path roughly parallel to the small hill, dodging among the rocks, trees, and hillocks and keeping away from the torches; and in this manner they made their way slowly across to the other side of the island.

Suddenly she stopped and pulled him with her to the ground. He lay there, quivering, trying to see where the danger was coming from, but nothing was clear in the darkness. To his left was a patch of bushes, to his right some rocks and then the slope leading up the eastern shoulder of the small hill. Ula whispered into his ear.

"There are some people on the summit. We will have to slide across to those rocks. We are exposed here. Keep down."

She started to wriggle on her belly toward the rocks. He followed, crawling over the ground as best he could. They reached the rocks and crouched behind the largest of them.

"I still haven't seen anybody," he whispered.

She eased her head above the rock, then lowered it again.

"Look now," she whispered back.

He peered over the rock and this time saw two figures moving on the peak. They were not carrying torches.

"Can you see them?" she hissed.

"Yes."

"I feared they might be there."

"What do you mean?"

"They're guarding the water supply. They have often tried to catch me by waiting there."

He thought of the mere on the other side of the hill, presumably the destination Ula had had in mind for them.

"How have you managed to get water in the past?" he said. "I mean, if they're watching the water supply?"

She nodded toward the eastern shore.

"One of the streams spills out into the sea down there, and it's possible to climb up the overhang of the cliff and catch it as it comes out. But it's very dangerous. Too dangerous for you. We will have to get our water somewhere else." She turned toward the great hill. "We must go this way after all."

He heard the fear in her voice again. She nodded toward a grassy mound just down from the rocks.

"We must get behind that. Let me go first, then you follow."

She looked around her and up the hill, then scampered across to the mound and disappeared behind it. He ran across and joined her. She peered up the small hill again.

"I don't think they saw us. Come on."

And she set off again, this time toward the center of the valley and the great hill beyond, guiding him as before between the torches. Once again she took him down paths and across terrain he had not seen before until finally, almost midway across the valley, she stopped at the edge of a hollow bordered by rocks and bushes.

At the far end was a cairn.

This was clearly not one of Ula's hiding places. The top only reached as high as his waist. But he could guess what she used it for and was not surprised when she removed some of the stones to reveal a small cupboard she had created inside. She reached in and pulled out a lidded bowl similar to the one she had produced in the other cairn.

"Here," she said, holding it out.

"You first," he said.

"No, you."

He took the bowl from her, smelled the water, then drank about half. Then he handed it back to her. She took it, raised it to her mouth, then lowered it again without drinking anything.

"Kit?" she said.

He gave a start.

"That's the first time you've ever called me by my name."

"I don't know if it is your name."

"What do you mean?"

"I don't know who you really are."

She held the bowl out to him again. He shook his head.

"You haven't drunk your bit yet," he said.

"I'm not thirsty."

"Yes, you are."

She pushed the bowl toward him.

"You need this more than me," she said. "And I can get water more easily than you."

He hesitated.

"Drink it," she said. "Do it for me."

He drank the rest of the water, then put the bowl down on top of the cairn.

"What were you going to say?" he asked her. "When you said 'Kit' just now?"

"I was going to say you must be careful."

"You weren't going to say that. You were going to say something else."

She was silent for a moment, then she said, "I'm frightened."

"So am I."

They looked at each other. Her face was dark, but her eyes were like two flames.

"Your eyes are burning," he said.

"So are yours."

She reached out and took his hand.

"Something's happening to the world," she said. "I can feel it."

"So can I."

"It's happening now. But I don't know what it is."

"Maybe it's the Apocalypse," he said.

"Maybe it is."

He looked past the flames of her eyes and saw more flames break out in the darkness. A fire had started on the summit of the great peak. Ula caught the direction of his gaze and turned to look, and they stared together at the blaze now hissing and leaping into the night. By its light they could see the pile of stones at the highest point of the hill.

And the naked man standing next to it.

He looked more terrifying than ever. He seemed huge now, even from down here in the valley.

"He is the Devil," Ula said. "He is pure evil. You must not go to him."

Kit heard the voices calling him up the slope.

"You're not like him," she said. "You're different. You're Kit."

"I am like him." Kit stared at the man. "I don't know how. I don't know why. I just feel I'm . . . the same as him."

"He is deceiving you."

Kit let go of Ula's hand.

"Don't go," she said.

"I must."

"You will be lost."

"And what if I am lost?" He looked hard at her. "What does it matter? My life's over anyway. It was over the moment I picked up your prayer boat. I've got nothing to live for without Mum and Dad." He shook his head. "Why should I fear the end of the world when my world's ended already?"

She looked down.

"I will pray for you," she said.

"To the God who doesn't exist?"

She looked up at him again, the flames in her eyes brighter than ever.

"I will pray to any God who will listen," she said.

He set off toward the great hill. He didn't look back. If he saw her face again, he knew he would waver. He kept his eyes on the figure at the top of the hill, the ugly creature now visible for all to see. But to make doubly sure that no one on the island could miss him, the man stretched out his arms to the side in that now familiar gesture and gave the great roar that Kit had heard before.

"Waargh!"

The cry resounded over the valley with unnatural force. A swarm of gulls rose into the sky over the eastern cliffs. Kit looked around him and saw torches moving fast toward the hill.

"Waargh!" came the cry. "Waargh! Waargh!"

More gulls rose screeching into the air. From over the sea came the long, eerie cry. Kit walked on toward the hill. The voices round his head were now louder than ever. They were no longer whispers. They were murmurs, they were mutters, they were shouts, they were screams. He was trembling and he couldn't stop. He glared up at the figure far above him.

"I don't want to be like you!" he snarled. "I don't want to be like you!"

"Waargh!" bellowed the man.

"But I am like you!" Kit went on glaring at the figure. "I bloody well am like you!"

"Waargh!" came the roar. "Waargh!"

And now he could hear other roars, the roars of islanders racing toward the hill. It was only a matter of time before one of them saw him. He stumbled on, still growling up at the figure on the peak.

"So how did you get from the rock to the hill? Eh? How did you get there? Did you fly with the birds? Does that mean I can fly too?"

He couldn't fly. He could barely walk. His body was so painful and weary it took all his energy just to trudge. He forced himself on toward the end of the valley, aware of the torches moving closer. Then he heard the first shout.

"Over there!"

It came from somewhere to the right. He turned and saw two men with torches tearing across a clearing toward him. He started to run toward the base of the hill. More shouts rang out. He glanced over his shoulder and saw that three women had joined the men, and all five were now pelting after him.

He was breathing hard already and struggling to keep going. He glanced up at the peak. The fire seemed brighter now and the man's body immense, far greater than it could possibly be. But he had no time to look more closely. He had to keep running.

He heard more shouts behind him. One of them sounded like Uddi's voice. He didn't look back but plunged on over the rough ground until he reached the foothills of the great peak. Now he checked over his shoulder. A crowd of islanders had formed in his wake. Not all were there—some were still hurrying in from other parts of the valley—but he could see Uddi, Zak, and Brand among them. Torin, too, was there, the only one without a club. Brand gave a great shout and the islanders surged forward.

Kit drove himself on up the hill. He didn't want to go to the figure. He wanted to throw himself on the ground and give himself up to the clubs. But something too powerful to resist was drawing him up the slope. He stumbled on, unwilling to look up, unwilling to look back, the voices growing louder and louder about his head. Halfway up the hill he stopped and checked over his shoulder again.

The islanders were barely fifty yards behind him.

"Waargh!" came the cry from the peak.

He pushed himself on up the hill, determined to lengthen the gap between him and his pursuers, but now the pain in his body was beginning to tell, and his legs and lungs starting to protest.

A spout of flame shot up from the fire on the summit.

"Waargh!" bellowed the man.

An answering bellow came from the islanders. It sounded so close that Kit looked in a panic over his shoulder again. Uddi and Zak had pushed ahead of the others and were no more than thirty yards behind.

"Waargh!" came the roar above him.

He blundered on toward the summit. The voices in the air grew louder. He put his hands to his ears and tried to shut them out. But it was no good. They were roaring inside him as well. He saw Uddi and Zak and the others stampeding up the slope. He saw the naked body glistening above him. He looked up at the sky and screamed into the night.

"Take this away! Take this away!"

The only answer was a screeching of birds.

He clenched his fists and raced on toward the summit.

19

Something struck him hard in the back. He
stumbled to the ground but picked himself up again. He saw
a spent torch rolling back down the slope. He turned and saw
Uddi and Zak glaring up the hill at him, and just behind
them the main body of the islanders. Someone else threw a
torch. It missed. He stared down at the faces below him. The
islanders had stopped now and were staring back up at him
with loathing.

He started to back toward the summit. For all the terror of
the naked man, he knew he had to watch the islanders. Yet he
felt the man's presence behind him as he moved closer. He felt
the energy that poured through the misty eyes. He wanted to
turn; he wanted to look at the man.

But he no longer dared take his eyes from the islanders.

He went on backing up the slope. The voices in the air
grew louder still. From his left came the crackle of the fire.
From behind him came the man's great roar.

"Waargh!"

More of the islanders threw torches. All fell short. He
reached the summit and stopped. He knew the man was just

inches behind him. But still he could not turn. He could only watch the islanders. And as he watched, he felt his fear turn to defiance.

"You can't hurt us!" he screamed at them. "We're too strong for you!"

The islanders growled back at him. Brand took a step forward.

"Go back to the pit!" he bellowed.

"You go back to the pit!" shouted Kit. "You're finished here! Your world is over!"

Brand raised his club.

"Kill the Devil!" he roared. "Kill the Devil's cub!"

Kit stretched out his arms to the side just like the man behind him.

Yes, he thought. Kill me. I'm ready.

The islanders charged up to the top. Kit stretched out his arms as far as they would go. All he wanted now was a swift end. The air was thick with shouts and stamping feet and the shimmering voices now wailing about him. He felt the man's stillness behind him, so different from his own quivering defiance. The islanders closed upon them and raised their clubs.

Then, to Kit's astonishment, they dropped them to the ground.

He stared. Their faces had suddenly changed. Anger was gone. Hatred was gone. In their place was terror. Then one of the women cried out.

"My God! My God!"

And the islanders turned as one and fled back down the slope toward the valley, screaming as they went. Kit stared after them, breathing hard, then lowered his arms and turned to the man. And as he did so, his eyes fell for the first time upon the cove, and he saw what the islanders had seen as they poured over the summit.

Figures in their hundreds were moving up the northern slopes. He shuddered at the sight of them. He knew at once what they were. He had seen them before as cold shadows. He had heard them whispering all around him. But now they were flesh and blood. They had faces, features, bodies, breath. He saw men, women, children, all screaming into the air in thin spectral voices.

They were carrying stones toward the summit.

He watched in horror. There were figures everywhere, some down among the ruins shifting stones across to piles around the embankment, others taking stones from these piles and carrying them up the slope. He stared in dread at this ghostly procession. Some of the figures were only yards from the summit and he could see them clearly. They were dressed in the simple garb of the islanders, yet he knew they were from another age. He looked on, trembling, but they did not look at him. Their faces had a fixed stare, as though they had one thing only on their minds.

He soon saw what that was. They were building the pile of stones here on the summit using bricks from the old ruins. He watched as the first figures reached the top, placed their stones on the pile, then set off back down the slope. A chill passed through him as they swept by.

He turned, shivering, toward the man.

"I wanted to die," he murmured. "I wanted to die so much."

The man did not answer. Kit took a step closer to him.

"Why won't you set me free?"

The man reached out a hand and tapped him lightly on the chest.

Kit felt a strange twisting movement, not on his skin but deep inside him. It came from somewhere far down, like a coiled serpent rising from the bottom of the sea, and it swirled up, up, up, along his spine and through into his head. He saw a cascade of color, a splintering of light.

Then he slumped to the ground.

He did not lose consciousness. Consciousness surged into him, more consciousness than he could bear. It rushed through him like a river bursting its banks. He saw wider, farther, deeper, higher. He saw fire, he saw fury, he saw serpentine shapes. He saw glittering eyes all around him, and then mouths, thousands and thousands of great, cavernous mouths opening, crunching, devouring worlds, planets, universes. And then somehow these myriad eyes and mouths became one and there was just a void. A great, watching void.

He stared into it and felt himself disappear.

How long he lay there he did not know. He only knew that it was days. He felt night go and dawn come, and then night again, and then dawn, and then night again, and on and on, it seemed, as though time had no meaning anymore. And during this time that had no meaning he felt the disintegration of all he knew. The world he had once believed in slipped away. The sound of the gulls, the smell of the sea, the touch of the breeze slipped away. His body slipped away. His thoughts slipped away.

He became nothing.

Yet even into nothing there came new realities. He sensed movement within him again, silent, shadowy movement. He saw pictures in his mind. He saw figures in the cove. He saw a dark, moving shape in the water. He saw a man floating in the sea, a naked man, face down. He saw a great wave rushing in toward the land, a wave that ate up the sea, ate up everything in its path, a wave growing, growing, growing, hurtling past the great rock and on into the mouth of the cove. He saw buildings there, stone buildings.

He saw chimneys smoking, fires burning. He saw fish stocks in baskets. He saw people cooking, washing clothes, careening boats. He saw them looking up in terror. He saw them running. He saw a wall of green and white plunging over them, over everything, a huge, watery monster thundering up the cove, over the banks and on up the slope, reaching toward the summit. And then slowly, spent at last against the body of the hill, drawing back into the sea, leaving only a wreckage of stones.

And then there was nothing again.

Save the light of dawn. And Ula's face looking down at him.

"You're alive," she said. "I feared you were dead. You had stopped breathing."

He opened his mouth to speak, but she put a finger to his lips.

"No, just lie there."

And so he lay there looking up at her, awareness of himself slowly returning. He smelled the sea again, he heard the gulls, he felt the hard ground beneath him. He saw Ula's eyes watching him. He turned his head and looked from side to side. The fire that had been burning there was dead. The man and the shadowy figures were gone.

All that was left was a huge cairn.

He stared at it in the gray morning light. It was a massive thing, a tall, conical structure at least forty feet high, beautiful in its proportions and the perfect placement of the stones. The sides looked smooth and almost shiny as the sun's rays caught them. The top of the cairn was now the highest point on the island.

"We must find you some food and water," said Ula.

He stood up and took some slow breaths. He felt strangely light. For a moment it almost felt as though he had no body at all. He squeezed his skin, blinked his eyes, felt his pulse. All was normal. Yet he felt different, somehow trans-figured.

He saw Ula watching him. She seemed wary of him, and he could understand that. He was wary of himself right now. He thought of his hilltop vision and tried to make sense of it. Some parts were clear; others were not. And it was these that disturbed him.

He looked down into the cove and saw that the ruins had vanished. Nor was there any sign of the man.

"He's gone," said Ula, picking up his thought.

"Are you sure he's not on the great rock?"

"I haven't seen him there. I haven't seen him anywhere." She paused. "And the Skaerlanders have gone too."

He looked round at her.

"They've gone?"

"Yes."

"All of them?"

"Except old Wyn. I've seen her down in the village. But none of the others. I think they've gone."

"When did they leave?"

"The night you first came up here and stood with the man against them."

"Did you see all that?"

"I saw everything. I came up the slope too."

"I didn't see you."

"No one saw me. But I saw you. I saw the man. I saw the spirits of the dead carrying the stones. I saw the Skaerlanders run away down the hill. I saw you fall down when the man touched you. I thought you were dead, but I was too fright-ened of the man and the spirits to go to you while they were still there. I waited until they were gone."

"When did they go?"

"An hour ago. In the darkness before dawn. I didn't see what happened. I just saw them slip back down toward the cove. When I came up here at first light, they were all gone. It's as though they've disappeared into the sea."

He said nothing. Ula went on.

"But the Skaerlanders left during the first night. They ran back to the village without stopping. I've never seen faces so full of terror. They loaded up the biggest boats with all the food and water they could find and then put off. I saw them in the distance when the light came. I think they've all gone. I've seen no one except for old Wyn in the days since they left."

"How long was I lying up here?"

"Four days."

"Four days!" He stared at her. "Are you sure?"

"Yes," she said. "And the man and the spirits were building the cairn all that time. They didn't stop day or night. I watched them."

Four days. It didn't seem possible.

He wandered over to the cairn, trying to work out how they'd managed to get the stones to the top without some kind of scaffolding. Then, as he drew nearer, he saw that the outer smoothness was an illusion. The stones had been placed with beautiful symmetry, but the exterior was not smooth at all. There were plenty of jutting edges to climb on.

He turned and stared down the northern slope of the hill. And as he did so he realized that just as he felt different, so too did the cove. The coldness, the whispering, the shadows, the figures—all were gone. It was as though the man had taken those things with him.

"The figures," he murmured. "You said they were spirits of the dead?"

"Yes."

216

"What do your island stories say about them?"

"I'll tell you later. When you've had some food and water. Can you walk?"

"Yes."

"Good. Come on."

And they set off down toward the valley. But walking felt strange. He felt as though part of him was still lying on the summit. He stared at himself. His arms and legs moved, his eyes turned this way and that, yet the essence of him seemed somewhere quite apart. He squeezed his hands into fists and tried to will his body to come back to him.

"You're somewhere else," Ula said after a while.

He didn't answer. He had no answer. She looked across at him.

"Where have you gone?"

"I'm right next to you."

"You're like a ghost."

"Thanks very much."

"You move like a ghost. You speak like a ghost."

"I haven't heard many ghosts speak, so I wouldn't know."

Yet he knew she was right and that his flippant answer was a poor attempt to cover his unease. They walked on in silence and eventually came to the base of the valley.

"Which way?" he said.

But she was already leading him down one of the narrow tracks to the right. They soon came to a clearing studded with cairns and boulders. In the middle was a small fire, nearly dead.

"Did you light that?" he said.

"Yes," she said. "Sit by it and get warm."

He sat down on a low rock, his mind roaming once more through the images he had seen on the hilltop. Ula rekindled the fire, then disappeared behind him. He didn't look round.

He could hear her fumbling with the stones from one of the cairns and could guess what she was doing. A moment later she reappeared with an open bowl. He looked inside and saw some loose pieces of cooked meat.

"What's that?" he said. "Some kind of bird?"

"Never mind. Just eat it."

He put a piece into his mouth and started to chew. It was nothing like any meat he'd ever had before, but it tasted good. Ula watched him in silence. He held out the bowl to her, but she shook her head.

"You must eat too," he said.

"It's all right. I've got some more."

"You're not just saying that to make sure I get enough food?"

"No, I've got some for myself."

She ran back to the cairn and soon returned with another bowl.

"This is the last of it," she said.

He glanced over and saw that her bowl had the same kind of meat in it, and no less than he had. He waited until she had started eating, then turned back to his own bowl.

"So you're not going to tell me what I'm eating?" he said.

"No."

"Probably just as well."

"You must eat as much as you can," she said. "You've had nothing for four days."

"I bet you haven't had much either in that time."

"No. I've been watching the summit."

"Did the islanders leave any food behind?"

"They left some of the geese for Wyn. We can kill one later. And they left the sheep and goats, obviously."

They finished their meat in silence. Then Ula looked at him.

"We must drink now," she said.

"Have you got any water here?"

"No. We must go to the village."

"At least we don't have to worry about getting caught. We can drink straight from the mere."

"The what?"

"The mere. The lake thing. The water source."

"Yes. Wyn won't be able to stop us doing that. Are you ready to go?"

"Yes."

They set off across the valley. The morning sun was bright now, yet Kit found himself shivering; though the food had grounded him to some extent, he still felt strangely disconnected from his body. He pushed himself on even so, his eyes on the small hill at the far end of the valley. It was strange to think that the village on the other side was now deserted, save for a harmless old woman.

"You were going to tell me about the spirits of the dead," he said.

"They were islanders."

"I thought so. I could see it in the way they were dressed."

"They died here many centuries ago," she said. "It's the island story that's most often told. I didn't tell it to you before because it has always frightened me."

"But the spirits are gone now."

"Yes, I know," she said. "I can feel they're gone. And I've seen their faces now. I'm no longer frightened of them. I feel sorry for them."

"I was frightened of them too," he said. "Especially when they were just cold shadows and I didn't know what they were."

"No one knew what they were," said Ula. "So no one

liked to go to the cove. But everyone suspected it was the Skaerlanders who died there long ago. I can tell you what happened now, if you want."

Kit remembered the pictures he had seen while lying on the hilltop.

"There was a wave," he said. "A great wave."

Ula looked round at him in surprise.

"How did you know that?"

"It rolled in from the north," he went on. "Past the great rock and straight into the cove. And all the people living there were drowned. Their boats were wrecked, their houses smashed into ruins. The wave thundered up the hill and then finally lost its power and started to draw back into the sea. And as it did so it pulled all the people and their possessions with it."

She stared at him.

"How do you know this?"

He shrugged.

"I just do. It's the great wave you told me about, isn't it? The one the islanders have always feared most."

"Yes."

"The Devil's revenge."

"Yes."

They walked on toward the small hill.

"So what was it revenge for?" he said.

"Can't you guess?"

"I think I can."

"Tell me."

"They were the first islanders," he said. "They murdered him because they believed he was the Devil. They clubbed him to death and threw him off the rock. And this was his revenge. Is that what the island story says?"

"Yes. It says our ancestors killed the Devil, and the Devil

sent a great flood in the form of a huge wave and almost all were drowned. Only those few who were on the other side of the island survived. And they had to start a new community. But the Devil's revenge did not end with the wave. There's been starvation and pestilence and many other terrible things throughout the centuries since. And the number of births has gone down with each generation so that the community has gradually wasted away. All this is blamed upon the Devil."

He glanced at her.

"And do you still believe that man's the Devil?"

"I don't know what he is," she said. "Not now."

"What about me? What do you think I am?"

"I don't know."

He bit his lip.

"Are you still frightened of me?"

"Yes."

"I don't want you to be."

"But I am."

They walked in silence for some time.

"Ula?" said Kit eventually.

"Yes."

"Why did the first islanders think the man was the Devil?"

"The island stories don't tell us. They just say that the Devil came and stood on the rock. And the islanders knew they had to kill him or be destroyed."

"But they were destroyed anyway by the wave. Most of them at least."

"Yes. The Devil was too strong. And now he has won again. The world of the Skaerlanders is over forever."

"But he's made the island good again," said Kit. "He's released the spirits of the people who killed him. It's like he's forgiven them."

"Forgiven them?"

"Yes. Doesn't it feel like that to you? They killed him and they suffered for it, but now he's forgiven them and let them go. And that big cairn is a kind of monument." Kit thought for a moment. "What will happen to the islanders in the boats? Where will they go?"

"I don't know."

"To look for another island? Another world?"

She shook her head.

"There is no other world for them."

They drew closer to the small hill. His body still felt uncomfortably light, and he was thirsty now. He thought of the water just a short distance ahead. Yet even water and the prospect of more food and a peaceful island could not fill him with happiness. Whatever he'd said to Ula about the island being good again, he knew that he was walking into a desolate future without Mum and Dad.

And something else was wrong, something bigger even than this. He wasn't sure what it was. The hilltop vision pressed itself upon him again, and he found himself staring beyond the island toward the horizon.

"We're nearly there," he heard Ula say.

But he didn't answer. He could only think of the pictures in his mind. He went on staring toward the horizon, suddenly deeply unsettled. There was an energy in the sky that he didn't like. They reached the bottom of the hill and started to climb. He looked toward the summit and remembered the way the man had suddenly appeared there and defied the islanders in the village.

But that man was now gone.

The pictures went on racing through his mind. They reached the top of the hill and looked down over the village. It was strangely silent. There were only two boats left in the harbor, one large, one small, both unweatherly. The sheep and goats were still in the enclosures, but there were hardly any geese left.

"Come on," said Ula. "We must drink."

They hurried down the slope to where the mere over-flowed and splashed down over the rocks toward the cliffs. Kit knelt down and drank, long and deep, and as he drank he felt the void open up inside him again. His vision on the hilltop had started with a feeling of water bursting the banks of his mind. And now as water coursed into his body, he felt the same opening of himself, the same clarity, the same naked fear. He stared once more toward the horizon. And then he spoke.

"It's not over."

He didn't know what he meant. He saw Ula watching him as she drank. Then her eyes moved from him and seemed to fix on something down in the village. He turned to look. And there, down by the harbor's edge, was the fig-ure of old Wyn.

She was beckoning to them.

20

"What does she want?" he murmured.

Ula said nothing. She was watching the old woman closely, and with obvious dislike.

"We don't have to go to her," she said eventually.

"She's got something she wants to say."

"That doesn't mean we have to go to her."

Kit scooped some more water into his mouth, his eyes on old Wyn. She was now hobbling past the cottages toward the hill. She certainly looked no threat. Her movements were labored, her steps wobbly. She stopped after a while and leaned on her stick, and beckoned to them again.

"I'm going down," he said to Ula.

"I don't trust her."

"Neither do I, but she can't hurt us, can she?"

"Not on her own."

"You said there was no one else left on the island."

"I haven't seen anybody but her. And the boats looked full. But they were a long way out to sea." Ula was silent for a moment, then she said, "I still don't want to speak to her. I hate her. And she has good reason to hate me."

"Why?"

"It doesn't matter."

He looked round at her.

"Why?" he said again. "Tell me."

"She is Uddi's mother. And she had another son."

"Had?"

"Yes. I killed him."

He stared at her.

"I told you I was evil," she said.

"But why did you kill him?"

"He raped me," she said simply. "So I stove his head in with a rock."

"Bloody hell!" He found himself looking at her with a mixture of respect and trepidation. Then he said, "It doesn't make you evil. Getting back at a man who raped you."

"I have done other evil things. Many other evil things."

He saw old Wyn beckoning again.

"I'm going down," he said. "Just to find out what she wants. You stay here."

"No, I'll come."

They set off down the slope toward the village. He felt better for the food and water, but his body still seemed unnaturally light, as though a gust of wind might blow it away at any moment. The old woman watched their approach. She had not moved any farther now that she'd seen they were coming down, and was simply leaning on her stick, waiting, her eyes narrowed to slits.

He studied her as he drew nearer. She was repellent to look at and he didn't trust her any more than Ula did, but he didn't fear her. He was more wary of the cottages they were passing. The islanders appeared to have gone, yet he couldn't help checking the doorways on either side of them for any movement within. He noticed that Ula was doing the same.

But there was clearly no one here.

He felt Ula touch his arm as they drew close.

"Be careful," she said in a low voice. "She means us no good."

He nodded but walked on. The old woman was only a short distance away now. The sun was bright upon her face, and he could see her small eyes watching them as they approached. She made no attempt to hide her disgust at the sight of them.

They stopped a few yards from her.

"What do you want?" he said.

She simply went on watching them. He tried again.

"Why didn't you leave with the other islanders?"

The old woman squeezed the handle of her stick. But this time she answered.

"I am too old for boat trips." She sniffed. "I might as well die here as die at sea."

"What do you want to say to us?"

She watched them again in silence. He glanced at Ula, then back at the old woman.

"We're not going to stand here all day waiting for you to speak. If you've got something to say, say it."

"Your parents . . . ," she began.

He took a step toward her.

"What about them?"

"You might as well know."

"Know what? Tell me!"

The old woman watched him drily.

"Tell me!" he shouted.

"We should have killed them." She sniffed again. "I wanted us to kill them. But nobody listened to me."

"Where are they?" He strode up to her. He wanted to grab her and shake her until she told him. "Where are they?"

She looked up into his face with a contempt so deep he wanted to squeeze the life out of her. He even felt his hands reach for her neck. She ignored this and went on, still watching his face.

"They're tied up and gagged." She spoke without emotion. "We've been starving them of food and water. They won't last much longer, thank God."

"Where are they?" He seized her by the shoulders. "Where are they?"

But now he felt Ula's hand on his arm. Reluctantly he let her pull him back a few yards.

"Kit," she whispered. "Ask yourself—why is she telling you this? She has no reason to want to help you."

"But I've got to know!" he hissed back. "I've got to know!"

Ula turned toward old Wyn.

"Why tell him this now?"

The old woman shrugged.

"They're going to die anyway. He can get rid of the bodies and save me the trouble."

"You bloody—" Kit started forward but Ula pulled him back.

"Don't," she breathed. "She's trying to provoke you. She's got nothing left to do but hurt you in any way she can. Don't let her."

Kit shook himself free and strode up to the old woman again.

"Where are they?" He thrust his face close to hers. "If you don't tell me now, I promise I'll kill you."

"As if that would frighten me." She stared back at him, her eyes almost mirthful. "I'll tell you because I choose to. Not because of your insolent threats."

He waited, his hands clenching and unclenching. She

watched him for a few more moments, then spoke again.

"They're in the chapel."

He pushed past her and raced off down the slope. But he'd barely gone a few yards before he felt Ula's hand round his arm again.

"Wait!" she said, running alongside him. "Stop!"

He didn't stop. He couldn't stop.

"I've got to check!" he panted. "I've got to check!"

"I know, I know, but stop! Just for a second!"

He stopped, with an effort.

"Don't try and hold me back," he warned her.

"I won't, but listen. You must be careful. Don't just run in. You don't know what's in there."

"Did you look in the chapel when you searched the island for them?"

"No. I looked in the cottages, but I never thought they would keep your parents in a place they regard as sacred. That's why I'm suspicious. I don't think they would do that. They would feel it's tainting a holy place to have your parents in there."

He looked back toward the chapel.

"I've got to check it out," he muttered, and ran on.

He didn't know whether she was still following. Certainly she wasn't running beside him anymore. But he couldn't think of that now. All his attention was on the chapel. The southeastern point of the island drew near. There was the timber store he had hidden in. And here at last was the chapel, raised on its knoll above the sea. He ran up to the door and stopped outside, his heart pounding against his chest.

He could hear nothing save the wash of the sea against the great slabs of rock below. He glanced over his shoulder and saw Ula standing by the timber store, watching uneasily. Old Wyn had not moved from where they had left her, but she was watching too. He took a deep breath and reached for the door.

But at that moment it opened from within.

A hand yanked him inside and then let go. He tumbled to the chapel floor and rolled over it. He saw shadowy figures as he fell. He scrambled to his feet and looked across. Uddi and Zak were standing before him. Brand was just behind them, moving to the door to cut off his escape.

There was no one else inside the chapel.

"Where are they?" he demanded. "Where are my mum and dad?"

Uddi stepped forward, seized him by the neck, and threw him back down to the floor. Kit scrambled up again, ready for the next attack, but the man merely sneered at him.

"We're not here to talk about the dead." Uddi waited for a moment, as though for those words to sink in, then glanced over his shoulder at Brand. "Is she out there?"

Brand peered out of the doorway.

"Yes. She's by the timber store." He closed the door and came over to join the other two men, his eyes now on Kit. "And what a fitting friend she makes for this creature. The Devil's whore for the Devil's cub."

"She's not a whore!" Kit snapped.

"She's a whore!" said Brand. "She's the bedfellow of any-one who wants her."

"Except Uddi." Kit glared at the man. "He had to try and rape her, didn't he? Just like his brother did. But I suppose rape's fine round here, is it? Among all you holy people?"

Brand snorted.

"Women who lead men astray deserve nothing better."

"She's not a woman! She's a girl!"

"She's what she is." Brand's eyes narrowed. "And you are what you are."

The men started to move forward, keeping well apart to cover all escape. Kit backed toward the center of the chapel. He'd taken in little so far beyond the fact that Mum and Dad weren't here. He looked quickly around him.

There was only one way out and that was the door. The chapel was simply a large windowless room. There was no pulpit, no altar, nothing remotely churchlike, just a circular space about eight feet in diameter in the middle of the room surrounded by tiered chairs facing inward. He looked back at the three men edging toward him.

"What did you do to my mum and dad?" he said, still backing toward the center.

They didn't answer. Suddenly the door opened. For a moment he felt a mad rush of hope. But it was only old Wyn. She leaned against the doorway, watching. The men didn't look at her, but Zak called over his shoulder.

"Is she still out there?"

"Yes. By the timber store."

"Keep an eye on her. We'll deal with her later."

Kit felt the back of one of the chairs against his legs. On an impulse he picked it up and swung it over his head. Uddi threw himself forward. Kit brought the chair down as hard as he could, but he was too late. Uddi's weight drove him back over the floor, the big man floundering on top of him.

"Keep hold of him!" roared Brand.

But Uddi already had him in an iron grip. Kit struggled but it was no use. He could feel all the pent-up hatred of the man in those clenched hands, just as he could see it in the eyes and the gritted teeth. Zak ran forward and the two men picked him up and carried him to the center of the ring.

Then threw him down.

"Show him as he is!" commanded Brand.

Uddi and Zak started to tug at his clothes. He tried to

resist but it was no good. They were too strong, too determined. They ripped off his T-shirt, his shorts, his briefs, his socks and shoes, and then they stood back and leered down at him. He shivered, naked, on the floor.

"Look at him," said Brand with a curl of the lip. "Made in his master's image."

Kit drew his knees into his chest and held them there. He saw Uddi and Zak step to the sides of the chapel. They returned a moment later with thick hairy ropes. Brand stepped closer.

"So is the Devil going to come and save you?"

"You don't know he's the Devil."

Brand glanced at his companions, who were now swinging the ropes. Then he turned to Kit again.

"We know who the Devil is. He gives himself away by his appearance."

"His appearance?" Kit snarled. "What? Because he's ugly? What if he was good-looking? Does that mean he couldn't be the Devil?"

"You're playing with words," said Brand. "We're not fooled by your trickery. The outer appearance is only one sign. The Devil's works tell us what he is."

"And what works are those?" said Kit, scowling. "He's cleared up some old ruins. He's built a big cairn. He's released some miserable spirits from the island. What's so bad about that?"

"You know nothing." Brand's eyes were full of scorn. "You're so filled with corruption you can't see the truth. The Devil has spread his evil since the beginning of time. The world is now so sated with darkness it cannot be healed. This island was once sacred. But the Devil came here, too. He brought plague and famine and persecution. Our crops failed. Our fish stocks failed. Our water dried up. Our women found they could not conceive. The Devil did all this. The island was a place of virgin purity. He came here and he defiled it."

"He came here and your ancestors killed him."

"He is the Devil. He must be destroyed."

"But what if you're wrong?" shouted Kit. "What if your ancestors were wrong? What if he's not the Devil? What if he's just a man standing on a rock?"

All three men laughed.

"A man standing on a rock!" Brand's voice was laced with derision. "And how did this so-called man get to the rock? Did he fly? Did he swim? Where's his boat?"

Kit saw the ropes swinging, swinging.

"How did the stones catch fire?" Brand went on. "How did the spirits become flesh and build the cairn? How did the waves become so violent? How did his familiar reappear in the sea? How did he die centuries ago only to come back now in all his foul nakedness?"

Kit said nothing.

"He is the Devil," said Brand. "He is your master. But you will not be saved."

"Neither will you," retorted Kit.

"We are already saved. God is our redeemer. We have no fears of the Apocalypse."

"So why have all the other islanders left?"

"Because they're cowards."

"Including your parents?"

"They are cowards too. But none of them will prosper. They have deserted God and God will desert them. There'll be no salvation for them."

"There'll be no salvation for you, either," Kit muttered. "You're doomed. Your world stinks. It's not a world of purity and goodness. It's a world of lies."

"Kill him," murmured Zak. "He's evil."

"If I'm evil," said Kit, "you're evil too. You think you're good. But you don't know what good is."

Zak threw back his fist to strike. But Brand stopped him.

"You're right," he said in a strangely muted voice. "We're not good. There can be no good in this tainted world. Everyone and everything has been stained by the Devil and his servants. Even this island is now beyond repair. But we are the torchbearers of the one true God and our redemption is secure. The Devil will not defeat us. We will defeat him. Now . . ." Brand took a slow breath. "Where is your master?"

"How the hell do I know?" said Kit.

He had barely uttered the words before the rope ends came lashing down on his back.

"Ah!" he shrieked. "A-ah!"

He writhed over the floor, desperate to escape the stinging ropes.

"Enough!" called Brand.

The ropes stopped.

"A-ah!" Kit rolled onto his side and curled up in a ball.

"Where is your master?" said Brand again.

"I–" Kit paused. "I don't know."

The ropes came whistling down again.

"Ah!" This time they were worse. Faster, harder, deeper. They seemed to cut through his body, his mind, his resistance. "He's . . . he's . . ."

The ropes stopped.

"He's . . ."

But he had nothing to say.

"Continue," said Brand.

And the ropes swung down again. He rolled about the floor, moaning, unable to think, speak, do anything. Then again, the ropes stopped. Into his moans came the sound of Brand's voice.

"It makes no difference whether you tell us or not. God is on our side. He will destroy your master, and he will destroy you."

Kit twisted his head round and glared up at the three men.

"There is no God," he spat. "There never has been a God. There never will be a God."

He waited for the ropes to start again. But they did not. There was a long silence, then Brand spoke again.

"There is a God," he said quietly. "But he is not for you."

The man turned to the others.

"Take him outside. But cover his loins. They offend me."

They pulled his briefs and shorts roughly on him, then dragged him out of the chapel and round to the seaward end of the building. He knew little of this. He saw only a blur of images: sea and sky, rock and stone, Wyn's shrewish eyes, his socks, shoes, and T-shirt scattered on the ground. Then the ropes that had whipped him were being wrapped round his wrists and tightened, and more ropes were lashing his ankles together, and he was being lifted upright, his lacerated back against the hard stone wall at the seaward end of the chapel.

He was breathing fast now, dangerously fast, as he realized for the first time what they were doing. He struggled to break free but it was no good. He had nothing left. They stretched his arms out on either side of him and bound his wrists to pegs driven into the top of the wall, then they lashed his ankles to another peg at the base and let go.

His body sagged under its own weight.

And it began.

21

He felt a crushing pain in his shoulders and arms. His body, which had felt so light, now dragged against the ropes like a heavy boulder, stretching his limbs with it and grating his bleeding back against the rough stones. His feet tore against their bindings. His hands and wrists chafed. The pain in his shoulders grew worse as his muscles stretched under the pressure of his body. He cried out, certain that they were going to dislocate at any moment.

Somehow they did not, but the pain continued as he sagged farther down the wall. The agony in his wrists and arms became acute, and as his body pulled farther down he found himself gasping for breath. He struggled to find some purchase with his feet so that he could push himself up the wall and breathe.

But it didn't work. He was too cleverly bound. The peg that held his legs in place was at ankle level, and his feet were tied just below it. He tried to twist his feet round and find something in the wall he could use to lever himself up on, but that too didn't work.

The pressure began to build in his chest and lungs. He

gulped in what air he could, but it was only a partial breath, a snatch at what oxygen he could get. He couldn't swallow enough, and he was finding it hard to exhale, too. He tried again to push himself up the wall and breathe. But his arms were already tired as they fought against the weight of his body.

Dimly he took in the figures below him. They stood before him, Brand, Uddi, Zak, and Wyn, watching with satisfaction. He tried to scowl back at them, to show defiance, hatred, fearlessness. But he knew he was a pathetic spectacle, writhing here at their mercy. Brand stepped closer and looked into his face.

"I will ask you again. Where is your master?"

"I . . . I told you . . ." Kit had so little breath in his lungs he could barely whisper. "I . . . I don't know."

"Tell us and we will untie you."

He glared down at the man.

"I don't . . . know . . . and . . . even if I did, I . . . I wouldn't tell you."

Brand gave a chilly smile.

"Then your end will be a slow and painful one."

Kit didn't try to answer. He had no doubt they would have left him strung up here even if he'd told them what they wanted to know. He felt utterly alone. Mum and Dad were dead, and he was convinced the naked man had left the island. There was no sense of his presence anywhere. Even the eerie cry had gone.

A wave of cramps rippled through his body, bringing with them more pain. He gasped and cried out, and writhed under the ropes in an effort to free himself. But the cramps went on. Again he tried to breathe. Again he managed only a small gulp of air.

He scrabbled with his feet against the wall again and

somehow pushed himself up a few inches so that he could take a fuller breath. But the effort cost him dearly, and when his body sagged back down the wall, the pain in his chest was worse. He cried out again and went on trying to breathe. But it was no good. He was slowly suffocating, and there was nothing he could do.

Zak and Uddi moved closer, triumph in their faces. Zak leaned forward and opened his mouth, showing his shattered teeth.

"Don't think death will be the end for you. It's only the start. The place that's reserved for you after death will be a million times worse than this."

And he spat over Kit's chest.

The two men turned and set off with Brand round the side of the building, leaving Wyn behind. She stepped forward. He glowered down at her. It was as though they all wanted to enjoy the freak show. Yet somehow this frail old woman was even more chilling than the others. She had a ruthlessness in her eyes that even Brand could not match. She stood there just a few feet from him, looking him up and down as he writhed before her, struggling for breath.

"Did you think you could win?" she said.

He said nothing.

"Heaven's not for scum like you," she went on. "The Devil has his hole, and we're going to send him back there with all his grubby servants."

She traced the end of her stick round his chin as he gasped for breath.

"Go . . . ," he muttered. "Go . . . go . . ."

"To hell?" she said. She took her stick from his face and leaned on it again. "I don't think so."

And she started to laugh.

The sound of it froze him. It was a laugh without humor.

He turned his head away, unable to look at her, and went on struggling to breathe. But the struggle was growing worse. Every wrench of his muscles felt like a knife tearing through him. His mutilated back was raw from chafing against the wall. He could feel blood running down his spine.

He didn't know how long he would last. He knew he would die. There was no way he could survive this. He could only pray that it would be quicker than Brand had said. Uddi returned and set about building a fire with Wyn just a few yards from him. He watched them through bleary eyes.

They started a blaze and set up a spit, then Brand and Zak appeared with a newly plucked goose, and they began to cook it. He turned his head away again. The strain on his wrists was now so great he felt his sagging body would tear itself from his hands. He could neither inhale nor exhale without the greatest effort, and he was starting to black out for short periods of time before the urge to breathe and the pain in his muscles jerked him back to consciousness.

The smell of the goose wafted over him. He found his eyes had closed again and forced them back open. The islanders had been roasting the bird for a good while and were now slicing some of the cooked pieces off the outside and eating them. They had bowls of water, too, and they were drinking his health as they ate and laughed at him.

"Help me," he murmured. "Someone help me."

But he knew no one could help him. No one could even hear him.

The islanders went on with their feast, then eventually stood up. They looked jubilant and happy. Uddi and Zak picked up the uncooked portion of the goose and carried it on its spit round the side of the building. They returned a moment later, and the four of them gathered up the drinking bowls. Then they came forward once again.

Kit stared at them. He had no doubt they intended some further mockery, but all he could think of was the bowl that Brand was carrying, the only bowl with any water left in it. The islanders stopped in front of him.

"So now we leave you to your death," said Brand. "But have no fear. We won't be far away." He gave an icy smile. "We have every hope of catching a second fish today."

Kit opened his mouth and tried to gulp in some air. But his eyes were still on the bowl in Brand's hand. The man caught his glance and smiled again.

"Water?" he said. "You want some water?" Brand turned to his companions. "Shall we give him some water?"

The others laughed. Brand looked back at Kit and the smile faded.

"We'll leave you some water. I'll put it down here for you. Drink as much as you want."

He placed the bowl down at the base of the wall and straightened up again.

"Prepare yourself," he said. "The worst is yet to come."

And then they left.

Somehow he stayed alive. But he had lost all sense of time. It seemed to be hours that he hung there writhing against the wall, gulping in what air he could, his body so heavy and so weak he could barely move it. He was so short of oxygen that he was blacking out again and again. His back was a bloody mess from grating against the wall, cramps were still rippling through him, he was aching with fatigue, and his muscles were strained almost beyond endurance. He could feel his heart laboring, his lungs struggling for air.

He didn't know where Brand and the others were. He had heard no sound of them since they left him. He peered out through blurred eyes and saw the sun well past its zenith. The sea was still, but he noticed a mist rolling in from offshore.

More cramps tore through him. He gasped and struggled to breathe again. He saw the mist rolling in closer. It was coming in fast, a great cloud of gray. He remembered the mist that had closed around *Windflower*. How long ago that seemed.

His mind was whirling now. He saw a jumble of images. He saw pictures from the past. He saw a spring day. He saw *Windflower* in the yard. He saw Mum in dungarees painting the hull. She looked round at him and poked her tongue out playfully. He saw Dad up the mast doing repairs.

The mist rolled in closer, swallowing the sea.

He saw their old house, he saw his school, he saw his bicycle. He saw the corner shop and Mrs. Armstrong. He saw her cat walking along the windowsill. He saw the paperboy on his bike. He saw Mrs. Harrison mowing the lawn. He saw the naked man.

But only in his head.

Something soft touched his feet, something light and quick. He struggled to look down. His eyes had closed again, and he hadn't realized it. He opened them and saw Ula kneeling by his feet, her hands fumbling with the ropes that bound his ankles.

No, he tried to say.

But the words would not come. His throat was too dry. He opened his mouth and tried again. But not even a moan would come out.

No, his thoughts called to her. *It's a trap.*

But she went on tugging at the ropes round his ankles. She did not look up at him. She was fiercely focused on the task. She pulled at the ropes, harder, harder. He struggled again to call out.

It's a trap, it's a trap.

But still she went on struggling with the ropes. He gave

240

a gasp and she looked up suddenly. Their eyes met, but she only held his gaze for a second before returning to the ropes. He gave another gasp and tried to call to her again.

It's a trap.

But again the words wouldn't come.

The mist drew closer still. He could see it down below the cut of the shore, almost as far as the slabs of rock below the knoll. The sea was now completely hidden. He looked back down toward Ula and to his horror saw figures creeping round both sides of the building. Somehow he croaked out a word.

"Run!"

She heard him and jumped to her feet, but even her quickness could not save her. Uddi's arm was round her waist and before she could bolt away, he had swept her off the ground. Zak closed in from the other side, followed by Brand, and she was quickly surrounded.

He heard a shout of triumph from Uddi. Ula was kicking and squirming in his arms, but Kit knew she had no chance. They wouldn't let her go this time. Zak had caught hold of her too, and he and Uddi carried her off round the side of the building. Kit watched in despair. He knew they would kill her. But what they would do to her first he could not bear to contemplate.

He saw Brand walking leisurely toward him. He stared down at the red-haired man with all the defiance he could muster. But he knew it wasn't much, and certainly Brand wasn't impressed.

"You see?" The man looked him over. "Your master won't save you."

Kit struggled in his throat to find something to spit. But there was nothing there. Brand seemed to understand and laughed.

"There's nothing you can do. You'll die here and we'll leave you for the birds to pick clean. Then we'll throw your bones into the sea, together with the girl's."

Brand bent down, tightened the ropes that Ula had loosened, then straightened up again.

"God is good," he said.

And he walked off.

Kit heard the sound of Ula's screams round the side of the building. They went on and on, and then they faded away. He closed his eyes and tried to block out the world, the pain, the thoughts, the memories. Darkness was flooding through him, a darkness that seemed to spread from inside him. But he was ready for it. He wanted it so badly now. Dimly he heard more screams. They were far away now. He hoped Ula would die quickly. And perhaps even he might be able to die now. He heard himself speak in a voice that was barely a breath.

"Take me," he said. "Please take me."

And something did take him. He felt himself lifted, just an inch or two, but that was enough. Air flooded into him so violently he choked with the pain of it. He gasped and spluttered and gulped in more air. His muscles, released for the first time from the strain of his body, fell limp. He felt himself drop down, not against the ropes but against this strange new support. He opened his eyes.

Mist was all around him. It had rolled right over the shore, right over the knoll, engulfing the chapel itself. The naked man had moved a rock up to the wall and climbed on it, and with one hand he was holding Kit up to take the strain from the ropes. With his other hand he was pushing the water bowl to Kit's lips.

Kit drank; and then tried to speak.

"Run," he murmured. "They'll catch you."

The man didn't answer. He simply dropped the empty bowl to the ground and started unhurriedly to untie the ropes. He freed the hands first. Kit gasped as they fell loose. He had no strength to stop himself flopping forward over the man's shoulder. The man seemed ready for this and simply caught him, then eased down and untied the ropes at the bottom and stepped back from the wall.

Kit saw nothing but naked skin. His face was pressed into the small of the man's back. He could not move. He did not want to move. He felt the man start to walk. He did not know where they were going. He knew only that they were walking into mist, walking into some realm he had never been to. The footsteps went on, *thump, thump, thump,* heavy and firm. He felt his body bounce slightly over the man's shoulder, but the shoulder was firm just as the man's body was firm. He could feel it breathing. He could feel the muscles moving. He could smell the sea. He could hear the ripple of waves. He could feel the man's smooth back brushing against his cheek.

His own body seemed a thing apart now. It was almost as though he was watching himself from some other place. He saw his arms hanging loose over the man's legs, dangling from side to side with the motion of walking. He saw his head hanging just as loose, his eyes closed, his mouth gaping. He saw the man's arm firmly clasped over him.

And they went on walking through the mist, walking he knew not where. Dusk was falling. That much he knew. The mist remained and all light was fading. He heard nothing now, not even the sound of the waves. He had no sense of land or sea. There was nothing but mist and the approaching dark. He tried to think, tried to make sense of where he was, who he was, what he was. But he knew nothing anymore. Nothing of himself, nothing of this man, nothing of anything at all.

"Are you God or Devil?" he murmured.

He wasn't sure whether he was talking to the man or to himself.

No answer came, but he'd expected none.

God or Devil, it didn't seem to matter right now. Everything was mist. And then suddenly there was more than just mist. He could feel something hard under him. The arms that had held him were still there, but they were laying him down now. He opened his eyes and saw the man's face, framed by mist and the darkening sky.

"Where am I?" he said.

But he knew. He was on top of the great rock. He didn't need to look. Somehow it made sense that the man should bring him here. He did not know how he had reached this place. But so much that would once have seemed impossible seemed possible now. The boundaries of what he had believed in had long since fallen away.

Yet still he knew nothing. Especially about the face staring down at him.

"Who are you?" he murmured. "Why won't you tell me?"

The sky darkened further around the strange, ugly face. With an effort Kit reached out and touched the man's hand.

"I don't . . . I don't believe . . ."

I don't believe in God, he wanted to say. But words were too much effort. He was so weak now he could barely breathe, even when there were no ropes to prevent him. The man did not speak, but Kit did not expect him to. And in a strange way the absence of words was reassuring. The man's silence was so much part of him it seemed to merge quite naturally with the silence all around them.

And the silence up here was profound. He could hear it pressing upon them, a vast, almost blissful peace. He could not even hear the sea, though he sensed its presence below them. He cried now. He cried deeply, more deeply than he had ever cried before, even that time in the cave. He cried for Ula, he cried for Mum and Dad, he cried for himself. He cried for all the world. He even cried for the man. He didn't know why. But he cried for the man.

Night fell. The hours passed. He wanted to sleep, but he could not. He was in too much pain. His body throbbed all over, and he could barely move. He looked up and saw the man still kneeling at his side, watching in silence. Kit stared into the strange eyes. They were unusually bright. He remembered how they had changed color, how they had been gray and then black, and then gray again. They seemed almost fiery now. And the energy he had felt from them before was flowing out of them again.

"I want to believe in you," he murmured. "I want to believe in something good. But I can't anymore. Everything I thought was good is gone now."

He went on searching the eyes, then turned his head to the side and stared into the darkness.

"They will be here soon," he said.

22

They came in the night in a long black boat. They came, just as their ancestors had done centuries before, to destroy evil and reclaim the land for the one true God. They rowed out of the harbor at the south end of the island, past the breakwater, past the cottages, and on toward the bluff at the northeastern tip, still hidden from view in the foggy murk. They pulled in silence, their hands wet and cold in the chill before dawn, the only sounds their grunting breaths, the grinding of oars, and the murmur of water against the bow as it cut a path through the milky sea.

Kit sensed them even before they neared the rock, and he knew the man had sensed them too. Neither had moved during the night. He had lain there on the summit, his mind drifting in and out of gray, misty realms, yet every time he had opened his eyes, he had seen the man's face above him exactly as it had been before: a dark form shrouded by night and fog, yet lit around the eyes by two yellow flames that rose, snakelike, toward the thick black hair.

"They're near," he said to the man. "I can feel it."

The man went on watching him. His naked body seemed

to glisten in the darkness. Kit reached out and touched the shimmering skin, then ran a finger along one arm and up over the shoulder to the neck, and then over the birthmark all the way to the face. The ugly face that he himself possessed. The man's eyes did not shift from him. Kit stroked the man's cheek.

"We're the same," he murmured. "I am whatever you are."

He took his hand away and let it drop beside him. He saw the man's head turn toward the island. And then he heard it too: the sound of oars somewhere below the rock. The man's head turned back, and he went on looking down at Kit. Kit stared back up at him.

"Let them kill me," he said softly.

The yellow eyes seemed to grow brighter.

"Let them kill me," he said again. He breathed slowly out. "I've got nothing to live for anymore."

He heard the oars again, closer. The mist drew in around the rock. Yet far above him he could see a faint lightening of the sky. Dawn could not be far away. He closed his eyes again and tried to compose himself. There would be no escape this time. What the man would do, he did not know. But there was no hope for a wounded boy. They would probably club him to death and throw him over the edge.

He felt strangely calm about this. It should be a quick end. He was so weak now it would only take one blow to smash the life from him. He didn't suppose they would torture him again. They would want his blood, pure and simple, and he was happy for them to take it. He would not resist. He was ready for the darkness.

He heard more sounds, the unshipping of oars, the knock of a boat against rock, then silence. They were making their way along the twisting ledge that spiraled round the outside of the rock to its flat top. He started to picture them with their clubs, yet even as he did so he found other pictures forcing their way into his mind; pictures he was surely seeing for the last time. He saw *Windflower,* and Mum at the helm in her yellow oilskins, and Dad up on the foredeck fiddling with the anchor chain. Then more pictures: Dad in the cockpit handing round chocolate, Mum sunbathing on the cabin top. A bright, sparkling sea. Sails bulging with life.

He opened his eyes and saw Brand, Uddi, and Zak at the far end of the rock.

They were standing there, mist swirling around them, all three with clubs. Their faces had an intensity of purpose he had never seen before. Kit spoke hurriedly to the man.

"Save yourself. Forget me."

But the man leaned down toward him, pulled him into his arms, and stood up. Kit looked up at him.

"Let me die," he whispered. "Let me die."

The man merely pulled him closer into his chest. Kit saw the islanders step forward. The man faced them, still holding Kit in his arms. From below came the sound of voices. Kit listened, even as he watched the islanders approach. It was the whispering voices he had heard on the island, but now they were reaching up from the sea. A moment later he saw shadows twisting over the top of the rock.

The three men stopped just a few feet away. Their faces were dark with hate, but they were looking around them now. The shadows were everywhere, wriggling like eels among the snarls of mist. Kit listened to the voices again. They were different from before. They were no longer desperate, no longer in pain. They were angry. And now he heard a new voice.

Ula.

It came from far below him. He felt a stab of anguish at

the thought of her. She could not possibly be alive. She must be a ghost too, another spirit voice. He heard it again. She was shrieking up to the top of the rock, shrieking his name.

"Kit! Kit!"

The islanders raised their clubs and rushed forward. Kit felt the man's arms tighten round him. He braced himself for the first blow. But before any of the clubs could land, the man stepped calmly backward.

And suddenly they were falling.

He saw everything as though in slow motion. He was still clasped in the man's arms, and he was gazing upward at the shocked faces of the islanders as they peered over the top of the rock. The man's body was beneath him, the strong arms still locked around him. He felt the night sky, the mist, the shadows all whirling about them, the voices whirling with them.

They splashed into the sea and went straight down.

He felt his body break apart from the man's and keep on going, down, down, as deep as the deepest sea, it felt, into a darkness that took away all will to fight on. Even the thought of Ula's voice in that other land of light and air could not induce him to return. He would open his mouth now and drink in the sea and give himself up to this watery deliverance.

Then he felt something hard in his back.

He felt hands pushing him, up, up. He resisted them. He did not want to go up. He wanted to go down, stay down, never come up. But the hands went on, pushing, pushing, pushing. He knew who it was. He could not see the man. He could see only darkness. But he knew the man was there, forcing him up toward the surface.

He reached down and tried to brush the hands away from his back. He didn't want this. He didn't want life. But the man's hands were not to be moved, and they went on thrusting him up. His eyes were open now and water was streaming past them, black water, gray water, then lighter, brighter water, and now foam and froth and swirling white. And then suddenly his head was clear of water and his mouth was gulping air.

The man broke the surface too and stayed close by, treading water, his arms round Kit. The great rock was barely twenty yards away. It was a miracle they had not hit any of the outlying teeth as they crashed into the water. The mist was still thick but dawn was breaking and by what light there was Kit could see a rowing boat bobbing over by the far side of the rock. There was a small figure at the oars.

Ula.

She looked over her shoulder and gave a shout.

"Kit!"

He tried to shout back but could only gasp.

"Kit!"

It was obvious she couldn't see them in the water. He tried again and this time managed some kind of a shout.

"Here!"

It was enough. She was soon rowing across toward them. But now to his horror he saw a second boat, a long black rowing boat that had appeared round the other side of the rock. Even in the mist he could see who was in it. Uddi, Zak, and Brand, each with a pair of oars, and old Wyn in the stern, her hand on the tiller. There was no matching them for speed, but Ula had a head start and was only a few feet away.

"Here!" he called again.

He felt the man's arms tighten around him. The little boat drew nearer. Ula spun her round and stopped her, then hurried to the side.

"Come on," she said, leaning down. "Reach up to me."

He reached up somehow and felt her hands seize him; then, as she pulled and the man pushed, he slid over the gunwale into the boat. It was the smaller and more rickety of the two craft that had been left behind in the harbor. The other, though rickety itself, was much larger and was now driving toward them at great speed, the oars sweeping back the sea with savage force.

"Sit in the stern," Ula said to him.

She helped him there and then turned back to the gunwale. He could see she was nervous of the man and didn't know what to do. But the man was already climbing aboard. She glanced quickly at the islanders, then back at the man, and made to sit down at the oars. But the man simply nodded her toward Kit and sat down at the oars himself.

There was no time to argue, and Ula didn't bother. She sat down in the stern with Kit. He was glad of it. He could hardly sit upright, and his lacerated back was stinging from the salty water. She put her arm round him, and he leaned in toward her. She stroked his arm.

"It's all right," she murmured. "It's all right."

The man had started rowing, not toward the island or even toward the rock, but out into the sea, into the mist. With an effort Kit turned his head and saw the other boat forging on after them. He turned back to Ula and dipped his head into her shoulder.

"They'll catch us," he said. "There's nothing we can do."

"It doesn't matter," she said.

"I thought you were dead."

"I managed to escape. They were starting to torture me, but I bit Uddi's hand and got the knife off him. Then I stabbed him in the leg."

"What about the other two?"

"I threw the knife at them. It didn't hit them, but it made

them step back and gave me time to run away. They must have been chasing after me when the man came and rescued you."

She looked warily at the naked figure still rowing them out to sea.

Kit closed his eyes. There was nothing to do now but wait. He let his head ease closer into Ula's neck. There was that smell again, that rich animal smell he had picked up before on her. Perhaps it would be the last smell he knew before the smell of death.

"How near are they?" he said, his eyes still closed.

She didn't answer at first. Then she spoke.

"I don't like the sea."

He opened his eyes. She was right. The restlessness was back, the feeling of something large and invisible moving nearby. He listened for the sound. And there it was.

The long, eerie cry.

The figure went on rowing, his own eyes fixed beyond them, his face without expression.

The cry came again, long and mournful.

And close.

Kit turned now and looked. The other boat was only a short distance behind. He could see Brand's back, the thick, red hair moving this way and that as he worked his oars. Then the head turned to look, and their eyes met. But not for long. There was a command from the stern that even Kit heard from here: Old Wyn screaming at her bow oar to keep pulling and not to waste time looking over his shoulder. And Brand turned back to his rowing like a chastened schoolboy. Kit stared at the naked man again.

He was rowing fast too, but with no sense of urgency or fear. Perhaps it was because he knew the little boat would be outpaced and there would be a fight, so he was conserving his energy. Kit did not know. He cared nothing for his own life now. He cared only for Ula. The thought of her dying out here or being captured again and suffering some terrible death back on the island was more than he could bear. As for the man . . .

The man would do what the man would do.

And Kit had no idea what that was.

"I don't like the sea," said Ula again.

He stared at it. The surface was moving in strange rippling swirls, but the restlessness was coming from farther down. He sensed a trembling in the deep and long aching tremors that seemed to reach up from far below. He heard a splash of oars, a shout of triumph from Wyn; then, to his horror, the naked man suddenly stopped pulling, spun the boat round so that the bow was facing their pursuers, and stood up.

The larger boat crashed into theirs. The little boat dipped under the impact, driving Kit back against the stern. He felt Ula's arm tighten around him. The man had kept his balance and was still standing by the thwart facing the other boat, but the islanders were now clambering aboard. Brand was first over the bow, followed by Uddi and Zak, all three screaming and flailing their clubs. The boat dipped and rolled under their weight, but they took no notice and struck out at the figure standing by the thwart.

He gave no resistance. He simply stood there and let the clubs fall. One struck him on the side of the head, another on the back of the neck. He fell over the thwart, face down, his hands on the bottom boards. The islanders gave a shout of triumph.

"Kill him!" screamed Wyn from the other boat.

"No!" shouted Kit.

He was struggling forward in spite of his pain. He felt Ula's hands pulling him back but he ignored them.

"Don't kill him!" he shouted.

He was on his feet now, and so was Ula, her arms round him to hold him back from what she knew he wanted to do. And he was indeed trying to reach forward and stop the punishment. But the clubs went on raining down on the man's body.

Then suddenly they stopped.

The three men straightened up and stared about them, a look of terror on their faces. Kit looked about him too, and then he heard it, the heavy rumble deep in the water, a sound the sea never made. He looked at Ula and saw her face dark with fear, as dark as the faces of the islanders, as dark as the blood running down the back of the motionless body before them.

But now the body was starting to move.

Slowly, like a wounded leviathan rising from the deep, the man straightened up until he was standing again before the islanders. He seemed suddenly to tower over them, as unnaturally large and imposing as he had been when Kit saw him on the rock and on the hilltop. The islanders stared back, their clubs hanging down.

Then the sea rose behind them.

Kit saw a rush of waves, a heaving chaos of green water and white foam, and then a body, a vast black body bursting from the sea right beneath them. Before he could see more, the boat lifted under him and threw him into the air. He heard a splintering of timbers, a confusion of screams, then the crash around his ears as he hit the water face down. As he did so, he saw through the driving spume a long translucent body slipping past not five feet below him, black and smooth and terrifying.

He splashed his arms and kicked with his legs and somehow made it to the surface. A hand seized him and pulled him backward.

"Ula?" he spluttered, looking round.

But it was Uddi.

"Evil filth!" snarled the man.

His hands closed round Kit's neck.

"Gah!" Kit tried to push himself away but it was no good. The hands were tightening and forcing his head back into the sea.

"Gah! Gah!"

He splashed again and tried to break free, his eyes frantically searching for help. But he saw only chaos. The islanders were gone. The naked man was gone. The boats were gone. Only wreckage was left. Then he saw Ula swimming toward him.

"Kit!" she shouted.

"Gah!"

The hands were growing tighter. He reached out and caught Uddi's wrists and tried to tear them from him, but the grip only grew tighter still. Ula called out again.

"The stab wound! It's in his thigh! His left thigh!"

Kit saw a change in Uddi's face at the sound of her words: first uncertainty, then a greater determination to finish the job. The pressure round his neck grew worse. He ran his hand over Uddi's leg, feeling for the wound—then suddenly he found it. He squeezed hard.

"Ah!" Uddi gave a shriek of pain and let go. As he did so, Ula caught Kit by the arm and pulled him clear.

"Wait!" shouted Uddi, splashing awkwardly in the lumpy water.

But Ula and Kit were now several feet from him. Kit was slipping down again as weariness and pain overwhelmed him once more. He felt Ula's arm tighten round him.

"No," she said. "Don't let yourself slip down."

"I can't," he murmured. "I can't . . . hold myself up."

He saw Uddi still splashing in the water. But the man had seen his discomfort too.

"So you're going to die after all," shouted the man. "Just like your master has died." Uddi looked about him. "You see? He is gone."

"Just like your people!" retorted Kit. "God's chosen children! They've all drowned too. And you're going to drown with them."

"Yes, I'm going to drown." Uddi splashed a few more times, then looked defiantly back. "But I go to a better place than you."

And without another word he leaned back and slipped from view.

Kit had no time even to gasp. Ula was already pulling him away.

"Come with me," she said. "He may be pretending to die. He may be swimming underwater."

He let her pull him away from the spot. Then, when she was sure it was safe, she stopped and they trod water again.

"I didn't think he would come for you," she said. "He was not a good swimmer. Nor were the others. But it was as well to be sure."

"You think he's dead?"

"Yes."

He looked into her face.

"And now you must let me die," he said.

She shook her head.

"You must," he said. "You can still survive. You might be able to swim back to the rock. And from there to the island. I'll never make it, even with your help. If you stay with me, you'll have no chance."

But she wasn't listening to him. She was listening to something else.

"What is it?" he said.

Then he heard it too. The deep rumble in the sea again. He felt Ula's arm tighten around him.

"Come on," she said. "Let's search for some wreckage to hold on to."

And despite his protests, she hauled him with her across to where the boats had been.

But the search was fruitless. It didn't seem possible that they should find nothing at all. But everything—both bodies and wreckage—had either floated off into the mist or sunk without trace. Kit knew now that all was lost, and probably even for Ula. She had to let him go now. She could not hold on to him and at the same time swim round looking for something buoyant to hold on to.

"Let me die," he said again. "You must. I want you to."

"I'm staying with you."

"But—"

"I'm staying with you."

She turned and stared into the mist.

"I think the rock's that way. What do you think?"

"I agree."

And she pulled him with her through the sea. At first he marveled at her determination, but his admiration soon turned to despair. He had to stop this. She was never going to make it with him as a burden. He started to pry her arm from him.

"What are you doing?" she said.

"You can't do this," he muttered. "I'm not letting you die because of me."

He felt her arm tighten again. He tugged at it with more force.

"Ula! Let me go!"

"I won't let you go. I—"

She broke off, her arm still round him. He saw her eyes staring past him.

"What is it?" he said.

She didn't answer. She just went on staring. He turned and looked.

Floating behind them was an oar. It was one of the big sweeps from the long black boat that the islanders had used.

"Come on," said Ula.

She pulled him across to it and hooked his right arm over it.

"Keep hold of it," she said.

"Okay." Kit stiffened suddenly. "There's the other oar. The one that goes with it. See it?"

"Yes. Let's see if we can get to it."

But the second sweep seemed to be moving by itself.

It drew closer and closer until finally it was just a few feet from them. Kit reached out and caught hold of it. And as he did so, his mind flew back to that misty night in *Windflower,* and to the little prayer boat. For here, too, was a floating object clasped by another hand. He stared past the oar into the sea and saw an arm reaching up to it from below, and then a body, and a face, staring up at him through the water. Then the hand let go and the body and face slipped away into the deep.

"My God," he murmured. "My God."

"What is it?" said Ula.

"Didn't you see?"

"See what?"

"The man. The naked man. He was in the water. He was giving us the oars."

"I saw nothing." She was already busy arranging the sweeps. She slid the second oar under Kit's free arm so that the two oars were now wedged into his armpits.

"Are they supporting you?" she said.

"Yes. But what are you going to do?"

"Swim behind and push you."

"You can't do that."

"What else can we do? It's the only way. If you move to the front of the oars and try to kick as much as you can, that'll help. I'll hold on at the back and kick from there."

"It's asking too much of you."

She looked him hard in the face.

"I don't want you to die," she said.

"I don't want you to die either."

"Then let's swim."

So they swam, Kit at the front with an oar under each armpit and his hands clasping the blades, Ula holding on to the oar handles and pushing from the back. But it soon became obvious that this wasn't going to work. Kit's weight on the oars was pushing both them and him down into the water, and though he wasn't going to sink, he was preventing forward momentum.

"Stop," said Ula. "This is no good."

"It's because of my weight," said Kit. "Let me take the oars out from my armpits and just hold on to them with my hands."

"But can you do that? Have you got enough strength?"

"I don't know. But let's try."

They set off again, this time with Kit holding on by his hands alone, and at once things were better. It was still a strain and he feared for Ula pushing at the back, but at least his body was less of a drag in the water now. His back was stinging again from the salt, but the weariness was worse. He kicked his legs as best he could, but he knew his contribution was meager compared with hers. She said little now, and he knew she was focusing all her energy on getting them to safety. Then suddenly he heard her voice from behind him.

"You spoke to God," she said.

He looked over his shoulder at her.

"What?"

"You said 'My God' a while ago."

"It was just an expression. It didn't mean anything."

"Oh."

They swam on, searching for a glimpse of the great rock. But even after what felt like an age in the water, there was still no sign of it. Daylight had come, but the mist was thicker than ever. For all Kit knew, they could be heading back out to sea.

Then suddenly the fog parted and the sun burst through, and they saw at last where they were. The cove was dead ahead, and the rock was about a quarter of a mile behind them. They must have passed within yards of it without knowing it was there.

"We can get there," said Ula. "If you can just hold on. Can you do it?"

He stared toward the shore. It was about the same distance from them as the rock, but he felt so tired now, so ready to give up, even though Ula was doing all the work.

"I can do it if you can," he said.

23

Yet even as he spoke, he felt his body resist. He had been managing a few kicks and his hands still clung to the oars, but the strength was leaving him. Ula was still swimming with the same powerful resolve she had shown all along, but she quickly noticed the change in him.

"Do you want to stop for a minute?" she said. "You can hook the oars under your armpits and rest."

"No," he said breathlessly. "Let's continue. I mean, if you think you can keep going. I'm sorry. You must think I'm useless."

"I don't think you're useless. I think you're brave. But you're right. We should keep going. We must get to the shore quickly. I don't trust this sea."

He knew what she meant. The water was calm, but the feeling of restlessness was still there. He could hear that rumble in the deep again and feel the tremors reaching up toward the surface. Ula kicked her legs and they moved slowly off again. He was almost weeping with shame now at the thought of what he was putting Ula through, but all he could do was cling to the oars as best he could while she pushed him on toward the shore.

But their progress was poor now. Even with Ula's fiery spirit the land seemed to remain as far away as ever. Moreover, as the minutes passed, it became obvious that the current was pushing them to the right of the cove. If they didn't get back on course, they were in danger of being swept past the island altogether. He tried desperately to kick again. He was still aching with weariness and pain, but he kept going somehow and with Ula now redoubling her efforts, they at last drew closer to the shore.

But they were still too far to the right. He could see the cove clearly now, well to the left of them, and the rocky scar, and dead ahead the western shore of the island stretching away.

"Aim for the long rock," Ula said. "We can land there if we have to."

It was obvious she meant the scar. He had no wish to go there—he wanted to land on something less dangerous—but he said nothing and went on kicking. He heard the rumbling in the sea again and looked back at Ula.

"Keep going," she said.

It came again, and with it the deep tremors in the water. He felt something glide underneath them. He knew what it was without even looking. But he stared down even so. The black form was slipping past just a few feet below. It was closer than it had ever been, and for the first time he saw it clearly. It was a sea snake of supernatural proportions, at least twelve feet across and a hundred in length. He saw nothing of its head, just the long black body and a strange feathery mane along its back. It vanished as quickly as it had come.

He shuddered.

"Did you see it?" he said.

"Yes," said Ula, kicking harder than ever.

The rumble came again. Kit looked over his shoulder, scanning the sea for further danger. He saw nothing out there but the great rock rising from the water.

"Keep kicking if you can," Ula said.

They drove themselves on. Kit was now close to exhaustion, and he knew Ula must feel even worse, yet they had clawed back some of the ground they had lost and the scar was almost dead ahead. He could see waves breaking over the end of it.

"Come on," Ula urged him. "We're nearly there."

He tried again to kick. His legs moved after a fashion, then hung limp.

Kick, he told himself.

He kicked, and kicked, and kicked.

The black form slipped beneath them again, so close this time it seemed almost to brush their feet. He felt a swell in the water that lifted both them and the oars onto a breaking wave. But while the movement startled them, the impetus hurled them forward a few more precious feet.

The rumble came again.

They kicked on toward the shore. And now at last he was starting to believe they might get there. Not only that, but they were clawing back even more lost ground. Whether it was their efforts or a change in the tide, he did not know, but it looked as though they might even make the cove itself. The scar was already slipping past to the right.

"Aim for any part of the shore," Ula said. "Whatever's nearest."

They drove themselves on. It looked certain now that they were going to make the cove but the caprice of the sea made it hard to tell exactly where they would land.

"Hold on," Ula said. "We must go where it takes us."

He knew she was right. They couldn't fight the sea,

especially now that they were both so tired. They kicked on, pushing themselves feebly forward, and gradually it became clear that the current was taking them to the shingle beach. Kit stared toward it through salty eyes. He had long since come to hate this beach, yet it had never seemed more welcoming than now.

He felt more tremors in the sea. They seemed to reach out through every bubbling wave. Kit knew they had to get to the shore soon. But the shingle beach was close now. It might even be shallow enough to stand. He let his body sink and probed for the bottom with his feet. He felt nothing—and then to his horror found his weakened hands losing their grip on the oars.

"Kit!" shouted Ula.

He dropped like a stone into the water. It was as black as the sea around the rock but this time he fell only a few feet. The bottom rose to meet him, and he hit it with a thump that jolted the breath from him. He felt his body shape to inhale and in a panic kicked himself off the bottom. Then Ula's hand seized him by the hair and pulled.

He broke the surface and gulped in air, splashing his hands about him. Ula had let go of the oars and was still holding him by the hair, but she let go of this now and put her arm round him instead.

"Hold on to me," she said. "We're nearly there."

And she kicked her legs and pulled him with her toward the shore, now just a few yards away.

"You mustn't die on me now," she panted. "Not when we're this close."

He said nothing. His eyes were on the beach, and he could think of nothing else. At last they felt the ground under their feet. They stopped in the shallows on the very spot where *Windflower* had been moored, and then looked at each other, shivering, breathing hard. Ula still had her arm round him, but she took it away and stood back. He reached out and pulled her to him again, and they held each other tight. Then Ula let go of him and turned toward the beach.

"We must get away from here. Up the hill."

"I can't," he muttered. "I've got to rest."

"No," she said. She glanced at the angry water rippling against their bodies. "We must."

Kit was watching the sea too now.

"What's happening?" he said. "What does it mean?"

"I don't know. But we must get away from the cove."

"But—"

"We must, Kit. Come on."

She took him by the hand and started to wade toward the beach. He followed reluctantly. He knew she was right, but he could barely walk for pain and exhaustion. She tugged him up the shingle as far as the embankment.

"We're safe here," he said. "We're out of the water."

"No, we must keep on."

"But—"

"Kit, come on!"

She started to scramble up the embankment.

"Ula!"

"Kit, come on!"

She reached the grass and looked down at him.

"Kit! You must!"

He started to climb slowly up the rock. She caught his hand and helped him to the grass.

"Come on," she said quickly. "Up the hill."

"We're safe here. We must be."

"Up the hill."

And she started to pull him with her. He stumbled after her, barely keeping his footing.

"Let go of my hand," he said. "You're pulling me off balance."

She let go of his hand, but he could see the impatience in her face.

"Run on ahead," he said. "I'll follow as best I can."

"No, you won't. You'll slump to the ground. And I won't let you."

She took his hand again and held it tight.

"Come on. Whatever speed you can manage."

And she led him on up the slope. He didn't speak now. He could barely think or feel. He was beyond even fear. All he knew was weariness and pain of a kind he had never known. He knew Ula was right. Left to himself he would have slumped to the ground and stayed there. Even now, with her hand tugging him up the hill, he just wanted to let himself fall.

"We're high enough now," he said. "We must be safe."

"Keep going."

"But I can't face this bloody hill again."

"You must."

"We're out of the sea now. What's the danger?"

"I don't know," she said. "But something feels wrong, and I'll be happier when we're on higher ground."

He heard the rumble in the sea again below them. And he knew she was right.

He climbed on, slowly, painfully. Ula was clearly suffering too, though she made no complaint. He marveled yet again at her spirit and strength. Without her he knew he would be dead. He felt a sudden determination not to let her down.

Come on, he told himself. Climb.

But with every step he found this determination tested. They were barely a quarter of the way up the hill, yet they seemed to have been struggling for ages. He knew Ula would be at the top by now if she hadn't been burdened with him. He clenched his fists and drove himself on. Up on the summit the great cairn rose into the sky, its crafted symmetry a strange contrast to the ruggedness of the hill.

He heard another rumble from the sea, a deep, disquieting sound. Ula squeezed his hand more tightly. They climbed on up the hill, both still shivering from the sea, and as they did so more sounds reached them. He heard a rushing in the air, then another slow rumble, farther off this time. But it seemed more ominous than all the others.

Ula glanced at him, and he caught the fear in her eyes.

"Are we safe yet?" he said.

"Keep climbing."

He didn't argue. His body was now so desperate for rest that every step was a trial. But their efforts had not been in vain, and they were now a good way up the hill. Ula stopped at last and turned to look back down over the cove. Kit stopped and turned too, then flopped to the ground.

"I can't go any farther," he gasped. "I just can't go any farther."

She didn't answer. She was staring toward the horizon.

"What is it?" he said.

"I don't know." She was silent for a moment. "But I don't feel safe."

"You're not going to ask me to climb any higher, are you?"

"Not if you don't want to."

"I just can't. I . . ."

Something in her face stopped his words. She had narrowed her eyes and was still gazing across the sea.

"Ula, what is it?"

She said nothing. But her mouth had dropped open. He

hauled himself to his feet again and stared with her. And then he saw what she had seen: a low green cloud stretched right across the horizon. It seemed to be growing with every passing second, and it was racing toward the island at frantic speed. And then suddenly he realized it was not a cloud at all.

It was a wave.

"My God," he said and started to struggle farther up the hill. But Ula caught his arm.

"There's no point. It will be here in seconds."

They held on to each other and watched in terror. Never had Kit seen such a thing. This was beyond any tidal wave he could have imagined. How high it was he didn't know. It seemed to dwarf everything. It engulfed the great rock and surged on toward the island like a mountain of destruction.

And then it struck.

There was a crash that seemed to shake the whole island. The scar, the bluff, the cove, the lower slopes of the hill all disappeared under a flurry of foam and angry green water. But still the body of the wave went on, gorging the hill as it drove on up the slope toward them. They stood there trembling as it raced on toward them, up, up, up, still moving fast, still full of dark, raging energy.

"Ula!" He pulled her close to him. "We're going to die!"

"I know." She held him tight. "Be brave."

But they had both misjudged the wave. It was gradually losing energy as the slope sapped its power. It was still moving up the hill, but it was slowing down all the time. About twenty feet below them it stopped and started to slide back down to the cove.

But it was not finished yet. The main body of the wave had not broken on the island and was still thundering across the sea toward the opposite horizon. Kit watched it with a shudder. Nothing would be able to stand in the path of such a wave, certainly not the islanders who had set off in the boats a few days ago.

He slumped to the ground again, and this time Ula slumped with him. They watched in silence as the water fell back over the cove, hissing and swirling as it went. A few minutes later the sea was calm again, and the cove looked exactly as it had done before.

Yet it felt different. He looked at Ula.

"I know," she said. "It's like it's been cleansed."

He smiled at her and she smiled back, the first smile he had ever seen from her. It was a strange, somewhat hesitant smile.

"Thank you," he said. He touched her arm. "For saving my life."

"I haven't saved your life yet. You need to get warm and eat something quickly."

"So do you."

"We must move again," she said. "If you can manage it."

"I'll try."

"Brand and the others didn't eat all the goose they cooked in front of you. They stored it away. We can start with that. And we must light a fire. Can you make it to the village?"

"What choice do I have? I can't stay here."

"You'll be able to rest back in the village." She took him by the hand. "And there's no more danger from the Skaerlanders."

But as if to mock her words, there was a scornful shout behind them.

"What a pretty sight! The Devil's children holding hands!"

Ula was on her feet in an instant, but Kit had to struggle

to his. He stared up the slope and saw a figure standing on top of the cairn.

It was Torin.

Kit gave a long sigh.

"Oh, God," he said. "Will this never end?"

Ula said nothing. She was staring up at Torin with an expression that Kit found hard to read. The old man went on watching them for a moment, then suddenly he bent down, picked a stone from the top of the cairn, and flung it to the ground.

"Hah!" he shouted, but this seemed to be to himself rather than to them. He was already bent over the cairn again, picking out another stone. He found one, straightened up, and threw it down after the first. "Hah!" he shouted again.

Down came another stone, and then another.

Kit caught Ula by the arm.

"We must stop him."

But she shook her head.

"There's no need. It's just a gesture. It would take him months to destroy a cairn this big." She paused. "But we should go up."

"He'll try and hit us with the stones."

She laughed.

"He couldn't hit us if we were standing right next to him." She glanced at Kit. "But it's best to be careful. So we'll keep out of his range."

She set off up the slope. He struggled after her, fighting the pain and exhaustion again. All he wanted to do was lie down and stay down. He felt Ula take his hand again, and even in his weary state he was aware of a certain defiance in her manner, which seemed to be directed toward Torin.

But the old man didn't seem the slightest bit interested in

them anymore. He was still busy throwing stones down from the top of the cairn. There was already a substantial scattering of them around the summit and the top of the slope.

But Ula was right. For all his efforts the old man was no danger to the cairn. It was too big to be threatened by him. And as they neared the top of the hill, it seemed Torin himself had finally realized this too. His feverish vandalism had almost ceased, and he was just standing there looking about him, and then at them as they approached.

Kit felt Ula's hand grip his more tightly, as though to make sure he had no thoughts of letting go. He gave hers a squeeze to reassure her. She glanced at him and gave a half-smile, then leaned across and whispered to him.

"Don't go any nearer than I do. Stop when I stop."

"Do you think he's dangerous?"

"Not at all. Just climbing up the cairn will have been an effort for him. And then throwing all these stones. He'll be exhausted."

"I know how he feels."

She squeezed his hand.

"You've been through much more than he will ever understand," she said.

He let her lead him toward the cairn. She stopped by the charred remains of the fire that the naked man had lit there. Before them, scattered around the base of the cairn, were scores of discarded stones. Yet the cairn itself seemed as imposing and magnificent as ever. They looked up at the old man forty feet above them. He stared at them for a moment, then bent down and picked up another stone.

Kit instinctively started to pull back, but Ula's hand tightened round his to restrain him. He checked himself and stood his ground. The old man watched them, the stone still in his hand.

"So here we are," he scoffed. "At the end of all our worlds."

"I thought you'd left the island," said Ula coldly. "Where did you hide?"

"Where even you wouldn't have found me." The old man could not conceal the pride in his voice. "I was in one of the caves along the eastern shore. It was either go in the boats with the others or join the hunting party with Uddi, Zak, Brand, and Wyn. Neither option appealed to me, so I chose solitary penance instead. And apart from being hungry and thirsty, I fared very well. Better than all the others, to be sure. And better, it would appear, than both of you."

They said nothing. Torin looked down at the stones lying at the base of the cairn, then threw the one he was holding on top of them.

"So this monstrosity is your temple, is it?" he said with a sneer. "Your holy citadel?" He gave a dry laugh. "How fitting for a God of rubble. That's about all he's worth."

He picked up another stone and flung it down with the rest.

"And what's your God worth?" shouted Kit.

"More than stones!" came the answer. "More than shadows and big waves!" The old man glared down at him. "My God is worth everything. My breath, my blood, my spirit."

"Maybe my God's worth the same!"

Kit felt Ula's eyes turn upon him, but he kept his own on the old man. Torin gave another laugh.

"You see? You don't even know! You say 'maybe'! Your God is a Maybe God!"

"Whatever he is," Kit said, "he's better than a God whose followers know no love!"

"Love!" Torin scoffed again. "Your love is just a love of people. It means nothing. The only love that matters is the love of God. All other love is a weakness that leads to attachment and fleshly desires. Look at you both! Holding hands!" The old man surveyed them with scorn. "Fall in love if you wish. Grieve for your parents if you wish. It will count for nothing."

"My parents!" Kit let go of Ula's hand and started forward.

"What of them?" said the old man.

"You killed them!"

"We didn't kill them."

"You mean—"

"But they'll be dead by now."

Kit felt Ula's hand on his shoulder.

"What did you do to them?" he shouted at the old man.

Torin shrugged.

"We did what we have done for centuries. We took them to a barren rock beyond the horizon and left them there to die of hunger and thirst. The Skaerlanders have not always been hotheads like Uddi and Zak. We generally prefer to take evildoers and outcasts to the rock and leave them there for God to deal with. Your parents will be food for birds by now."

Kit ran up to the cairn, choking back the tears.

"Where's the rock?" he demanded.

"I do not choose to tell you."

"Tell me, you bastard!"

He shook his fist at the old man.

"Tell me where it is!"

But the old man merely sneered down at him.

"Why grieve for human life?" he said. "It's quite worthless. Your parents are gone. Forget them."

Kit opened his mouth to scream back. But Ula spoke first.

"What of my parents?"

Kit whirled round in surprise and saw her staring up at the old man.

"What of my parents?" she said. "I've asked you enough times who they were. Surely you can tell me now."

The old man's scorn did not fade. If anything, it grew deeper than it was before.

"They were two of the most evil people you could meet," he said. "Your wantonness came from your mother. She was as licentious and headstrong as you are. It's lucky for everyone that she died so soon after you were born."

Ula took a slow breath.

"And what of my father?" she said heavily.

The old man snorted.

"Your father was more wicked still. And his greatest sin was that he managed to conceal his evil from the community throughout the whole of his wretched life. They even thought him a holy man. But there's no concealment from God, and justice is swift both here and in the afterlife."

"When did my father die?" said Ula.

Torin laughed.

"Even as you watch," he said.

And then he jumped.

Ula gave a scream. Kit ran and pulled her back, but they were in no danger. Torin hit the ground some way from them. His head hit one of the discarded stones with a sickening crack, and his body rolled down the slope for several yards before one of the outcrops of rock stopped it.

Ula raced down the hill. Kit struggled after her and finally reached the outcrop where the body lay. She was bent over the old man, cradling his head in her hands and talking to him in a low weeping voice.

But it was clear at once that Torin was dead.

24

They carried the old man back to the summit and buried him under a small cairn, which they built from the stones he had hurled to the ground. Then they stood back and looked down at the grave. Neither spoke, but Kit noticed Ula was mouthing some kind of prayer as she stood there weeping.

He, too, was weeping, but not for Torin. He was weeping for Mum and Dad and for himself. Even as he had helped Ula build the cairn, his eyes had been searching the sea for some sign of the rock where they had been taken, though he knew this was pointless. The old man had said it was beyond the horizon. He looked at Ula, trying to gauge the right moment to ask her about it. She looked up suddenly from her prayers as though she'd picked up his thought.

"I don't know where the rock is," she said. "I'm sorry."

He looked down at the ground and felt more tears flood into his eyes. Ula hurried over and held him. She was still crying herself. He reached out and pulled her closer to him.

"I'm sorry too," he said. "About your parents, I mean."

"I never knew about the rock," she said. "Probably they would have told me when they thought I'd become an adult."

"Sounds like they treated you too much like an adult. The men, anyway."

"That was my fault. I was angry. Nobody would tell me who my parents were." She held him close to her. "They would have known who my mother was, even if they didn't know Torin was my father. But no one told me about my mother. I was just told she was a bad woman. So I became a bad woman too. To be like her. And to defy them and everything they believed in."

Kit felt his body swaying with exhaustion and he knew he was close to fainting. Ula picked this up at once.

"Come on," she said. "We must get to the village. We can rest there."

"But I've . . . I've got to . . ."

"I know. You want to go and look for your parents. I understand. But listen, Kit—" She looked him hard in the face. "You can't go today."

"I've got to."

"You can't. You're too weak to move. You must eat and drink first, and rest and get warm. And you need your boat."

"I know." He had been thinking of *Splinters* and wondering whether she had come to any harm in the cave. And he'd been dreading the climb down the cliff to get to her. "I don't know if I can . . . I mean . . ."

"I'll get the boat for you," she said. "But . . . I must rest, too."

"I know. I . . ." He turned and scanned the sea again. "I understand. It's just that I . . . I've got to try and find them as soon as I can."

"You must eat and drink and rest first. And set off tomorrow morning."

"I've got to go today."

"You can't. By the time we've gotten to the village and eaten and rested, and I've brought the boat round to the harbor, it'll be night. You can't search for the rock in the darkness." She took him by the arm. "Come on. I'll help you to the village."

They set off down the hill. And the moment he tried to walk, he knew she was right. Now that they were no longer swimming or running for their lives, his body seemed to have given up. He plodded on, left foot, right foot, plod, plod, plod, his dazed eyes fixed on the ground. Without Ula he knew he wouldn't be able to walk at all. He could barely stand upright without her holding on to him. They shuffled down the hill and finally, after what seemed an endless trudge, they reached the bottom.

"We'll rest for a minute," she said.

He started to slump to the ground, but she held him up.

"No, not like that. You won't get up again. This way."

She led him down a narrow track to a clearing with a small cairn in it.

"Sit on top of that," she said.

He sat down, breathing slowly.

"Please tell me this is one of your cupboards," he murmured. "Please tell me you've got some water in it."

She didn't answer but he saw with relief that she was indeed bending down at the cairn. She removed some of the stones and pulled out a small earthenware pot with a lid. She removed the lid and smelled the contents.

"It's all right. Drink it."

He drank some of the water, then handed her the pot.

"I can wait," she said. "Drink the rest."

He drank the rest without argument.

"Come on," she said, taking him by the arm.

"Can't we stay here a bit longer?"

"No, we must get to the village."

"But—"

"Kit, I'm worried you might die."

He said nothing. His mind had drifted away to a rock in the middle of the sea, and to a sight that made him shudder.

"Kit?" Ula's voice broke into the picture. "Kit, are you listening to me?"

"What?" he said dully.

"Kit, you're in danger. If you don't eat and drink and rest soon, you might die."

"I don't care if I do."

"But what about your parents? How will you look for them if you're dead?"

Even in his distracted state, he knew this was a trick. A kind, loving trick, to be sure, but a trick nonetheless to get him moving again. She was right, though. He couldn't find Mum and Dad if he were dead. He looked back at Ula, then hauled himself to his feet.

"Well done," she said.

He stood there, swaying before her. She took his arm again.

"Come on. We can rest soon."

But soon was not soon enough. Soon felt like a very long time. How long exactly he did not know. It seemed to take hours of fumbling and stumbling just to cross the valley, and then there was the other hill, the smaller hill, which now felt like a mountain. But Ula pulled him on. He could sense the urgency in her step and in her hands as they gripped him and kept him moving. And he, too, was now starting to feel the same urgency. Beyond this peak was a place where they could rest.

He knew that what she had said was true. He couldn't set

out today. But he would have to leave first thing tomorrow whether he was well enough or not. Every day was now critical. He tried to work out when Mum and Dad had been taken. It had to be at least seven or eight days ago. They could survive without food for that amount of time, but the lack of water would cause dehydration and lead to death much more quickly. And if Uddi and the others had done terrible things to them as well, it could be even worse. He started to shiver again as these images pressed themselves upon him.

"We're nearly there," said Ula.

He looked up and saw the top of the hill just a few yards away.

"Thank God," he murmured.

She glanced at him.

"You talk of God a lot these days."

"I still don't believe in him."

"Perhaps."

He frowned. She'd said that to him before, that time he first spoke to her in the cave. She'd said "perhaps" in exactly the same voice—a voice that seemed to cast doubt on what he'd said just before.

"No perhaps about it," he said.

And that had been his answer too, the very same words. It felt almost creepy to hear himself say them again. He hadn't repeated them deliberately. They had just come out. He looked round at her, but she seemed unconcerned by what he had said and was focusing on the summit just ahead of them.

They reached it at last and stopped. Below them the village looked like a dead place. The sheep, goats, and geese were the only living things he could see here apart from themselves. No figures moved on the slopes; no boats bobbed in the harbor.

They made straight for the mere and drank their fill, then splashed water over their faces and bodies. Then Ula took him by the hand and led him down toward the dining hall. He was shivering violently now; the pain in his body was growing worse and cramps were rippling through his muscles again.

She took him into the dining hall and sat him on one of the stools, then she disappeared through to the food store and returned a moment later with the remains of the goose that Brand and the others had cooked. Kit reached for it at once.

"Wait," she said. "They didn't cook the bird all the way through. They just cut pieces from the outside when they were done. Not all of it's fit to eat."

She took a knife, searched for a cooked portion of the bird, then carved off a slice and handed it to him.

"Eat," she said simply.

He thrust the meat into his mouth and devoured it almost without chewing. She handed him another piece, and while he was eating that, she fetched a bowl and put the carved slices in it for him to take. He felt almost demented with hunger and was soon wolfing down the meat.

Ula carried on carving, then after a while she stopped and set about starting a fire. He barely took this in. He was still obsessed with the food. But after a while he realized that she still hadn't eaten anything herself. He looked round and saw that she had set up the spit over the fire and was roasting the uncooked part of the goose.

"Aren't you going to come and eat?" he said.

"In a moment. When the fire's going properly."

But it was already going properly. He could see that. She had a fine blaze there. This was another one of her kind tricks—a trick to make sure he ate enough.

"I'm not eating any more until you come and share it," he said.

She came over at last, pulled a stool close to him, and reached for the bird.

"It's good," he said. "My God, it's good."

"There you go again," she said, stuffing some meat in her mouth.

"What do you mean?"

"Talking about God."

He said nothing. She stood up again.

"I've got to go and see to the goose," she said.

"I'll come with you."

They took their stools over to the fire and sat there warming themselves. Ula turned the goose, and as the bird cooked she cut more pieces off, and they went on eating until they were full. He felt his body droop forward. Ula caught him.

"Come on," she said. "Come and rest."

He let her take him by the hand and lead him out of the dining hall into the open air. The afternoon was drawing on. The sky was overcast and the air was still. She led him to the nearest of the cottages and pushed open the door. Inside was the usual spartan simplicity, but the hide on the floor was all he wanted right now.

"Lie there," she said. "Lie on your front if the wounds on your back are too painful against the ground."

He lay on his front and pulled the pillow under his chin. She placed the blanket gently over his back.

"Does that hurt?"

"It's all right."

"I'll be back in a minute," she said.

He felt strangely vulnerable without her, but she was soon back as she had promised. She was holding his T-shirt together with his shoes and socks.

"They left these on the ground by the chapel. I thought you'd want them." She put them down beside him. "Now rest. Sleep as long as you need to. I won't be far away."

And she disappeared again.

He put his T-shirt on, taking care not to chafe his back, then pulled the blanket over again and fell into a deep, foggy sleep. It was so profound he seemed to lose all sense of himself and felt frightened and disorientated on waking. And he woke often. The pain in his back woke him. The pain in his limbs woke him. The cramps woke him. His thoughts and memories and visions of Mum and Dad woke him. And each time he woke, he cried out like a baby.

Yet during these wakings he found Ula there. She had a fire burning in the cottage, and there was a pitcher of water beside him and a plate with some leftovers of the goose on it, and she had brought a hide and a blanket and pillow in for herself and was lying next to him. He rolled in and out of sleep, sometimes aware of her and of himself and the small smoky cottage, and sometimes aware of nothing save a deep, unconquerable pain. And then somehow even that went, and he slept on for what seemed like several hours.

When he woke the next time, he found Ula gone.

He sat up and looked about him, frightened at being left alone. The inside of the cottage flickered in the light from the fire. He reached over and pushed another log on, then drank some of the water and lay back on his side. He was still spent, still aching in every part of himself, and his thoughts kept racing to the rock in the middle of the sea.

He had to find it, even if it meant disaster. He had to know what had happened to Mum and Dad, whatever it cost him to see it. He tried to drift back into sleep but found he could not. He could think only of Mum and Dad, and now

Ula. He was starting to worry that she wasn't here. She had said she wouldn't be far away.

"Ula?" he called.

There was no answer.

"Ula?"

Again no answer.

He hauled himself to his feet and stood there for a moment, struggling for balance. He was still desperately unsteady on his feet, and his back was stinging acutely. He took some slow breaths, then stepped over to the door, opened it, and walked out. Night had fallen. He had been vaguely aware of it from inside the cottage, but he had no idea what time it was. There were stars visible but not many. The sky was still overcast. A deep silence hung over the island.

He stared about him, searching again for Ula. He didn't like her not being here. He was starting to feel panicky without her.

"Ula?" he called.

There was still no answer.

He started to walk down toward the harbor. The sea was still and moonlight was glazing the surface. He stopped by the quay and looked down at the water, then made his way along the breakwater to the end and sat down.

"Where are you?" he murmured, staring over the sea. "Where are you?"

He wasn't sure who he was talking to. There were so many people he yearned to see right now: Mum, Dad, Ula, even the strange man. He didn't know where any of them were. He had never felt so alone.

"Where are you?" he said to them all.

He heard a sound far out to sea. It was the long, eerie cry. Strange how comforting such a scary thing could be. It was almost reassuring to hear it. Yet it was a lonely sound, and it belonged to something he had no wish to see again. Monsters could not bring back Mum and Dad. Monsters could not make him well again.

Perhaps nothing could.

He went on staring over the sea, then the cramps forced him to stand up. He hobbled back to the cottage and looked inside again, hoping Ula would be there. But she was not. He felt panic closing around him.

"Ula, where are you?" he muttered. "Where the hell are you?"

She couldn't have left him. She had said she would get *Splinters* for him, but she wouldn't have done that in the darkness. And she'd have told him before she went off. He floundered up the slope toward the little hill. Perhaps she was up at the mere filling another pitcher. Or perhaps in one of the enclosures. Perhaps she was milking one of the goats. Or perhaps . . .

He was meandering about now, going nowhere, calling her name.

"Ula? Ula? Ula?"

He dropped to his knees halfway up the hill and put his hands over his face. He could feel himself breaking up. He could feel black despair all around him, covering all escape, wrapping him up like a cloak, wrapping up the faces of Mum and Dad and Ula, and then squeezing, squeezing, squeezing.

"No!" he screamed.

"Kit!" came a voice.

"No!" he screamed. "No! No! No!"

"Kit!" He heard the sound of padding feet. He felt arms reach round him and pull him forward. He felt a body close against his. He felt a hand stroking his head. He heard a voice whispering.

"Kit."

"No! No!"

"Kit, it's me. It's all right. It's me. It's Ula."

He knew who it was. He was clutching her now, terrified in case she left him again.

"Ula!" He was sobbing into her ear. "Ula! Ula!"

"It's all right."

"You left me!" He pulled at her. "You said you wouldn't be far away! But you left me!"

"I went to get your boat."

"You should have told me!"

"You were sleeping deeply," she said softly. "I didn't want to wake you. And I had to bring the boat round now. You'll be wanting to start early."

She held him close.

"I won't leave you again."

He dug his head into her neck. They held each other in silence and after a while he calmed down.

"I'm sorry," he murmured. "I'm sorry, I'm sorry, I'm sorry."

"It's all right."

She looked at him in the darkness.

"Come back to the cottage."

He was still crying.

"Come on," she said.

They stood up and she took him by the hand.

"I won't leave you again," she said.

They set off back to the cottage. The fire had gone down now, but there was enough life in it to be rekindled, and Ula soon had it blazing again.

"Lie down," she said.

He lay down on his side.

"Is it too painful to lie on your back?" she said.

He nodded. She lay down beside him, then stretched out her arm over his head. He leaned in toward her and she held him. He didn't sleep and neither did she. Her eyes were closed, but he could tell that she was awake. They lay there in silence, listening to the crackle of the fire.

"Ula?" he said some time later.

"Yes?"

"Will you come with me in the boat?"

"No."

She twisted round so that she could look into his face but kept her arm around him.

"When you leave this island," she said, "you won't want to come back. Whether or not you find your parents. You'll want to go back to your world."

"I know."

"But I've got my own world. It's this island. I can't leave this place. I'm the last person born on Skaer. And I'll be the last person to die here."

He said nothing.

"Do you understand?" she said eventually.

"Yes." He frowned. "I can't stay and you can't leave."

They looked at each other long and hard, and then he sighed.

"I know," she said, and she pulled him closer.

He lay there against her, breathing the sea from her skin.

"Maybe both our worlds are coming to an end," he said. "Maybe the Apocalypse is for my world as much as yours."

"That was what the Skaerlanders believed. I told you, this island was meant to be a kind of heaven, a pure place in an impure world. The one place left where the Devil has no control. Once this place is lost to him, the whole world is lost. So yes, the Apocalypse is as much for your world as it is for mine. That's what the island stories say."

"And what do you say?"

"I don't know anymore. I don't know about God or the Devil or anything."

"What about me? What do you know about me?"

She looked at him.

"I know nothing about you. Nothing at all." She smiled. "But I'm no longer frightened of you."

He smiled back.

"I'm glad."

He tensed suddenly.

"What is it?" she said.

"I thought I heard those whispering voices again."

"Can you hear them now?"

He listened but all he heard was the crackle of the fire.

"No, they've gone."

"Are you sure they were here?"

"No. Maybe I imagined it. But I heard the sea creature earlier. I didn't imagine that."

"I heard it too. When I was out on the water."

"Was the boat all right?"

"Yes, she was quite safe in the cave."

"Did you sail or row her?"

"I sailed her."

"Where is she now?"

"Moored in the harbor." Ula yawned. "In the morning I'll pack some food and water for you to take with you."

"Thank you."

He wondered why they were suddenly talking so formally. His words sounded stiff and awkward; hers sounded stiff and awkward. There was a pause.

"Ula," he said softly, and then stopped.

She reached out a hand and touched his face. He moved a fraction toward her. She let her hand stray round his cheek, then pulled him closer. He ran his fingers through her hair. She kissed him. Her mouth was warm and it tasted of the sea. He moved clumsily, his body still hurting in a thousand places and worn out with fatigue, but she was light and quick and gentle.

"Kit," she murmured.

She eased him out of his clothes; she slipped out of her own. She stroked his neck. She kissed his eyes. She touched his wounded back with soft fingers.

"Poor boy," she whispered.

She pulled him gently onto her.

"I can't," he said. "I mean—"

"It's all right."

"It's not that—"

"It's all right," she whispered. "I know. You're hurting. You're tired. You're frightened. Just lie there. Don't move."

But he was moving, in spite of himself. The warmth of her body took him over, and soon she was moving too. He clung to her now, without subtlety or skill, and his mind and emotions soared out of control; yet still she stroked him, kissed him, whispered to him as the dark, flickering room whirled about them.

Later, when they fell asleep, he found himself dreaming. He dreamed he was moving underwater through a vast, limpid sea, not swimming but somehow gliding after the naked man, who was moving just ahead of him. He himself was naked too, and after a while he realized that the two of them were not alone. Just as he was gliding in the man's wake, so a phantasmagoria of other naked beings was gliding in his. He saw Mum and Dad and Ula and Torin and Brand and Uddi and Zak and Wyn, and then all the other islanders, and now other people, people from his old life, and still more people, people he had never seen before, thousands and then millions and then billions of people all gliding like fish after him, just as he was gliding after the man.

"Why are there so many people?" he muttered in this dream. "And where is the man taking us?" He could feel panic rising. "How are we all going to get back?"

Something cool brushed over him and he woke with a start.

He looked sharply about him, then suddenly remembered where he was. The fire was dead and the cottage was dark. He had been woken by a breath of wind on his skin. He was lying on his side, his arm flung over Ula, who was fast asleep next to him. He saw her body twitch as another breath of wind wafted in. He pulled the blanket over them both and lay still.

But his mind was moving again, back to a rock in the middle of the sea and to a sight he dreaded. He heard the spirits of the dead whispering in the night again. There was no mistaking them this time. He looked into the darkness and spoke to them.

"Why are you here?" he murmured. "Why have you come back?"

Ula stirred and he thought for a moment that he had woken her, but she was only seeking warmth. He pulled her closer and she gave a soft moan, then slept on. He listened again to the strange wordless voices.

"Have you come back for me?" he said.

25

The morning brought more mist and a strange crimson sea. He stood with Ula on the quayside and stared out beyond the harbor wall.

"What does it mean?" he said.

"It means you can't set off," she answered. "You'll never find the rock in this mist."

He looked round at her.

"But you are going to set off," she said. "I can see it in your face."

"I've got to. I can't stay another day."

"No, I suppose you can't."

He heard the sadness in her voice. It matched the sadness he was feeling himself.

"Are they still speaking to you?" she said. "The whispering spirits?"

"Yes." He listened to them. "They're all around me. Why won't they go away? I thought they were free. I thought the man released them."

"Maybe they want to help you."

"I don't see how they can. I never hear any words. Just this jumble of voices."

He listened to them again as he ran his eye over *Splinters*. She was rocking in the swell and bumping against the quay.

"I'll get the provisions," said Ula.

"I'll help you."

"No, stay here. I can do it."

He frowned. He hated the thought of leaving her, even though he knew he had to, and he felt dreadful about the fact that she'd risen in the small hours without waking him, slaughtered another of the precious few geese she had left, plucked it, cooked it, and packed the meat for him to take with him, together with water and goat's milk.

How long these provisions would last he didn't know. He still felt horribly weak and his hunger and thirst seemed without end. Yet he knew he'd have to be sparing with what she gave him, not just for himself but for the slender possibility that he might just find Mum and Dad alive. Ula reappeared with two large bags. She put them carefully down on the quay.

"This bag has pots of water and goat's milk," she said. "And this one has meat in it."

He opened the bags and looked in. The pots all had lids bound tightly on with cord, and they were wrapped in hide to stop them breaking.

"Thank you," he said.

"Try to keep them upright."

They looked at each other.

"Thank you," he said again.

They reached out and held each other, both crying. Kit didn't try to stop himself. He wanted to cry. He wanted Ula to know how much he felt for her. Neither spoke. They just held each other and cried, and then, when the tears had stopped, they went on holding each other for several minutes more. Then Ula drew back.

"You must go."

She looked down at the ground.

"I'll never forget you," she said.

"I'll never forget you," he answered.

He gently lifted her chin with his hand and smiled into her eyes. She leaned forward and kissed him, then drew back again.

"Go," she said.

He climbed down into *Splinters*. He was breathing hard, struggling not to cry again. She passed down the bags, and he stored them on either side of the centerboard case, checking the pots of water and goat's milk to make sure they were wedged upright. His eye fell on the little prayer boat. It was sitting on the bottom boards just by the mast. He took it in his hand, stood up, and held it out to Ula.

She shook her head.

"It's yours," she said.

"Are you sure?"

"Yes."

"Thank you." He turned it over in his hand and examined it. "I'd like to keep it. It's all I have left of you."

"No, it isn't," she said.

He looked up at her.

"You have more of me than that," she said. "Much more."

He studied her face for a moment, then understood.

"Yes, you're right," he said. "I'm sorry."

"Take it with you," she said. "You may have to use it one day."

"I'll never let it go. Never ever."

"You may have to."

"What for?"

"To send a prayer yourself." She paused. "To the God who doesn't exist."

He saw she was teasing him and smiled, then looked at the prayer boat again.

"The God who doesn't exist," he murmured. "Yeah, I guess." He gave a sigh. "I don't really know what exists anymore. After everything that's happened, it's like . . . everything's just weird. I don't know if the man exists. I don't know if this island exists. I don't even know if you exist."

"I exist," she said quietly.

He said nothing.

"Kit?"

He looked up at her.

"I exist," she said. "Promise me you'll never doubt that. Whatever happens to you, promise me you'll never doubt that I exist."

He bit his lip.

"I promise."

"Thank you."

He stared past her at the island.

"So now you've got this place to yourself."

"Yes."

"What will you do after I've gone?"

"Try to survive for as long as I can."

"It won't be easy."

"No, it won't. The island was dying even before the Apocalypse."

He looked sharply back at her.

"So has the Apocalypse come?"

"My Apocalypse has come," she said.

"You mean mine hasn't?"

"I don't know. I'm not sure."

Kit looked up at the sky. It was a misty blue, but fiery streaks were reaching across from the east. He heard the voices whispering round his head again. They seemed to be urging him to move. But he could not move. Not yet. He looked back at Ula.

"You said this place was meant to be pure, like a kind of heaven, and that once it's lost to the Devil, the whole world is lost."

"Yes."

"Do you believe that?"

"The Skaerlanders believed that."

"But do you believe it?"

She looked up at the sky.

"I don't know what I believe," she said slowly. "But I know my world has come to an end. And . . . I'm frightened for yours."

Their eyes met.

"So what can I do?" he said. "How can I stop the Apocalypse? How can anyone stop it?"

She reached out and touched his face.

"Love," she said. "Love as much as you can."

He glanced down at the little carved boat.

"And pray?" he said.

But she gave no answer.

He placed the prayer boat under the stern seat, then shipped the rudder and hoisted the sail. It flapped gently in the breeze.

"Which way will you go?" said Ula.

"I don't know." He looked out beyond the harbor. The mist seemed to surround the island, and it was curiously illumined by the crimson sea. "It doesn't make much difference which way I head. I'll be guessing, whatever course I take."

He heard the eerie cry out to sea.

"I wish that thing would go away," he said.

"It won't," said Ula. "Not while the man's near."

"You think he's near?"

"He must be. Wherever the sea creature is, the man is never far away."

"I still don't know what he is," said Kit. "God or Devil. Or just a weird man. And that creature's a mystery too. I mean, I know it's a giant snake. But how does it make that cry? I've never seen its head break the surface. And how come it only appears when the man's around?"

She said nothing.

"Maybe the Skaerlanders were right," he said. "Maybe it really is his familiar."

"Maybe," she said. "Or maybe something more."

"Like what?"

"I don't know. Just . . . something more. I can't explain it."

He felt a strange movement in his spine, the same movement he had felt just before his hilltop vision. He shivered and looked down.

"I'm so frightened. I'm frightened I won't find Mum and Dad. Or I'll find them dead."

Ula touched his face again.

"You must hope, Kit."

"You said that once before."

"Yes, I did."

They looked at each other.

"Good-bye," he whispered.

"Good-bye," her mouth said.

But no word came.

He pushed *Splinters* off from the quay, then hauled in the sail and steered toward the mouth of the harbor. The boat was moving slowly in the light air, and he was glad of it. He was watching the small figure on the quay and drinking in this last sight of her. She didn't wave, didn't smile, didn't move at all. She simply stood there.

He reached the harbor mouth and saw the end of the breakwater ahead. He checked to make sure he was clear of the walls, then suddenly he was through and the sea was open before him. He looked back and saw to his horror that Ula was gone.

"Ula!" he shouted.

But then he saw her again. She had run down to the southeastern point and climbed up the knoll to the chapel, and now she was waving to him. He waved back, his eyes fixed on the bright, tiny form. He waved and waved and waved, and then the mist fell over him.

And she was gone.

So, too, was the island. He was alone upon a misty sea. Yet he didn't feel alone. The whispering voices were with him still, and somewhere to port he could hear the eerie cry. Both sounds chilled him in different ways, yet he knew that if he was to find the rock, he would have to resist these fears and keep searching.

But he had no idea which way to go, and he was already losing his sense of direction. He had assumed he was still heading in a southeasterly direction, but the sail kept flapping or crinkling along the luff, so either the wind was changing or he had blundered off course—whatever that course was meant to be.

The cry came again, still off to port. He remembered Ula's words.

"Wherever the sea creature is, the man is never far away."

On an impulse he altered course to port.

The whispering voices grew louder. He sailed on into the mist, listening for the eerie call in the distance. He had no idea whether there was any point to this. It seemed risky in the extreme to go looking for the great sea snake. But he had no better plan. *Splinters* slipped on, moving like a ghost in the flimsy breeze, and still the sea shimmered with its crimson face.

The mist, too, was starting to shimmer. It was not gray but a pale blue, and this was now being lit through by stabs of orange and gold that leaped, flamelike, from the surface of the sea. He heard the cry again, to starboard now, but a long way off. He altered course again. The sail flapped and set, and the boat moved on. The mist fell back a few feet, and he saw a pocket of clear air ahead. As he entered it he saw shadows rising from the sea.

"I know who you are," he called to them. "You're the spirits of the dead. But you don't frighten me."

Then the mist came down again, and they were lost from view.

He sailed on, straining his ears for the distant call. He had not heard it for some time, and he had no idea whether or not he was holding his original course. Then it came again, off to starboard and still some distance away. He altered course again. Here was another clear pocket, and here again were the shadows rising from the sea. He could see their bodies now, their arms and legs, their faces, their glittering eyes. They started moving round the boat in an endless stream, watching, whirling, whispering. He reached down and touched the prayer boat.

And sailed on.

The mist was changing further. The crimson of the sea was brightening and the haze brightening with it so that he felt as though he were sailing through a burning forest. The shadows, too, were changing. With every yard they were losing their darkness and turning to a silvery gray. Their voices were fading too, though he could still just catch them in the air around him.

But he was not listening for them. He was listening for the eerie cry. He had lost all sense of direction again, and he needed to hear it. There it was, dead ahead but still far off. He sailed on, his eyes on the shadows as much as the sail. The prayer boat was on his lap now. He pictured Ula making it. He pictured her finding the wood in the sea, drying it, carving it, putting the stones in the keel to weight it, then launching it. He pictured her mouth moving as she uttered her prayer.

His own mouth was moving too. But he was talking to the man.

"Where are you? Where are my mum and dad?"

He listened for the sea creature again but heard nothing.

"Why can't you take me to them?"

He stroked the prayer boat.

"Why can't you take me to them?"

The mist closed round him again, and the shadows vanished once more. *Splinters* moved quietly on, the only sounds the whispering in the air and the heave of the sea. A light gust struck the boat, and she heeled over. He eased off the sheet, anxious to keep *Splinters* on an even keel and not risk spilling the water and goat's milk. He shouted into the mist.

"Where are you, sea monster? I need to hear where you are!"

But no cry came back.

He eased off the sheet again and slowed *Splinters* down. The mist had grown thicker again and was now pushing in from all sides. He could hear the whispering but could see no shadows at all. He looked up beyond the mast and saw through a gap in the fog that the sky was turning crimson like the sea.

"Take me to the rock!" he shouted.

He didn't know who he was shouting to. He was just shouting.

"Take me to the rock! Take me to the rock!"

But still there was no cry from the sea.

He let go of the sheet completely and the sail hung idle. *Splinters* stopped and slumped in the swell. It was pointless going on without some sense of direction. He'd just be meandering around. He stroked the prayer boat again and murmured into the mist.

"Tell me where they are."

He heard the cry again, over to starboard, and it was nearer, much nearer. He felt a rush of fear but also of excitement. He hauled in the sail and set off again in the direction of the cry. It came again, nearer still. Suddenly he felt less safe. He could feel the trembling in the water, the clear sense of a vast presence nearby.

"Come on," he said quietly. "Call to me again."

The creature did, with a great mournful cry only yards away. Kit shivered at the sound and felt his hand reach for the prayer boat. There was a surge of water to starboard and a rush of gleaming black, then nothing but foam bubbling on the surface. *Splinters* rocked violently from side to side, and he threw an anxious glance at his cargo of provisions.

But there was no time to check that the pots were all right. Even before the boat had settled, there was another surge of water, this time across the bows, and the gleaming body broke the surface again and plunged back into the sea. He was trembling now, but he forced himself to clamber forward and check the pots.

They were all right and the lids were still on tight. None of the water or goat's milk appeared to have seeped out. He heard the cry again, and this time it was a massive sound right under the bow. He looked up in terror, expecting at any moment to see the body rear up and smash the hull to pieces or toss it into the air. But instead he saw a flurry of water ahead and then, through a gap in the mist, the clear outline of a rock.

He stared toward it. It was about a hundred yards away, an ugly gray rock about thirty feet high. It looked like an upturned tooth. He hurried back to the stern, seized the helm, and pulled in the sail. *Splinters* started to edge forward again. As she broke from the mist into another pocket of clear air he saw the silvery shadows around the boat again. They were still whispering, but their voices were fainter than ever. He took little notice of them. His eyes were fixed on the rock. But now the mist was closing in again, and the wind was failing too.

"Don't drop," he pleaded.

Somehow the breeze held and *Splinters* kept moving. The rock drew closer. He clutched the gunwale, terrified of what he might find. There was no sign of Mum and Dad from here, but the visibility was so poor it was hard to see much on the rock beyond the fact that it appeared to have no flat surfaces where anyone could lie down. He called out.

"Mum! Dad!"

There was no answer. He took a deep breath and sailed on. Here was the rock now, surrounded by mist. He ran his eye anxiously over it. There was no one on this side. He sailed round to the other side and at once saw a ledge near the top. It certainly looked large enough for two people to lie on, but it was too high up for him to see if anyone was there.

"Mum! Dad!" he called.

Again there was no answer. He steered *Splinters* in toward the rock. He was struggling to keep calm now. He knew he had to check the ledge. They might well be up there and too weak to call out or move. And it could be far worse. But he didn't dare think of that.

He brought *Splinters* alongside, climbed onto the rock,

and made the painter fast. It was good for the moment that the sea was calm and the air still. He clambered up the side of the rock, his heart beating furiously. The ledge was easy to reach, and in another few seconds he would know the worst. He clawed his way up to the lip and peered over.

They were not there.

"Oh, God." He felt tears start in his eyes. "Oh, God."

He beat the ledge with his fist. They were dead. He knew it. Maybe they'd taken their own lives in the end. Better that than just waste away here. He climbed over onto the ledge and stood there, searching for some trace of them. But there was none. He pressed his face into his hands and started to sob.

An icy breeze brushed his body.

He stiffened and took his hands from his face. Something was moving around him, something cool and light and quick. He stared and saw a silver cloud racing about him like a whirlwind, and he knew at once what it was.

The spirits of the dead were leaving him.

But even as they left, their rushing movements were pushing him round, round, round. He turned, unable to resist the vortex of silver light, and as the shadows whirled up into the sky and vanished forever, he saw, half-hidden in the mist, another rock just a short distance away.

And two figures lying on top.

26

Splinters ghosted toward the second rock. The sea was utterly still. The wind was barely enough to push the dinghy on. There was an unearthly silence all around. He didn't call out. He couldn't bear the possibility of another silence and what it would mean. He could not see them from down in the boat, but from the top of the other rock he had spotted no movement at all.

He sailed grimly on, his eyes on the rock. It was a misshapen thing, about the same height as the first rock but much wider all round. It had a flat peak and on one side, just a few feet down from the top, a ledge that appeared to lead into some kind of narrow cave. He was breathing hard again as he struggled with a turmoil of emotions. *Splinters* touched against the rock. He climbed out and made the painter fast, then dropped the sail, picked up a water pot, and with the help of his free hand started to clamber up to the top.

None of the scenes he'd pictured had prepared him for what he saw. The two figures were lying together, Dad behind Mum's back with his arm stiffly over her. They were so gaunt and thin it was hard to believe they could be alive. But then their eyes flickered toward him.

"Mum! Dad!"

He ran forward and knelt down beside them. Mum reached out a hand and touched his arm.

"Kit," she murmured. "Sweet Kit."

Her voice was so faint, he could barely hear it.

"Sweet Kit, sweet Kit."

She stroked his arm.

"Are you an angel?" she whispered.

He felt tears rush into his eyes again. The sight of Mum and Dad was almost too much to bear. Their hands were mottled and blue. Their lips were dry and cracked. Their eyes were sunken, their skin parched. He put down the pot of water and took Mum's hand. It felt cold. He closed both of his around it and rubbed gently. He felt Dad's hand reach over Mum's back and touch him on the arm. He took one of his hands from Mum's and held Dad's with it.

"I've got some water," he said.

He let go of their hands, took the pot, and carefully removed the lid. He was desperately thirsty again himself, and hungry, too, but he didn't care if he never ate or drank again as long as Mum and Dad lived. He felt Mum's hand on his arm again.

"Dad first," she whispered. "He needs it more."

He caught a shake of the head from Dad and nodded.

"No, Mum. You first."

He knew this was the risky part. Too much water too soon could be fatal for both of them. He raised the pot to her lips and tipped a trickle over them, then with his finger he smoothed the water over them and around her skin. Her mouth opened and a cracked tongue tried to lick the moisture from her lips. He tipped a little more and again smoothed it over her lips and her dry cheeks.

She breathed out with a sigh.

He tipped again, a tiny amount as before, but this time into her mouth. She coughed at once and he felt her body stiffen.

"Easy," he said. "Easy."

But the water stayed down.

"Dad," she whispered. "Dad . . ."

"I know."

He saw Dad's hand reaching for the pot.

"Dad," he said. "Not too much at once."

He saw Dad nod and handed him the pot.

"I'll get the rest of the things."

He fetched the two bags from *Splinters* and set out the pots on top of the rock. Dad was now sharing the water with Mum, each of them taking tiny sips. Kit crawled over to them and put his arm over their wasted bodies. Dad took the water from Mum and drank a little more himself, then put the pot down and pulled Kit closer. And the three of them huddled together.

"Kit," said Mum softly. "Kit, Kit."

None of them spoke for a while. They just lay there as the mist closed in around the rock and the fire in the sky grew dim. But Kit soon started to fidget. He felt sure they should be drinking more water. There was a listlessness about them, and they still looked dangerously close to death.

He sat up and moved all the pots in closer.

"These ones here have got water in them," he said. "These ones have got goat's milk. And these ones have got meat. You just take what you want when you need it."

"Thank you," said Dad. His voice was a whisper like

Mum's. He took a long, tired breath. "Are you all right, Kit? Are you hurt?"

"I'm . . ." Kit thought for a moment. He knew he couldn't tell them everything that had happened. Not yet anyway. They'd be even more distressed than they already were. He was glad that his T-shirt covered the worst of his wounds. "I'm okay," he said eventually. "But *Windflower*'s gone. I'm sorry. I couldn't stop it." He paused. "The islanders blew her up."

Dad's face clouded.

"My God."

"I know."

"So *Splinters* is all we've got left?"

"Yes."

Dad picked up a pot of water and handed it to Mum, then took one for himself and started to sip it.

"Well, I'd rather die in *Splinters* than die here on this rock."

"So would I," said Mum, sipping too.

"But you're not going to die," said Kit. He looked into their pale eyes. "You're not going to die. You're going to live. We're all going to live."

He thought of Ula.

"You must hope," he said.

Mum squeezed his hand.

"I never lost hope, Kit," she whispered. "Never once."

Dad pushed a water bowl toward him.

"You must drink something too. And eat something."

"I'll only eat when you eat."

"We probably won't be able to keep anything down yet."

"You could try."

So they all ate. Mum and Dad took only the tiniest morsels, but it was no use. The food kept coming up again.

"You eat, Kit," said Mum. "Please. You must eat even if we can't."

Kit was so hungry he wanted to gobble all the meat at once, but more than anything else he wanted Mum and Dad to eat. He wanted them to have all the meat themselves. So he took little for himself and tried to give the impression that he was having more. Mum and Dad went on sipping water, and he was glad at least of that.

But they were still horribly weak. He glanced down at *Splinters*. Some time soon they would have to set off. Their chances of survival at sea were slim, but they were even slimmer here on the rock. And the longer they delayed, the more danger Mum and Dad would be in.

He looked at them again. It was too early to suggest moving. They still needed to drink more and get some strength back. Perhaps they would be too weak even to move. He hadn't seen either of them try to stand up yet. How they had managed so many days on this rock he didn't know.

"How did you survive?" he said.

They looked at him with their weary eyes.

"Don't tell me if it's too tiring to talk," he said. "Save your strength."

Mum nodded across the water toward the other rock.

"They put us there first of all. Then they left us. But . . ." She took a few slow breaths.

"Easy, Mum. Tell me later."

"But we . . . we spotted this rock. And we saw it had a cave." She took some more breaths. "Where we might be able to get some shelter. So we . . ."

She stopped, out of breath, and Dad went on.

"We swam across. We did it on the first day while we still had some strength left. And it was just as well we did. We'd never have escaped that huge wave if we hadn't crawled through to the end of the cave."

Kit stood up and walked across to the far end of the rock. There just below him was the ledge he had seen from the boat. And as he craned over farther he saw the narrow cave stretching all the way back into the rock. There was barely enough room for two people to squeeze in, but somehow it had saved their lives. He straightened up again and walked back to them.

"Which direction did the wave come from?"

"The other side of the rock," said Dad. "We didn't know what it was at first. But we heard things in the sea that we didn't like the sound of, so we crawled into the cave to be safe. We'd just got right down inside when the thing struck."

"It was terrifying," said Mum.

They both fell silent, struggling for breath.

"Don't talk for a bit," said Kit. "Just drink what you can."

And then we must set off, he thought. But I can't tell them yet.

He stared behind him toward the other end of the rock and pictured the great wave thundering in, and Mum and Dad huddled inside the cave as the water roared and whirled round the entrance. It must indeed have been terrifying.

He heard the eerie cry far off.

"We heard that sound a lot, too," said Dad.

Kit looked at them.

"Are you strong enough to go?"

They didn't look strong enough even to stand up.

"We're strong enough to try," said Mum. She reached out a hand to him. "But you'll have to help us."

He quickly took her hand.

"It's okay. I want to."

"We're going to be a burden to you."

"We're together." He kissed her cheek. "That's all I care about. Are you ready to stand?"

"Yes."

He slipped his other hand under her back and started to pull her up from the rock. She could hardly move by herself. But she was light. She had lost so much weight that he lifted her easily. He helped her to her feet but did not let her go. She stood there for a moment, swaying, then her legs started to buckle. He caught her and held on.

"I'm sorry, Kit," she said. "You'll have to carry me to the boat."

"It's okay."

"But don't try and climb down the way you came up. Go down that way."

She nodded to the left and he saw a rough ledge leading down the side of the rock. It was a little narrow but certainly easier than the way he'd come up.

"I'm going to put you over my shoulder," he said. "Fireman's lift. Okay?"

"I might be sick down your back."

"Don't worry about it. My back's had a lot worse than that lately."

He eased her carefully over his shoulder and carried her down to the boat. The sea was still calm and the mist close around them. He sat Mum gently down on the thwart.

"Can you sit upright without my help?"

"Yes." She clutched the gunwale. "I'll be fine."

She gave him a smile.

"I'll go and get Dad," he said.

He found Dad already on his feet and struggling down the ledge by himself. But he looked horribly shaky.

"Dad!" he shouted. "What are you doing?"

Dad slipped at that very moment, but Kit leaped forward and caught him before he hit the ground.

"Ah!" groaned Dad.

"What's happened?" called Mum from the boat.

Kit helped Dad upright again.

"Are you all right?" he said.

Dad clung to him, his arms shaking. Like Mum he was lighter than normal, but he was still heavy enough to put a strain on Kit's weakened frame.

"Sorry, Kit," he panted.

"Are you okay?"

"I'm fine. Let's go."

"Is everything all right?" called Mum.

"He's fine!" Kit called back.

But it was clear that Dad wasn't fine. And he could tell that it wasn't just the lack of food and water or this little fall. It was something else. Dad had clearly been hurt in some other way, and perhaps Mum had too. He thought of Uddi and Zak, and what they could do to people in their power, and he shuddered.

He heard the eerie cry again.

He helped his father into the boat.

"Easy, Dad," he said. "Sit on the thwart next to Mum."

The boat dipped under their weight.

"I'll get the pots," he said.

He hurried back to the top of the rock, collected the pots that they hadn't emptied, and put them in the bags, then made his way back to the boat.

"Just stay there on the thwart," he said. "I'll put these on the bottom boards in front of you."

There wasn't going to be much room for his legs, but he didn't care. He wanted them to have the provisions in easy reach so they could eat and drink whenever they wanted. He untied the painter, climbed into the dinghy, and pushed off.

Splinters drifted out into the mist.

"I'm going to hoist the sail," he said. "Just keep still and mind your heads with the boom."

It felt so strange to be speaking to them like this. He felt almost like a parent talking to two simple children. But in the last few minutes he had sensed the change in them. The water had nourished their bodies a little, but their minds had slipped back into that listlessness he had noticed before. They seemed disoriented and were clearly still traumatized. He reached past them and hoisted the sail. It hung limp at first, then suddenly flapped.

"Come on," he murmured. "We need some wind."

And something came, just a whisper of a breeze, but enough to move them away from the rock. He stared back at the gray form vanishing in the mist, then turned forward again. Mum and Dad were not even looking at the rock. Their eyes were glazed and weary. He leaned forward and waited until he saw them focus on him.

"We're going to live," he said. "Okay? We're going to live."

Dad seemed to stir for a moment.

"Which way are you going, Kit? I'm afraid I don't know where we are."

"Neither do I." Kit stared into the mist. "But I can find the way."

And he sailed on, listening for the cry. Nothing came back. He thought of Ula again. He thought of her launching her boat. He looked about him for the little model. It was under the stern seat again, though he didn't remember putting it back there. He reached down and touched it, and started murmuring.

"Where are you? Where are you? Where are you?"

The cry sounded again in the mist. It was far off to starboard.

He altered course.

"More wind," he murmured. "We need more wind."

And the wind did pick up, though only a little. *Splinters* slipped on across the silent water. He saw Mum's head fall onto Dad's shoulder. They were leaning against one another, each with a hand round the gunwale. He was glad that the sea was so calm and hoped he wouldn't have to go about too soon.

But for the moment there seemed little likelihood of that. The wind was coming across the quarter, and the boat was moving on a comfortable broad reach. He looked down at the sea. It had lost that crimson quality and was now darkening into gray. The sky, too, when he glimpsed it through the mist, was heavy and leaden. Dusk was approaching and he braced himself for the long night's sail ahead. He looked at Mum's and Dad's withered bodies and wondered whether they would make it till dawn, and whether he would too. His hunger and thirst were now acute and his body shrieked with pain and fatigue.

The cry came again across the sea.

Mum gave a start, as though the sound had jolted her back to consciousness.

"Are you all right?" he said to her.

She was looking about her in a confused way. Then suddenly she nodded.

"I'm sorry, Kit. I'd forgotten where I was."

"It's okay. Do you want something more to drink? Or some meat?"

"I'll try some meat again and see if I can keep it down." She looked at Dad, whose eyelids were lowered. "Jim," she said softly.

He opened his eyes.

"You need to drink again and maybe try some meat."

He looked at her tiredly.

"Okay."

"Kit?" she said. "You must eat and drink too."

"You two first," he said. "I've got to steer the boat. I'll have something when you've finished."

To his relief, they both fell for this and started on the pots. They drank more water and some of the goat's milk, and this time managed to keep some meat down.

"Your turn, Kit," said Mum.

He picked at the meat and slurped at the water, but luckily the darkness had now fallen, and they didn't seem to notice how little he was eating and drinking. Night had come quickly, and there was still no sign of an end to the mist. If anything, it was growing thicker. He thought back to that first night when they had entered these seas, with the dense fog and the model boat bobbing past. He glanced down at it again and thought of Ula.

"Love," he murmured. "Love as much as you can."

"What did you say, Kit?" said Mum drowsily.

"Nothing."

He heard the cry again. It was still far away, though not so far that he couldn't tell which direction it was coming from. He altered course toward the sound.

"We'll go where you go, my friend," he whispered. "We have no one else to follow."

The mist and the darkness deepened. He could see nothing now beyond the bow, and barely even as far as that. The only clear things he saw were Mum and Dad sitting on the thwart facing him, their eyes closed. He checked the sail. The wind had picked up a little and though *Splinters* was moving faster, she was also rocking more, and he could see that Mum and Dad were holding on to the gunwales more tightly and having to brace themselves with the motion of the boat. He eased out the sheet and *Splinters* settled back.

They moved on through the night. Mum and Dad seemed in a kind of glazed slumber, half-asleep yet aware of the movement of the boat. He watched them carefully in case they slumped back or toward the side of the dinghy. But somehow they remained upright, leaning as before against each other and holding on to the gunwales. He was glad that they were at least getting some kind of rest.

But he needed rest too, and he had already found himself drooping over the tiller. Each time it happened, the boat started to come round into the wind and the change in motion jerked him back awake, fortunately before it disturbed Mum and Dad, but he knew it was going to be a struggle to keep awake all through the night. He reached down to one of the remaining pots of water and took a tiny sip.

"Stay awake," he told himself. "You've got to stay awake."

But the next thing he remembered was the sound of the sail flapping, and then a hand on his arm.

"Uh?" he muttered.

"It's all right, Kit."

It was Mum's voice. He opened his eyes and found himself slumped over the helm and *Splinters* head to wind. Mum was leaning toward him from the thwart, her hand still on his arm.

"You fell asleep," she said.

"I know. I'm sorry."

"I'll come and sit in the stern with you."

"But . . ." He glanced at Dad and saw him still sitting upright on the thwart.

"He's all right," said Mum. "And we'll keep an eye on him."

But even as she spoke, Dad started to change position. Somehow, even in sleep, Dad seemed to have sensed that Mum was moving, and now he lowered himself down until he was curled up half-over the thwart, his head hard up against the side of the hull, his hands and arms pressed against the bottom boards. He looked anything but comfortable in this contorted position, yet his eyes were still closed and he seemed not to have woken.

Mum sat in the stern on the other side of the helm.

"Let me take the tiller," she said.

"Are you sure you're strong enough?"

She looked at him with something of her old spirit.

"It's just a stick of wood as I recall," she said. "Unless they've changed the design recently."

He smiled. It was good to hear her bantering with him. She took the helm.

"Give me the sheet, Kit."

He handed her the sheet.

"Right," she said. "Which way are we going?"

But he no longer knew. He had been pretty certain before he fell asleep that he was following the sound, but now with the boat head to wind, he'd lost his bearings. To his relief he heard the distant call again.

"That way," he said, pointing.

She looked hard at him.

"Are you doing what I think you're doing?"

"Yes. I've been following the sound."

"And do you know what's making it?"

"Yes."

"So do we. We saw the creature several times around the rock."

She frowned, then reached out suddenly and stroked his hair.

"You've been so brave, Kit." She gave him a kiss, then looked up at the sail. "Right. Let's go."

And they set off again. He soon found himself slipping in

and out of sleep. Sometimes he felt Mum's shoulder under his head and the hard bony edge of the tiller moving against his side; sometimes he felt nothing at all but a black, dreamless void. Then, some time later, he woke to find Mum slumped over the helm herself, the sheet running free, and *Splinters* surging round into the wind. He seized the tiller and sheet and brought the boat back to a broad reach. Mum stirred and sat up.

"Kit?"

"It's all right."

"Did I fall asleep?"

"Yes. It's okay. I've had a rest. I'll carry on."

"I'm all right now," she said. "I can take the helm again."

"No, you rest."

He heard the cry again far away. It seemed a strangely comforting sound now. He kept hold of the helm and sheet, and they sailed in silence for a while, both now awake. Dad was still sprawled over the thwart and seemed to be resting after a fashion. But he still looked frighteningly frail.

"I won't let him die, Kit," said Mum.

"I won't let you die either."

"I'm not going to die," she said. "None of us are going to die."

He hesitated.

"Mum?"

"Yes?"

"What did the islanders do to you and Dad?"

"It doesn't matter."

"It does."

"No, Kit." She touched him on the arm. "It doesn't."

He looked round and saw she was watching him, and her eyes had a touch of steel in them. For a moment it made him think of Ula.

"We're together again," she said. "That's all that matters."

He said nothing. She stared away over the bow.

"A strange thing happened when we were on the rock," she went on. "I had this dream. I dreamed you came out of the sea and gave us water. But you had no clothes on. You were stark naked. And you were older. It was weird. It was clearly you, but you were a man."

"What happened in the dream?"

"You just gave us water out of a bowl and then slipped away into the sea without saying anything. But the really weird thing was that in the morning I felt a little better. And Dad said the same thing, even though I hadn't told him about the dream."

Kit reached down and touched the prayer boat again.

"I thought the world was going to end when we lost you," she said.

"It's not going to end," he said. "I won't let it."

Yet something was happening to the world. He didn't know what it was, but he could sense it all around him. The mist cleared as the night passed, and when day came, it brought with it another crimson sky and another crimson sea. Flashes of gold were racing through both, and he sensed a strange thunder in the deep.

"I don't like the look of this," said Mum.

Dad stirred suddenly and without warning stretched over the side and vomited into the water. Mum hurriedly moved forward and held him.

"I'm all right," he muttered. "I'm all right."

He splashed some seawater over his face and sat up on the thwart. He looked haggard, but he was at least alive, and despite throwing up, there was a little more color in his face. He gave a wry smile.

"I'm beginning to think being bankrupt wasn't such a

bad deal after all." He stared around him. "I don't know what all this means. I've never seen sea or sky like it." He yawned and stretched. "But it's definitely time I did my stint at the helm. Change places with me, Kit."

They changed places and Dad took the tiller.

"Which way are we going?" he said.

"We're following the sound of the sea snake," said Kit.

He waited for an acid response. But Dad merely shrugged.

"Well, that's novel. And where did you last hear it?"

Kit pointed.

"Okay," said Dad, and he headed that way.

They sailed on across the burning sea. They sailed all through the day and into the next night, following the eerie call. They drank all the water and goat's milk and ate all the meat, and threw the pots and bags over the side, and sailed on. And then at some point in that second night, they all stopped. No one quite knew how it happened. But suddenly, without a word being spoken between them, they all realized that they had nothing left.

No one steered. No one moved. They lay about the boat sprawled across each other, and *Splinters* drifted in the swell. The stars were out, and as Kit lay there in this drowsy dream-life he felt sure he saw a comet racing overhead. But there can't be a comet, he thought sleepily. I can't be seeing a comet when I'm lying in the cave with Ula. He glanced at her. She was lying right next to him, and her quick eyes were laughing. She leaned down and kissed him and stroked his cheek.

"Love," she said.

And he closed his eyes.

When he opened them again, he saw dawn breaking once more.

And the bow of a boat looming over them.

27

He stared. The sea and sky were already a fiery crimson, but he took little notice of that. All he cared about was the boat heading toward them. He heard a rumble of engines, then silence. The bow drew closer, and he saw the name *Elizabeth*. There was a sound of shouts above him followed by the padding of feet on the deck.

"Mum," he murmured. "Dad."

They looked blearily round at him.

"There's a boat," he said.

"Are you okay?" came a shout.

They sat slowly up. Dad peered under the boom for a few moments, then turned wearily back to them.

"It's a fishing trawler," he said.

"Thank God," said Mum.

There was another shout from the trawler.

"Are you okay?"

"Do we look okay?" Kit muttered to himself. "Do we bloody look okay?"

Dad hailed back.

"We need help!"

"Can you catch a rope?"

"Of course we can catch a rope," Kit muttered again. "What do they think we are? Stupid or something?"

But he wasn't thinking straight. His mind had been with Ula, and his dream had been so vivid that he'd felt she was there with him. Even at this most wonderful of moments, he could feel some resentment toward his rescuers.

A rope came flying across. Dad caught it and made it fast. Mum was already hauling down the sail. Kit pulled up the centerboard and unshipped the rudder. He felt he needed to be doing something, but suddenly there was nothing more to do but wait and watch the trawler pull them alongside. He saw worried faces staring down at them, mostly men, though there was one woman among them. And then suddenly *Splinters* was alongside, and three of the crew were climbing down to help them.

"Easy!" called a voice from the deck. "They look very frail."

He looked up and saw a grizzled, middle-aged man who was clearly the skipper. The man caught his eye but was too busy directing operations to give more than a brief, anxious smile.

"Help the lady out first," he called.

"No," said Mum. "Take my son first."

And Kit saw a hand reaching in his direction.

"Grab hold," said a man.

Kit did as he was told, and the next moment he was pulled into the man's arms and then lifted by more hands up onto the deck of the trawler. His feet failed him the moment he put them down.

"Watch him!" shouted the skipper.

Another of the men caught him as he fell.

"Keep him in your arms while we get the others out."

And the skipper turned back to the side. Kit called desperately after him.

"The dinghy! You won't let her drift away?"

"Of course we won't," the skipper called back. "We'll heave her up on board. Now just give me a minute while I sort out the others."

A few moments later Mum and Dad were on board, held, like him, in strong, capable arms. He stared vacantly about him. The trawler crew looked friendly enough, but they were clearly nervous, too. The skipper stepped forward.

"My name's Ross," he said. "Most of this crowd's my family, but I won't bore you with the names. There's obviously lots you need to tell me some time or other, but right now I think we need to get you into bunks and give you something to eat and drink or whatever you need. The boys'll get your dinghy on board. When we've got you as comfortable as we can, we'll radio for the air ambulance."

"Thank you," said Dad.

Ross turned to one of the young men.

"Baz, clear three of the starboard bunks. Take Nathan with you. Maggie, get some water and some fruit juice and something for them to eat. Nothing too heavy. Barny, Adam, Will—take the mast out of the dinghy and get her on board. Right, let's go."

And Kit felt himself carried past the hold and down below. He closed his eyes and tried to believe this was truly happening. Somehow it didn't seem real. He felt himself put down and opened his eyes again. He was lying on a bunk in a small cabin with an empty bunk above him and another double bunk opposite. He saw Mum being placed carefully on the lower bunk and then Dad on the one above her.

"Thank you," Mum said to the three men.

They nodded somewhat shyly and stood there for a moment, as though unsure what to do. Ross came in.

"All right," he said to the men. "No need to hang around. Go and help Barny and the others with the dinghy. Where's Baz?"

Baz appeared in the doorway.

"Go and radio for the air ambulance," said Ross. "Do it right away."

"Okay."

And the young man disappeared, leaving Ross alone with them in the cabin.

"You're all very kind," said Mum in a tired voice.

"No problem at all," said the skipper.

Kit watched Ross from his bunk. There was something reassuringly solid about the man, yet he seemed nervous in the extreme, and it was clear that he had something on his mind beyond their own immediate crisis.

The woman called Maggie entered with a tray of water, orange juice, and soft fruits.

"My daughter," said Ross proudly.

Yet the anxious expression remained on his face. And as Kit looked he saw the same anxiety on Maggie's face, though she was hiding it a little better.

"I hope my father's not making you talk too much," she said, putting the tray down.

Kit didn't answer. He was watching Mum and Dad. Exhaustion had mastered them and their heads were back, their eyes closed. He didn't suppose they'd even seen Maggie come in. She watched them too for a moment, then looked round at her father.

"Should we wake them just to get them to drink a little? Or should we let them sleep?"

"Let them sleep," said Ross. "But keep a close eye on them."

"Okay." Maggie turned with a smile to Kit. "But you're going to have something, young man."

She poured him a glass of water.

"Don't gulp it down," she said. "Take small sips."

He drank the water gratefully. It was cool and clean and beautiful.

"Drink some more," she said.

He drank some more. He, too, was exhausted and all he wanted was the oblivion of sleep. Yet the nervousness of the skipper and his daughter pressed itself upon him, and now, as the water started to clear his mind, he remembered the nervousness he'd seen on the faces of the crew.

"What's going on?" he said.

And yet he already knew. He thought back to his vision on the hilltop; to the things Ula had told him; and to all that he had seen and heard and felt. He saw Maggie look at her father and whisper, "Don't tell him."

"Tell me," he said to the skipper.

Ross looked at him.

"Tell me," Kit said again.

Ross scratched his chin and glanced at Maggie, and this time she nodded. He gave a heavy sigh.

"I'm sorry if I'm distracted," he said. "But we're all distracted right now. I don't want to scare you when you're in such a state. But I'm afraid there's nothing I can do about the timing. The thing is . . ." He gave another heavy sigh. "I'm worried sick. We all are. It's the sea and the sky. I've never seen anything like it. I don't know what's happening out there. But there's something wrong. I mean seriously wrong. It's been building up for days. And it's not just here. There's a heap of other stuff going on around the world."

Kit thought of the figure standing on the rock.

And the great wave crashing on the island.

"What other stuff?" he said.

"Volcanoes rumbling on several different continents. Earth tremors. No eruptions or full-blown quakes yet, but the threat of them in loads of places. Weird winds. Freak storms. There's nothing else but this on the news. And it's global. Something's cooking on a big scale. And now this sea and sky. I'm telling you, it scares the daylights out of me. It's got stuff in it I've never seen before. And I don't want any piece of it."

He stopped suddenly.

"I'm sorry," he said. "I don't mean to scare you. But you did ask."

"I know," said Kit.

The skipper patted him on the shoulder.

"You stay here and rest with your mum and dad. I'll make sure someone's with you at all times. But you'll understand if I get back on deck now."

Kit said nothing. His mind was on the pictures in his head. Pictures he didn't want to see.

"Maggie?" said Ross. "Can I leave them with you?"

"Sure," she said. "You get back on deck."

But before Ross could leave, a worried-looking Baz reappeared.

"What is it?" said Ross.

"Can't get the radio to work."

"What?"

"No signal. Nothing."

"I'll come and fix it."

But Baz didn't move aside.

"It's not the only thing that's not working," he said.

"What do you mean?" said Ross.

"Check your watch."

Ross glanced down at his watch, and his face took on a

bewildered look. Kit's mind went racing back to *Windflower* and the island. He tugged at Ross's shirt.

"Check your compasses, too," he said.

The skipper looked round at him.

"The compasses?"

"They won't be working either."

"He's right," said Baz. "They're not working. Nothing's working."

There was a sound of hurried footsteps outside, and the young man called Nathan appeared.

"Skip?" he said. "We've got a problem."

"What now?"

"The engines. Can't get 'em to start."

"Damn and blast!" Ross threw a glance at his daughter. "Maggie, look after our friends. I've got to sort this out."

And he hurried off with the others.

Kit leaned back in his bunk and saw the pictures in his head unfold. He saw the world. He saw the brink. He saw the void.

Maggie spoke.

"How did you know about the compasses not working?"

He forced his mind back.

"It's what happened to us," he said.

"Can you tell me about it?" she said. "Or do you want to sleep?"

"I don't want to say too much. I'm . . ."

"I know," she said. "You're exhausted. It's okay. We can talk later."

"I don't mind talking," he said. "For a bit, anyway."

"I understand. Just talk as much as you like. Do you want some orange juice?"

"Yes, please."

She poured him some, and he drank it slowly. Never had

orange juice tasted so good. He leaned back farther, his mind on the sea and sky.

"What about some fruit?" said Maggie. "You should be able to digest it. It ought to be eaten anyway. We've had it for a few days, and it's at the end now."

Like the world? he found himself wondering.

"No," he said aloud, answering his own question. "No, no, no."

"You don't want any fruit?" said Maggie.

But he was still thinking of the world. He clenched his fists.

I won't let it end. I won't let the Apocalypse come.

He saw the confusion on Maggie's face.

"I'd love an orange, please," he said quickly.

"Sure." She watched him for a moment, somewhat warily, then reached out and took an orange. "I'll peel it for you," she said, and she started working at the rind with deft fingers. He thought of Ula's quick hands and wished she were here now. Maggie handed him one of the pieces.

"Eat it very slowly," she said. "Really chew it before swallowing."

He chewed, and as he did so he heard feet running about on deck. Maggie glanced up at the sound, then back at him and smiled.

"Don't worry," she said. "They'll fix everything."

They won't, he thought. But all he said was, "The orange is good."

"That's one thing we have got," she said. "Plenty of good food on board. The fishing's been terrible, but at least we've eaten well."

He heard more feet running about on deck. He looked at Mum and Dad again to make sure the sound hadn't woken them. But they were still fast asleep.

"Why has the fishing been terrible?" he said.

"Hardly any fish stocks around these waters anymore. Dad's almost had enough."

More footsteps sounded on deck. Yet for all the running, a strange silence hung over the boat. And there was a stillness in the air, as though some vast energy were about to break loose. He thought again of the man on the rock.

"How long have you been at sea?" he said.

"Five days."

"Have you . . ." He hesitated. "Have you seen any large waves in all that time? I mean, really monster waves."

"Nothing *Elizabeth* can't handle. The weather's been weird and unpredictable, and it's been steadily building up to this horrible stuff we've got at the moment. But we've had no monster waves. And let's hope we don't get any. That's the last thing we need right now."

"The Devil's revenge," he murmured to himself. He didn't know whether Maggie heard him. She watched him in silence for a few moments, then leaned forward.

"Listen," she said. "I don't even know your name, but—"

"Kit. It's Kit."

"Well, Kit, you don't need to say more than you want. But . . . can you at least tell me where you've been?"

He pictured that strange, forbidding place.

"We've been on an island," he said. "We nearly got wrecked there. I ran our cabin cruiser onto a big rock, but we got her ashore. And then . . ." He tried to think how to phrase this. "Then things went . . . very wrong. We sort of fell out with the inhabitants. And, well, we had to come away in the dinghy and here we are."

He sensed that she knew he was leaving out most of the story.

"What was the name of the island?" she said.

"Skaer."

She looked at him blankly.

"Skaer?"

"Yes."

"I've never heard of it. And I know all the islands in these parts. I've trawled here with Dad since I was a kid."

He felt a new kind of unease creep through him.

"There's definitely no island of that name in these waters," she went on. "The nearest island's miles from here. You couldn't have come from there in that little dinghy of yours."

"We were two nights at sea."

"Oh." She frowned. "That's a bit different. Were you sailing all that time?"

"Pretty much."

"Even so, it can't be right. You said you fell out with the inhabitants, and the island I'm talking about is uninhabited. The nearest inhabited island is twice that distance from us. And you couldn't possibly have gotten from there to here in two days of sailing."

Kit looked away and felt his unease grow deeper. He heard more shouts above, more footsteps running about. He thought of Ula and felt her slipping away. He clutched at her image in his mind.

"What is this other island?" he said.

"The nearest one?"

"Yes."

"It's called Cairn Island. On account of all the cairns dotted about it and especially the huge one on the summit of the main peak."

He stiffened.

"Cairn Island?" he said.

"Yes."

"And you said it's uninhabited?"

"Yes."

Well, it almost was. If you added Ula to Torin's lot, that only made twenty. You could practically call that uninhabited. And now, with just Ula there, it was almost literally uninhabited. Maggie spoke again.

"No one's lived there for over four hundred years."

He felt a shudder pass through him. He said nothing. He couldn't speak.

"The island's been barren for centuries," she said.

Ula, he whispered in his mind. Don't go, don't go.

"I've got a book on it somewhere," said Maggie. "Hold on."

He didn't want to hear it. He didn't want anything to do with it. But she was soon back with a small book in her hand. He said nothing. He simply stared at the end of the bunk as she leafed through the pages. She gave a sudden exclamation.

"Amazing! Listen to this. You were right about the name. I'll read it to you."

Ula, don't go, don't go.

"'Cairn Island,'" she read. "'Originally known by its old dialect name of Skaer. Three and a quarter miles long by one and a quarter miles across. Once home to a strict religious sect but now barren and uninhabited for four centuries. The island is distinctive for the unusual number of cairns dotted about it, most particularly the extraordinary stone monument on the bigger of its two peaks. The large rock half a mile off the north end of the island has long been a hazard to shipping, but the recent installation of an automatic light-house has reduced the danger considerably.'"

She stopped reading.

"You're crying," she said quietly. She reached out and put a hand on his arm.

"Read me the rest," he muttered. "If there's any more."

"Just a little," she said. "Are you sure you want me to?"

"Yes." He took a deep breath. "Please."

She paused for a moment, then read on.

"'The island is a mysterious place. No one knows who built the cairns or why the original inhabitants left. The last-known person to live on the island was a hermit woman. It is said that her spirit haunts the island to this day. But it is a benign spirit, and the island, though barren, is a peaceful place and a well-known haven for birds.'"

She read no more. There was no more. And Ula had slipped away.

Kit tried to picture her in his mind. It was so easy to do. But what was he picturing now? An idea? An illusion? A desire? Yet he had felt her mouth on his. The imprint of her lips was still there. It was as real to him as the wounds that still ached upon his back. Maggie spoke again in a soft, low voice.

"Where have you been, Kit? Where have you really been?"

"I've . . ."

He thought of the island again. He thought of the Skaerlanders and all they stood for. He thought of the feet rushing about above him. He thought of the trembling of the earth, which he could feel even now reaching up through the sea. He thought of the end of the world.

"I've walked into the past," he said slowly. "And into the future as well."

Maggie stroked his arm.

"Wherever you've been," she said, "you'll be all right now."

She smiled at him.

"Listen, I'd better just go and check how they're doing

up there. Will you be okay for the moment? I won't be long, but I can send one of the boys straight down if you need somebody with you."

"I'm fine," he lied.

"Okay. I'll see you in a minute."

He said nothing as she went. He just lay there, staring ahead.

"Ula," he whispered. "Ula."

He closed his eyes and tried to hear her voice. And her words came back inside his head.

Promise me you'll never doubt that I exist.

"I promise," he answered.

But his heart was breaking. He heard a new sound, a deep rumble beneath him. What it was he didn't know, but it certainly wasn't the engines. He opened his eyes and sat up again. He saw Mum's eyes open too. Dad was still fast asleep, and Mum was only just awake, but she was watching him dreamily from her bunk.

"All right, sweetheart?" she murmured.

"Fine."

"Is that the engines I can hear rumbling?"

"Yeah."

"Oh, good." She reached out and took Kit's hand. "I love you," she said.

"I love you, too." He nodded toward Dad in the upper bunk. "And that old geezer up there."

She squeezed Kit's hand and then let go.

"Have they called the air ambulance?"

"Yeah, they've sorted it out."

"Thanks, Kit. Get some rest, won't you?"

And she drifted off to sleep again.

He climbed out of his bunk and stood there swaying on his feet, then slowly made his way out of the cabin and up to the deck. He was moving through a dream now, a dream disconnected from time and any reality he had ever known. He stepped onto the deck and saw the sea and sky on fire.

He walked toward the rail where most of the crew were gathered, staring out. He was still moving through the dream. Everything was dissolving around him, all life, all matter, everything that had ever been. He saw gold and crimson flames shooting from the water. He saw flecks of fire spitting down from the sky. He heard the rumbling beneath them grow into a roar.

He joined the group by the rail. Ross saw him and moved to the side to make a space for him.

"Are you all right, lad?"

Kit said nothing. His eyes were on the approaching flames.

"I've never seen anything like this before," said Ross. "If those flames get any closer, we've had it."

Nathan pushed through to the rail.

"Any luck with the engines?" said Ross.

"Nothing. They just won't move."

"And the instruments?"

"Not working."

"Damn!" Ross drummed the rail with his fist. "There's got to be something we can do."

"Pray," said Maggie.

Kit looked out over the blazing sea.

But what are we praying for? he asked himself. What kind of a world? If the Skaerlanders are right and the human race is beyond redemption, then maybe it's best to let the Apocalypse come and burn everything up.

But he shook his head.

"They're wrong," he murmured. "They're wrong, they're wrong, they're wrong."

He felt Maggie touch his arm.

"Are your mum and dad all right?" she said.

"They're sleeping."

"Is somebody with them?"

"No, they . . . I mean . . ."

"I think somebody should be with them. Whatever's going on out here."

"Yes," he said. "Yes, you're right. I shouldn't have left them. I—"

"It's all right. I'll go and sit with them."

He swallowed hard. Was he losing everything now, even remembrance of the people he loved most? He had lost Ula already. He couldn't lose Mum and Dad as well. And if this was to be the end, he should be with them.

But Maggie had already hurried off below.

He gripped the rail and whispered, "Don't let them die."

From somewhere nearby came the long, eerie cry.

"Bloody hell!" said Ross. "What was that?"

The crew members exchanged frightened glances. Kit stared over the rail and pictured Ula's face again.

Love, she kept saying to him. *Love, love, love.*

He turned and walked back down the deck to where *Splinters* lay, then reached under the stern seat and took the little carved boat. And then he walked down to the stern of the trawler, away from the rest of the group. Below him the sea was a swirl of crimson and gold. He could feel the heat rising from it. He stared at the tiny model. He did not know what to say. He remembered how Ula's lips had moved as she mouthed her prayer over Torin's grave. But he could think of no words for the God who did not exist. In the end he found only one.

"Go," he said.

And he dropped the prayer boat over the side.

It floated there, bright and clear, and did not move away at all. It stayed close to the trawler, so close that he could easily have climbed down again and picked it up. But then, as he watched, he realized that it was gradually slipping away. He kept it in view, anxious not to lose it too soon. But it was moving fast now, faster than he wanted it to, and suddenly he was struggling to see it.

And then it was gone.

The eerie cry came again. And then another sound.

The rumble of engines.

He heard a cheer behind him but didn't look back. He was still staring over the stern to the place where the prayer boat had been. Ross joined him.

"They've sorted it out," said the skipper. "Thank God for that. We can at least get ourselves moving. I've seen a gap in the flames just beyond the bows. We should be able to get through that, and with any luck we'll find clear water."

Kit spoke, but it was to Ula.

"I promise," he said. "I promise."

Ross gave him a fatherly squeeze.

"It's all been a bit much, hasn't it, lad?"

Kit said nothing and went on gazing over the stern. He heard footsteps behind him, then Baz's voice.

"We've got the radio back. And the instruments."

"Good boy," said Ross. "Call the air ambulance."

"I've already done it. They're on their way."

Kit pressed his hands together and pretended they were still holding the prayer boat. And for a moment it almost felt as though they were. He could feel the wood and even the tiny stones that Ula had taken from the shore and put into the keel. He heard Ross speaking to him again.

"We'll have to leave you for a bit while we get ourselves clear of this fiery stuff. Will you be okay here?"

He didn't answer. But they left him alone.

He stood there, close to tears. A few moments later he heard the sound of the engines revving up, and then the trawler began to move. The burning water started to slip by. He didn't look round to see the gap through which the skipper was going to take them. He was still trying to see the prayer boat. He was desperate to glimpse it one last time. He could see the spot where it had been.

But nothing more.

He felt a hand on each shoulder and found Mum and Dad standing on either side of him, with Maggie close by.

"I couldn't stop them," she said. "They woke up and when I told them you were on deck, they insisted on coming up to join you."

He looked from one to the other.

"Kit," said Mum. "Darling Kit."

She kissed him and put an arm round him. Dad leaned over and put an arm round them both. Then they pulled each other close and stood there together, watching the fire. It was drawing back now, slowly, slowly, and the trawler was moving on toward the gap.

Kit closed his eyes and thought of Ula again. He pictured her face. He listened to her voice. He drank in her warm animal scent. He opened his eyes and looked for the prayer boat again. He could just make out the spot where it had been, but that was all. Beyond it the curtain of flame was still receding toward the horizon.

The eerie cry came again.

He felt Mum and Dad draw closer. He squeezed them hard and felt their arms tighten round him. And as he thought of Ula again he suddenly felt as though she was holding him too. He could not see her. But he was sure she was there, right in front of him, her arms round him, her head tucked into the crook of his neck. He heard himself speak—but he did not know whose words they were.

"We can stop it," he murmured. "We can stop the Apocalypse."

He felt Mum and Dad and Maggie turn to look at him, but he didn't look back.

"It's up to us," he said.

He went on staring toward the spot where the prayer boat had been. He could see nothing there now save a flurry of sea, and then that vanished too. Yet not all was gone from the surface of the water. Something else was moving, something he was looking for, something he knew was there. It was distant now, but he caught it and held on to it as the trawler forged on.

The unmistakable figure of a man striding away across the sea.

About the Author

Tim Bowler was born in Leigh-on-Sea, Essex, England, and lived for many years in a house overlooking the Thames Estuary, where his first novel, *Midget*, was set. He is also the author of *River Boy*, which won the prestigious Carnegie Medal in England; *Storm Catchers*; and *Firmament*, which *Kirkus Reviews*, in a starred review, called "a gripping page-turner of immense and surprising beauty." He lives in Devon, England.

Visit Tim Bowler's Web site at www.timbowler.co.uk.